Flocking It Up

FLOCK AROUND
AND FIND OUT

JAYCE CARTER

ENTWINED PUBLISHING

Flock Around and Find Out
ISBN # 978-1-80250-721-8
©Copyright Jayce Carter 2025
Cover Art by Kelly Martin ©Copyright March 2025
Interior text design by Entwined Publishing
Published by Eternal, an Entwined Publishing imprint

Published in 2025 by Entwined Publishing, United Kingdom.

Entwined Publishing is a division of Totally Entwined Group Limited.

FLOCK AROUND AND FIND OUT

Chapter One

Sex toys got the job done, but times like now, I had to admit an actual cock—and the man attached to it—could still prove itself useful.

I didn't love giving blood, but somehow the sensation of fangs in my skin never failed to get me off. Did I have some weird kink?

If so, I really didn't give a fuck, at least not right now. It felt too damn good to care. And from the grinding of a hard cock against my lower back when he rolled his hips, I had to guess that Kelvin felt exactly the same.

He had his lips latched on my throat, the suction rushing shivers through my body, the swallowing sound far sexier than it had any right to be.

I arched backward against him, losing myself in so many competing sensations. It was always like this, though—always overwhelming and too much and not enough at once. No matter how many times we found ourselves like this, our bodies intertwined, our breaths a tangled, panting mess, it never failed to surprise me just how deeply I felt every last touch of his.

Kelvin withdrew his fangs and licked my neck, his saliva cool compared to my heated skin, a way of showing that he'd sealed the wound. It soothed the pain from the bite but didn't douse the flames inside me. If anything, it made me want him more.

My brain had turned into a mess — nothing but need and desire and heat. I dug my nails into his back, through his shirt, desperate to yank the fabric from him. I wanted him bare to me, without a stitch hiding him.

"Please," I begged, the word ragged and broken. Any other time, my wanton pleas would have humiliated me, but I was too far gone.

He grasped my chin and kissed me, his tongue still coated in blood, but I didn't give a fuck. I sought the warmth of his mouth, teased his agile tongue, anything to have just a little more.

"This is enough." The words came out rough through his panting breaths. They made me light-headed, made me want to hear him say far filthier things in that same tone of voice.

Except, I knew better. Even as far gone as I felt, I knew better. This was his line, the one he always drew.

I might like it any other time, but right now?

Right now, I was horny and his self-control sucked.

I'm not the sort of girl who has to rely on a reach-around. It was great when I got one, don't get me wrong, but if I didn't? I could handle my own shit just fine.

So I reached down, between our bodies, and slipped my hand beneath my skirt. The flowy fabric hadn't been the reason I'd picked this outfit, but it sure proved a benefit. I snaked my fingers into my panties to find my already-soaked cunt.

It reminded me that it had been far too long since I'd had someone stretch me just right, since I'd experienced that slight burn when a hard cock filled me. I had plenty of toys, but they didn't do the job the same way.

It hadn't been for weeks, not since…

A momentary vision of Harrison hit me, and I shoved it away.

I'd be damned if that mess fucked with my orgasm. It had hung around in my head for far too long, ruining my mood time and time again—I wasn't about to let it ruin this, too.

"You're killing me," Kelvin whispered, his words harsh, but he didn't stop me. "How do you expect me to hold back when you do things like this?"

"So don't hold back." I nipped his full bottom lip, biting it in retaliation for him denying me what I wanted.

"I already told you. If you want me, you have to tell me *before* I bite you. I won't do it, not when my bite has already fucked with your head."

Which he had told me, and somehow, he'd stuck to it no matter the temptation. No matter what I did, how badly I wanted him, he *never* crossed that line. He never touched me beyond the needed to make sure I didn't go through withdrawal from the venom in his bite.

It really was annoying how he could hold himself back and I had all but zero control.

Pathetic.

Thankfully, that remained at the back of my mind, hidden behind the waves of want that filled me. I teased my clit, the hardened nub begging for attention.

What wouldn't I give to feel Kelvin's lips on it?

I pulled back enough to stare at his mouth, the fantasy so real and reality so close but unattainable.

"I can't," he whispered, the words upset and thin. "You have no idea how much I want to push you back, spread your thighs, and lick you until you scream, Grey, but I can't."

"Why not?"

"I've already told you why—because I've already seen you stare at me like you hate me. I can't have that again. I'll wait until you're sure you want it, that you want me. Until then? I'll just suffer." He dropped his gaze, but the folds of my skirt hid the way my fingers teased my slit. "Fuck, am I suffering... This is why I don't usually do noble, because it's unpleasant. A hedonist like myself prefers enjoying life to the fullest."

"So why are you resisting?"

He lifted his gaze to mine, staring into my eyes in a way that shook loose my thoughts, that felt far more personal than the intimate way we sat, than anything else we'd done. "Because you're about the only thing in the world worth doing this right for."

And just like that, the asshole got me off with that declaration like I was some love-struck virgin.

This really is sad.

* * * *

Why was dressing in front of someone so much more embarrassing than undressing? I could strip down and not think twice about it, but somehow, standing here, in the center of the hotel room, putting my skirt back on felt like being on full display.

Kelvin made it no easier, sitting in the chair in front of the desk, staring right at me.

"We don't have to meet at places like this." He gestured at the hotel room.

"What? You think I'm going to invite you over to my house like some guest?"

He didn't react, and that made me feel worse. Had he pretended to be hurt, it would have been a sign the words hadn't hit. Him not snarking back suggested they'd stung.

"You could come to my place."

"Thanks, but I'll pass. My last time at your place wasn't that pleasant." I recalled staying there, with him, after I'd gotten framed for a murder I for sure didn't commit. It hadn't been a good time.

He pressed his lips together, then sighed. "I could rent a place, if you'd prefer."

The idea had me shaking my head. My headache and body pains had disappeared since Kelvin's bite, but the muscles in the back of my neck tightened, suggesting one was still coming.

"You want to play house?"

"It doesn't have to be playing house."

"It would be, though. We aren't anything like that."

"Why can't we be? I know you're angry still. I know you aren't happy about how things have gone, but can't we get past that? I've come to help you every time you've called for months, but you still can't even consider something more between us?" He stared straight at me, not breaking eye contact, not giving me a moment of space to think.

And it was *far* more terrifying than had he snarled and shown his fangs. Kelvin mad—that I could take. I could handle him yelling and cursing at me, wouldn't so much as flinch at that.

This, though? A moment of him being so fucking vulnerable?

Fuck this.

He let out a broken laugh, one dark and desperate. "I guess I put myself in this position. This is the finding out after fucking around, isn't it?" He got to his feet, then went to the closet and took out his jacket, sliding it on and buttoning the front.

"That's it?"

"I've waited this long. I have little choice but to continue until you understand. Are you ready to go?"

"I don't need an escort."

"I've never been much of a gentleman, but I'm not about to let you walk alone out of a hotel room that we used together."

And fuck, how was I supposed to argue with that?

I didn't have an answer, which was exactly why, fifteen minutes later, I found myself in the lobby of the hotel, Kelvin to my side.

The reason was obvious. No one came to a hotel in pairs at this hour for anything other than sex. With him all dressed in his suit, it probably appeared he was cheating on his wife, meeting some girl in the middle of the workday.

In reality, the middle of the day meant fewer chances that other vampires would see us, and this place had a good underground garage. That had been his only real requirement for the place, though he'd wanted to pick far better amenities than I did.

I would have been fine with something that charged by the hour, since I didn't plan to spend all that much time here and the ambiance didn't matter. Kelvin had fancier taste, though, so he wanted something nicer.

This place had been our compromise — something that probably didn't have bedbugs but also didn't cost a small fortune. In the end, I'd picked it, probably because Kelvin was still trying to win me over.

Good luck.

Turned out that no matter how nice someone seemed, how kind their actions, I just couldn't forget being forcefully bound to them—even if they'd done it for my own good.

My crow screeched in my head at the very reminder of the indignity. It valued freedom above all else, and Kelvin had snatched that from me, making me his thrall—or at least some twisted version of it.

It meant that even when I thought for a moment that I might be able to forgive him, that I might rethink how angry I was, that he could slip beneath my walls again, my crow reminded me, *no fucking way.*

The lobby had that old world money feel, with metal detail on the ceiling and over-the-top trim on everything. I held the key card between two fingers, then headed for the reception desk.

Somehow, checking out was always the worst part. It felt like they could see what we'd just been doing, since not many people checked out only a few hours after checking in.

Not that I cared all that much. What did it matter if they suspected we'd been having steamy, forbidden sex just before?

Jealous much?

I turned in the key, suffered through the suggestive stares—*they probably figure I'm a working girl*—then headed away from the prying eyes of the staff.

"Should we meet here next week again?"

I shook my head. "No. I'll just call you when it's time."

"Why? We end up meeting at the same time every week, anyway. It makes more sense to expect it at this point."

Except, I couldn't. Sure, I understood his reasoning, and yeah, it made more sense. If we knew we needed to see each other at this time, why not plan it ahead? It'd end up easier on us both.

I couldn't, though. "This way is better."

He sighed, the same sound as before, full of the same frustrations. "You can't even stand the idea of a planned time with me, can you? Is it me, or is it the schedule of it?" He ran his fingers through his hair, pushing the locks from his face.

It made me question, for just a moment, if he'd grow sick of this. So far, he'd focused on getting what he wanted, on winning me over, but what would happen if he changed his mind? If he decided this was too much?

I tried to picture a future where Kelvin *wasn't* there. Where I couldn't just call him up if I wanted. The truth was, if I couldn't see him, I'd suffer—not him.

It was a terrifying future I hadn't realized was possible before.

He set his hand on my cheek, his skin flushed and warm—probably from my blood. "Don't worry about that," he said, his voice sweeter than I usually heard from him, as though trying to make up for worrying me. "I'll be here no matter how long it takes."

I went to answer—though what I'd say, I had no idea—when a shout echoed through the lobby. Not a *'you cheated on me, you asshole'* yell of a woman who found her husband her with some woman, but instead one full of real fear.

I twisted to find someone barreling from the elevator just as the doors opened—a woman whose eyes were bloodshot and full of madness. Blood coated her hands and stained her shirt. She must have gotten hurt unless she was just a *really* messy eater.

Or both...

The woman was small, only an inch or two taller than me, but she rushed with the confidence of a football player going in for a tackle.

She'd have slammed right into me if not for Kelvin yanking me aside and out of the way with less than a second to spare. It left me falling against his chest.

Funny, he could have leveled the person if he wanted to, but instead chose to save me.

Probably since we were in public, and he didn't care for leaving evidence that might bite him in the ass later. It was best to keep a low profile at such times, after all. No one wanted humans getting a whiff of the real world.

The woman ran forward, toward the door, but before she reached it, a familiar figure stepped inside and before of her.

Galen.

It was hard not to notice him. Not because of his looks—he actually looked a bit like a computer nerd, someone who might get glanced over at any time. Instead, a glance at his face showed the immense power at his disposal, the incredible will of his wolf, that he became so impossible to ignore.

"Wonderful," Kelvin muttered, the word so soft that I doubted he'd intended for me to hear.

The woman skidded to a stop just before Galen, who stood as though entirely unworried. He didn't prepare for a fight, didn't appear any different from a man walking up to a stranger.

I took a step that way, wanting to warn him, but Kelvin held me tight. "Stay out of it."

Sure enough, Galen's voice rang across the lobby despite how quietly he spoke. "Stop this."

The amount of power in that voice sank into me, demanding even I obey. I rarely heard him use his powers, rarely saw this side of him. It reminded me that he did in fact rule over all the Weres in this area of the country, that he could force any of them to his will.

And the immediate reaction from the woman told me something else—she was a Were.

She dropped to her knees, tears filling her eyes, the anger draining away, fear replacing it. She sobbed out broken words and I could only catch *sorry* among them.

Galen crouched before her, balancing on the balls of his feet without effort. "You're tired, aren't you?"

She nodded.

"You knew you shouldn't run. There is no help out there, not for people like you." His words struck me as vicious, yet he said them without venom. Instead, there almost seemed a strange kindness in them, an acceptance, a truth.

"I don't want to die," she said.

"Do you want to harm others? Do you want to hurt those you care about? No? Then you know that the only place for you is in the pack."

His brows inched toward each other before he lifted his gaze, finding me so fast it felt as though he knew I was there. A new tension entered his body, different from before. He'd shown no fear or worry before, yet now? Now he seemed on edge. He moved his gaze over me—was he checking for injuries?—and when he seemed satisfied, he returned his focus to the woman.

This time when he spoke, a sharp edge rested in his words. "You could have done serious damage. This proves your lack of control, that I can't allow you to roam free."

"Not the cage," the woman pled.

He rose, then gestured toward her. For the first time, I noticed others behind him—three men in police uniforms—who came forward. Funny that he made it impossible to pay attention to anyone else. They grabbed the woman, who had started to fight, and hauled her out despite her screams. Another officer went to speak to a hotel employee, no doubt to smooth that over.

I'd known, of course, that Spirits had people in different positions of power to help keep our secret, but seeing it always unnerved me. I wasn't foolish enough to not recognize how dangerous too much power was, so the idea that we could affect law enforcement concerned me.

Galen didn't leave. He headed our way, his shoulders pulled back, his steps sure. Then again, he'd just faced off against a Were—he wasn't that worried about me, and he knew Kelvin wouldn't do anything here.

"Your strays are becoming a problem," Kelvin said, skipping pleasantries. "You should keep them on a leash."

"I'm taking care of my own. Last I heard, no Grave has gotten hurt by a stray."

"Yet that one nearly mowed over this crow, and I doubt either of us would have liked that."

Galen's nostrils flared, the only show of temper.

Leave it to Kelvin to get beneath Galen's skin.

"What was wrong with her?" I asked to derail whatever they had going on between them.

Galen turned his gaze from Kelvin and focused instead on me, his expression softening. "She's a stray. She can't control her beast, so she has to stay with the pack. She didn't listen to that and tried to run."

"She seemed afraid."

"No one likes to face reality when that reality isn't what they want and isn't likely to change." He shrugged, though a certain discomfort said he didn't like it.

Or perhaps he just didn't like *me* to see it.

"What'll happen to her?"

He didn't answer, and that sure told me the answer.

I recalled Trey, the werebear who'd had his mind ruined by a Sprit, the way that they'd expected to have to kill him. No doubt this was the same sort of situation.

A Were who couldn't control its beast was dangerous. In that state, the beast was agitated, vicious, reactive. I knew logically Weres like that couldn't be allowed to just go along as they wanted — they were far too dangerous.

Knowing something logical and accepting it was a whole different matter, though.

"You won't actually hurt her," I said with a soft laugh, as though I knew he was kidding even if he wasn't.

His gaze hardened, looking every bit the alpha he was. "If Kelvin hadn't been here, she could have hurt you. She could have slammed into you, could have taken you apart right here in the lobby."

"She wouldn't have."

"Did you see the blood on her? She injured three other people in this hotel alone, not to mention whoever else she ran into before that. She definitely could have hurt you, and that isn't something I'll allow. Don't worry about it, though, it isn't your problem." His gaze moved between Kelvin and me, a question there.

Kelvin didn't answer it and I sure didn't plan on it. Galen knew something was going on between us, but the last thing I wanted was to have to explain it.

Not only was that awkward as fuck, but it took me back to Kelvin denying me — as he always did — and how pathetically I'd begged.

Nope, that was not the sort of thing anyone else needed to know. It was humiliating enough just having Kelvin, Harrison and me know.

"When do you plan to have this situation dealt with?" Kelvin pressed.

"I'm working on it."

"Should we convene the council? If you can't deal with it on your own, I'd be happy to offer my people to clean up your mess."

I never knew that an offer of help could sound that threatening, but leave it to Kelvin to manage that little gem.

And of course, Galen took it exactly as intended. "No, thank you. I believe we can take care of it." He looked at me once more, though his expression was more guarded this time. "Call me later, Grey. I'll have to deal with this, but afterward, I'd like to see you."

I nodded, unsure what else to say. Seeing Galen wasn't uncommon, and it had been a few days. Still, agreeing with Kelvin behind me felt odd.

Especially when I drew such distinct lines with Kelvin.

Galen offered one more glare Kelvin's way before turning on his heel and walking out, not glancing back. I had to admit, he managed to look pretty bad ass...

As soon as he left, Kelvin let out a soft snort. "Well, as fun as that was, I'm afraid I need to get back. I have work to take care of."

Which, of course, reminded me that he did manage to drop everything for these little get-togethers, and I should probably be more thankful than I felt. He could have said no, after all.

So instead of causing more problems, I offered a smile. "Yeah, sure. I've got shit to do, too. Well, thanks." I took a step back, ready to bypass the whole awkward goodbye thing. A walk of shame was bad enough, but the goodbye just before was downright painful.

Before I could shuffle away, though, Kelvin caught my wrist and pulled me in close. I expected a kiss, something passionate, the way he always did. His voice reached my ear, instead. "Be careful around Galen. The Weres aren't in a good place, and their territory isn't safe."

With that, he released me and stepped away, then turned toward the elevator that went to the underground garage, his warning ringing in my ears.

The warning against the Weres didn't feel personal, not like he just hated Galen—which he did—but instead like he knew things going on that I didn't.

My phone rang, getting my attention. I pulled it from my pocket and looked at the screen to find the caller.

Porter.

I answered, wondering what weird and horrible luck had me talking to these three men one after another.

"Hello?"

"Can you meet me right now?"

So much for niceties.

I almost said no, just to play hard to get—and because it felt weird to see him while I still likely had Kelvin's scent all over me—but Porter had never reached out like this. He'd helped me when I'd needed it, but he hadn't ever been the one to make the first move. He was more aloof, less concerned with me or the rest of the real world. The curiosity was enough to get me to agree. "Sure. Where at?"

A quickie at a hotel, a feral Were, and now a druid asking for my help?

Well, wasn't today shaping up to be one weird fucking day?

Chapter Two

The oasis was impressive, really. We lived in the desert, which meant there wasn't much greenery anywhere—save for the massive golf courses that spanned far too many square miles. They served for all the green space we usually got, except for these rare patches that almost didn't make sense.

Why on earth was there an oasis here? The sign had said Big Morongo Canyon and the number of trees had impressed me, especially since more of them sat beyond the parking lot, beyond the small strip where I'd parked my car.

The high desert sat only a fifteen-minute drive away, including a road that wound through the mountains, but I rarely made the trip without reason. It always felt farther away.

If they had shaded pockets of trees like this, however, it might be worth hitting up more often.

I walked along the path—a white walkway with nice slats that lifted me up about a foot from the ground level and was probably done that way to allow animals to scurry beneath.

It didn't shock me that Porter would meet me here. It felt like a very *him* place to be, after all. In fact, seeing him in town, around others, would have felt like the strange thing.

I took the turns he'd told me to, following the path he'd explained. A right at the first turn, then follow that until just past a rusted car. It almost felt like someone pranking me as I walked through the space and headed off in search of him.

Sure enough, however, I spotted a familiar figure sitting on a bench on the side of the path, right where Porter had said he would be.

"Figured I'd find you somewhere off the path," I said, far more out of breath than I should have been.

"I don't like to disrupt things more than I have to."

"Aren't you a Nature, though? How is it disrupting?"

He patted the spot beside him and I took a seat. "Even things part of nature can leave too great an impact on the surrounding areas. This is one of my favorite spots locally, and I would hate to be the cause of issues here." He paused, then added softly, "Plus, the caretakers of this preserve watch like hawks and I don't want to piss them off."

I peered up slightly. "Is that why the no horns thing?"

"I can't have them out when I'm around humans, so I usually hide them unless on my own land or very far out."

The conversation drifted away for a moment, and I found myself loath to break the easy silence. The sounds of water running somewhere near, the buzzing of some flying insect, the occasional croak of a frog, it was all a rather nice way to spend an afternoon.

In fact, I wondered why I hadn't done this before, why I hadn't given myself the time to relax, to take a break more often, especially out here. Sure, there was a slight scent of rot—it happened when water sat still for a while, and given the lack of rain around here, it tended to do that—but it was still one of the better afternoons I'd had.

What does that say about me and my life?

"You've spoken to the Weres?" Porter asked.

And just like that, I knew my afternoon wasn't going to remain this pleasant. "Sort of."

"Then you know what's happening."

"Just because I heard something doesn't mean I know what's going on. There are more strays, right?"

Porter stared out at the tree line rather than at me, and I wondered what he saw. Was his vision better? Did his honed senses somehow draw his gaze to things that I missed? Was he looking at lots of little creatures out there? I wasn't sure, but I was rather curious about it all.

"Yes. However, the thing that the other clans seem to miss is that we are all connected in a way we don't fully understand. What befalls one spills onto the others. The Weres are suffering, but it is not confined just to the Weres."

"You've lost me."

His lips curled at the side into a slight, indulgent smile. "I've detected Were energy in a few animals."

That got my attention.

The energy in each of the clans should never cross to another clan or to animals, and it never remained in small amounts like that. If it infected a person, it took over.

"So there are Were animals?"

"No. They weren't changed, but that energy infected them like an illness. I have not yet found it in a Nature, but this is a situation that has never occurred before. There is no way it isn't connected, that it doesn't have something to do with the Were problem."

"So why haven't you told Galen?"

The expression on Porter's face implied he really would rather not do that. Or that he'd prefer to go have dental work for fun rather than talk to Galen.

Which I could understand if we were talking about Kelvin or Ruben, but Galen was almost the life of the party compared to the others. Or, rather, he was the least likely to try to kill someone.

I'd take my few wins where I could, honestly.

"Galen's looking into the Were problem. You need to ask him—he might know something."

"Have you learned nothing from your time on the council? We do not work well together. It simply isn't something that we are intended to do. We naturally repel one another, something that spawns from our very spirit energy. We can't help it, and nothing will change it."

I kicked my feet out, sighing at the speed with which they decided to give up. Weren't these supposed to be men who ruled the entire spiritual world, at least in this area? Why would they act so afraid of just a little meeting?

Babies.

"Well, I work with you all just fine and I'm a Spirit," I reminded him, as though he might have forgotten the fact.

"You are, but you are a type that we have never encountered before. You don't seem to follow the same rules as the rest of us."

"That sounds like a bullshit excuse," I snapped. "That's like when people tell artists that they're so talented but totally ignore all the work it took for them to get like that. I work with you all because I have to, because I've always had to. I never had the luxury of just sitting back and saying, 'it's too hard.'" My cheeks warmed at my little tirade.

It was the truth, though. They'd all come into this world with battle lines drawn, with allies and enemies.

Me?

I'd had nothing. I'd had to carve my own way, to figure out how to survive in a world where nothing was on my side.

So, I wasn't about to listen to Porter as he bitched and moaned about just how sad it was that he had to be here, all by himself, that working with Galen was just too much of a challenge.

Suck it up, cupcake.

"Very well," he said after a moment, giving in much faster than I would have thought. I would have complained for longer before I ever actually listened to good advice—maybe he wasn't as stubborn as I was. "Will you set up a meeting for us?"

"Me? I figured you'd go to Ruben for that."

"I prefer to stay as far away from Justices as possible." He shuddered. "They have an unnatural energy that I don't like to come into contact with. Besides, if we go through Ruben, it all becomes official information, and I suspect Galen is attempting to solve this issue on his own, without council intervention. He would likely appreciate if we spoke on our own."

* * * *

The idea was good, or so I thought until that night, when I sat down at my worn kitchen table, in my little house, with two of the most powerful Spirits drinking coffee out of my coffee cups—the ones with naked men on them.

Yeah…this wasn't how I'd thought my night would go.

The men hadn't spoken since they'd arrived. They'd both walked in without appearing nervous, but had clearly been on guard.

They weren't really supposed to be in the Null space, where my house was, but that didn't seem to matter if I invited them. So long as they didn't fight, it was seen as a necessary breach.

Which reminded me again how little the rules seemed to actually matter. I got nailed every time I even bent one, but others got to break them all they wanted and get away with it due to some loophole no one told me about.

Next time Ruben got on my case about a rule, I was going to try the same tactic to get out of trouble.

Still, the fact no one spoke made the tension thick and uncomfortable. It felt like when my parents had come over to my little one-room studio when I'd first moved out, when they'd hated it but didn't want to admit such a thing. We'd sat there with this exact silence, full of all the things they wanted to say but didn't dare.

I knew that silence, especially because I never kept what I shouldn't say to myself. I always blurted it out carelessly. It went to show that I wasn't a great example of keeping quiet, of being good, of understanding tact.

However, since that silence had never been one I liked, I broke it first. "I know my coffee is good, but could we get to the point? I want to get to sleep at some point."

Galen offered me a glare, like I'd broken some unspoken rule I didn't know about. Maybe he was trying to intimidate Porter with the silence? One look at Porter said it wouldn't work.

Still, after a moment, he sighed and set his cup down. "You asked for this meeting," Galen said.

Porter set his down as well, as though that somehow signaled something between the two of them. Maybe this was the language of men?

Fuck knew I didn't understand it.

"I've detected Were energy in a number of animals in the wilds."

The widening of Galen's eyes, just for a moment before he hid it, went to show he hadn't known and that he didn't like the news. He wiped the look away, again telling me this wouldn't be an easy conversation.

Both sides had questions and information — information that could help the other side and questions the other side could answer — but neither wanted to come out and say any of it. They didn't want to give away their advantage, to offer anything to an enemy that might use it against them.

This was why wars broke out, because people valued their stubbornness and presumed strength over the need to work shit out.

"Are you sure?" Galen asked.

"Completely. Do you have any idea how this could have happened?"

"Are Weres trying to make animals into Weres?" I asked, thinking I'd come up with a brilliant idea. Maybe Weres were trying to turn animals to make them into weird little Were pets?

Or so I thought, until the expression of *both* men said it was one of the dumbest things they'd heard.

Neither addressed me, as though I hadn't spoken at all, like that protected my ego.

It was a good guess.

"Could this be connected with the increased number of strays?" Porter asked.

Galen shot me a dirty look, as though *I'd* been at fault for blabbing. I had, but it was rude to assume. He turned his gaze back to Porter. "I don't see how it could."

"Why are there more strays? They're usually rare, are they not?"

Galen didn't shift in his seat, probably to avoid giving away his discomfort, but I knew him well enough to read him easily. He hated this conversation. "Strays have always been uncommon. Normally, new Weres are located easily by sense, and they are drawn to other Weres. Strays, however, don't have that draw. They lack the ability to control their beast, and because of that, they can't join a pack. Without any of that, they end up dangerous and typically must be put down."

"So are there more Weres being changed or are more of them changing into strays?" I asked.

Galen tapped his finger against the side of his cup. "Both, I think. In addition to the strays, some of our older Weres seem to be losing themselves and going feral. They're struggling with control. Because of that, those afflicted have started to change others more often than is typical. I don't know why. I can't explain it. I've found no evidence of drugs, of spells, of mind control. Some Weres simply seem to be losing their sense of control." Galen finished the words with a huff, a sure, rare sign of his frustration with his lack of progress.

Then again, he'd always been a type-A, take control sort of person. He was the kind who wanted to fix shit immediately. He didn't want to risk not knowing an answer, to let it stagnate.

So I had no doubt he'd already done all he could to figure out what was going on and had hit nothing but walls.

Which wasn't a good sign. If Galen couldn't discover the problem with his own wolves, what chance did we all have?

"Is there anything that links the Weres who this happened to? Is it just wolves?" I asked.

He shook his head. "No. It's all types of Weres. I haven't seen a connection between any of them yet. They're happening in equal numbers regardless of type, age, or anything else. The only difference is that it is a far higher number of brand new Weres. There have not been any changed Weres in the past three months who have changed normally. Every one of them have become strays."

I rested my chin on my palm, thinking about that, about what it could mean. Why would it be all of the new wolves? Was there a reason? "Are they all violent?"

He hesitated at that question. "They're all driven by their beasts, unable to control them." At my look of confusion, he went on. "Our beasts are animalistic. Violence is a human concept, something that comes from the choice to harm others without a reason. Animals react based on situation. So have people gotten hurt? Yes, they have, but not because the strays are targeting anyone, not because the strays are evil or plotting. They revert to their animalistic urges and drives. Loud places, busy places, shows of dominance, these all can trigger a reaction."

I nodded, sort of understanding what he meant. I recalled when Trey had been driven mad, when he'd lost himself. He hadn't hurt people just to hurt them, but he'd reacted without the logical ability to think his way through a situation.

And the idea of a whole host of Weres in that same position was absolutely terrifying. The damage they could do, the carnage...

I understood fully what Kelvin had meant, why this was such an issue.

"Do you have any such Weres for me to examine?" Porter asked.

Galen lifted one side of his lip into a snarl. "I see no reason to have a Nature in my territory."

I tossed the crumpled napkin in my hand at Galen, striking him in the temple. He would have managed to deflect it easily if he hadn't had all of his attention on Porter. It went to show he didn't view me as the threat at all. "Don't be like that."

"It's a fair point," Porter offered. "We don't like entering each other's territory when avoidable."

"Well, too bad. This is a problem that will affect us all, right? Isn't it better to combine our resources and try to figure it out together?"

And fuck had I never thought I'd be the 'let's work together' cheerleader, yet here I was.

"Fine," Galen muttered, sounding less than thrilled with the idea. "Two days from now, come to my house. I'll have a few different subjects at different points in the progression."

Porter nodded, then stood.

"Where are you going?" I asked.

"We've done what we came for. I will see you both in two nights." With that, he left, not even a goodbye.

Rude much?

Next time he came over, I'd make his coffee with salt instead of sugar as a petty payback.

When the front door closed behind him, I let out a deep breath. Dealing with them together exhausted me.

On their own they were tiring, sure, but together? It took juggling egos and I'd never been graceful enough for that bullshit.

"Sorry to drag you into this," Galen said, his voice soft, having lost the sharp edge it held during the meeting. It went to show how differently he spoke to just me, how differently he treated me.

"Sounds like it's not just a you problem," I pointed out. "And it isn't like you haven't been there for me with enough of my problems."

"The difference is that you never let me help. You never lean on me, even when I want you to."

"Well, take me to dinner when it's all worked out, okay? But be ready—I want to go to Korean barbecue and you're going to have to do all the grilling and I'm going to get the biggest, most expensive set on the menu." My stomach growled at the very thought of it.

He chuckled but made no move to get up, to leave. Instead, he seemed to settle in more. "You were at that hotel with Kelvin."

I refused to appear uncomfortable about it. We were adults, right? There was no reason for me to act like I'd done anything wrong. Consenting adults could fuck like bunnies if we wanted, and I owed him nothing.

Try as I might, however, I couldn't quite get that idea to sink in. "Yeah," I answered.

He shook his head. "I'm not trying to make you feel bad. I get the circumstances of what's happened. There are certain biological realities when it comes to vampires, to anything."

"Way to sound like an awkward father giving his teenager the sex talk."

"Well, what else do you want from me? It *is* awkward." He sighed, then went on, again softening his voice. "I'm trying to tell you that I understand, that I'm not blaming you. I don't like it, of course, but I understand why it's needed. The last thing I'd want is for you to suffer from withdrawal."

It would have been so easy to let things go there, to let him think it was that simple, but that felt dishonest. "It's not just the bond," I said.

"I know." At my lifted eyebrow, he went on. "I wish I could say that it was just a physical need, that it's nothing more than a feeding that occurs because it has to, but I know better. You've always had a connection with him beyond that. I don't like it, of course, but I accept it."

"How? How can you just accept that when you said you want me to become your mate?"

"Because I know you. You aren't the type to be tied down, not to just one person or one thing. You never have been. If I were to try it, I'd only end up hurting you."

I frowned, oddly unsettled by his statement. Was he giving up? It wasn't that I wanted him to sit there and pine over me, to keep wanting me even if I weren't available or anything.

Well, I mean, who didn't want someone else to love them unconditionally?

But that was different. I was just disappointed because despite us never really getting past the enemies-to-lovers thing—or at least annoyance-to-lovers thing—I'd always held a bit of hope that we would.

I hadn't realized that until I was faced with losing it. I'd never really considered how much I cared about Galen or how he'd spoiled me by always being there, no matter what. The idea of losing that...hurt.

"You're worrying over nothing," he pressed. "I didn't say I wasn't interested anymore, didn't say I was giving up."

"But you said—"

"That I know you won't settle down with one person, and after taking enough time to think about that, I'm okay with it."

That stopped me. Sure, Kelvin was fine with me fucking whoever, because he was a filthy pervert. Harrison had somehow seemed okay with the whole thing, probably because it was partly due to my issues with Kelvin.

But Galen?

Strait-laced, by the books Galen? He was okay with some weird harem idea? With me screwing around as I wanted? I couldn't quite figure that out, couldn't make sense of it. He was the sort to be possessive and difficult and domineering, but he was telling me he was fine with whatever this was?

I wasn't sure if I liked that or not.

It almost felt like him saying he didn't care all that much.

Which made no fucking sense, but when had I ever?

"So you're fine with anything?" I asked.

"No, not anything. I'm not a doormat, Grey. I just have come to understand that the way Weres do it isn't the only way. I trust my instinct enough when it tells me that you're it for me, that you are meant to be my mate. It wouldn't lead me wrong, after all. So beyond that, what our future looks like, that might change. It might not be exactly what I expected, what I thought it would be, and that's okay. Before I changed, I didn't expect to become a werewolf. This wasn't at all the future I saw for myself, but that doesn't mean it's wrong. It doesn't mean that this didn't work out."

I blew out a long breath. "You sure put a lot of faith in instinct."

"You learn to when you're like this, when you have an entirely different being inside you. My wolf—my beast—it isn't me. It isn't a part of me. It is a different creature who shares my skin, and instinct is one of the things that guides us both, that helps us work together. You have a different being inside you as well—your crow. You have to figure out how to coexist."

I thought again about Trey. I hadn't seen him since that night, since I'd saved him and he'd saved me and we'd somehow managed to survive it all. How was he doing? Was he still suffering?

The damage done to him had been reversed, at least some of it, but that didn't say how much of a recovery he'd make. It might not be enough, after all.

"He's doing okay."

I jerked my gaze to Galen at his very right guess. "How'd you know what I was thinking?"

"Because as much as you may hate it—I know you. Trey's doing better than expected. The damage wasn't all reversed, of course, and he still struggles with his control, but he isn't in danger of execution anymore."

"Is he back in school?"

"No. He can't stop his shifting, so even in a school with mostly Spirits, he runs the risk of having issues if he turns into a bear all of a sudden."

"They should just make him a mascot—all fixed." The joke lacked any real feeling, but that was fine. I made it more to defuse the situation, to lessen the anxiety inside of me just a bit.

And the guilt…

"He doesn't blame you," Galen tacked on, voice soft. "None of it was your fault."

"I got him targeted. If I hadn't gone to that school, if I wasn't looking for the drug dealer, they never would have done that to him." My voice cracked as I admitted it, hating the truth of the statement.

"You can't blame yourself for everything that happens. Stick to just the things you do, not the unintended consequences. If you blamed yourself for everything else, you'd never get any sleep, given what chaos you tend to have around you." His joke was no better than mine, but it somehow helped. The bit of levity eased the guilt inside me, or at least let me ignore it for a short while. I didn't have to think about what was going on, what I'd done, none of it.

He stood, then took both cups into the kitchen. The ease with which he walked around my house surprised me, but Galen seemed at ease everywhere, didn't he?

He was solid in a way few things really were. He showed up when I needed him, never backed down even when a smart man would. He'd been my first introduction to my new life, to the Spirit world, and in the years since I'd changed into what I now was, he'd never wavered in that support.

It made me wonder what my life would be like if I lost that, if I no longer had him at my back.

I couldn't fathom it, honestly. That was how important he'd become to me, how vital to my everyday life.

Which made me wonder again why I always resisted, why I pushed him away, why I fought against what seemed inevitable.

Before I could talk myself out of it, I walked up behind him as he rinsed the cups in the sink. I wrapped my arms around him, his frame leaner than one would expect from the alpha of all the Weres. I rested my forehead against his back, breathing in his clean, wild scent.

"Grey..." he said, his voice deeper than before. Every word vibrated through his back, the warning soft.

"Is this what instinct says you should do?" I whispered. "I mean, I don't have the same instinct you have, but I know what *my* passenger is saying."

The same thing my crow had said for the past five years—that Galen was dangerous as fuck but I should climb on and enjoy the ride, at least for a while.

He shuddered, then set the cups in the drying rack. With all the energy rushing through him I would have expected him to just toss them aside, shattering them if he had to. Who really cared, after all? What was some ceramic in the face of what we had both wanted for years?

He gripped my wrists.

This was it. Would he turn us both and plant my ass up on the counter? Fuck me here in the kitchen?

In front of my precious dishes?

Sounded like a good end to a weird day to me!

Except he pulled my arm away from him, didn't grab me again. He moved out of my grasp. "I should get going."

Wait...what?

For a moment I wondered if this was some kinky game, then I remembered this was Galen we were talking about. I was pretty sure the idea of kink might just make him faint.

"You don't have to," I said, trying to press, to play coy but also make it clear that I was being extremely easy at the moment.

"Yeah, I think it's best."

Shot down.

That was embarrassing, really, a rejection that final, that sure. The only thing worse would be if he took a look at my naked body and then noped out.

Was it because of Kelvin? Because of earlier?

I'd showered!

I managed to keep my mouth shut and not blurt that out, since I doubted it would help my case at all. Galen wanted to leave instead of sleeping with me, and no matter how little I liked that, I had to accept it.

So I plastered on a smile to hide the cracks in my confidence. "Sure. It's been a long day. Guess I'll see you in two days."

He nodded, took a step toward me, then paused and shook his head. "Sleep well," he offered in a rush before leaving just as Porter had.

It left me there, alone in the house, wondering just what the hell had happened.

Was I losing my touch? I scratched my head and figured that there was nothing I could do to work it out right now. It wasn't like I could control how he felt, what he wanted and what he didn't.

Was it annoying and confusing? Fuck, yes, it was. I had no idea how he could tell me he wanted me even if we weren't exclusive, that I was end game for him, then turn me down when I was actually finally offering myself to him?

I huffed out an exasperated breath then headed up to bed.

The truth was, I doubted I'd *ever* really understand men. There was no reason to let that get to me now.

A good night's sleep could fix almost anything.

* * * *

Galen

You idiot. I rested my forehead against the wheel of my truck, having parked about a block away after leaving. Dragging myself out of Grey's house had been one of the hardest things I'd ever managed to do. Everything inside of me had demanded I stay, that I get closer, that I cover her in *my* scent.

I'd told her I was fine with not having her all to myself, and I had meant it, but that didn't erase the need to possess her, to ensure she was actually mine.

A deep growl filled the cab of the truck, low and dangerous.

Stop it!

I wrestled with my beast, with the prowling wolf inside me that scratched at the inside of my body, that wanted out, wanted at Grey. I'd protected her from it — from me — for five years now, ever since I first saw her and knew immediately that she was mine, that I had to have her no matter the cost.

And I'd spent the five years since trying to protect her — from a world determined to hurt her and her determined to destroy herself.

Here we were, and she *finally* gave me a chance to move beyond where we'd always been, and what did I do?

Run away.

I curled my hand into a fist and slammed it against the center console, the plastic giving instantly. That was the risk with Weres, and the reason so many of the stronger types drove such beater cars. We tended to lose our tempers often.

Not me, though. Never me. I had always been careful to keep control, to never allow myself to get out of hand. The risk was too great for that to happen, and I didn't want to risk those around me.

However, something about Grey had always spoken to my beast in an uncomfortable way. It wasn't easy, didn't calm me. If anything, it served the opposite. It riled me, made me want to possess her at any risk, no matter the consequences.

And as tempting as it might have been to fall into that, to just allow myself to get carried away by that feeling, I couldn't.

So I'd left even when I hadn't wanted to, had walked away even when everything inside me had screamed to grab her and not let go.

But I couldn't risk her.

No matter what I wanted or how badly, I couldn't risk her seeing this, or what might happen if I truly lost myself. So instead, I'd ran. That hurt expression plagued me, reminded me that even if she had the mouth of a pissed-off mechanic and the right hook of a bar fighter, she was still someone who could get her feelings hurt.

And I was probably one of the few who could do that to her.

Better a bit of pain now, though, than worse later. Better for me to upset her now than have her end up six feet under later.

So even though everything inside of me wanted to go back to her, even though my instinct screamed in my head, I pressed my foot down on the gas and guided the truck away from her house, back toward my own.

I needed to figure this out before it ended up doing some real harm, before I risked Grey with it. I'd done things I wasn't proud of, had made plenty of mistakes, but I refused to think that seriously hurting Grey could ever be one of them.

No matter what, I had to find a cure and protect her.

Chapter Three

I twisted my hand to open the portal that gave me access to the delivery bay. It felt strange and yet familiar, something I'd done for so many years but had rarely used recently.

I had to admit, it felt good.

Did I love being a delivery girl? No, I really didn't. It hadn't been my dream growing up as a child to turn into a package bitch for supernaturals, but I doubted many people became what they wanted.

Well, Tony Lutes had said he'd be a gynecologist when he was twelve, and fuck if that boy didn't end up there. I knew because he'd been on the other side of the stirrups during one awkward checkup one year. Judging from the way he'd dragged himself around, however, I didn't think it had gone the way he'd hoped. Instead of being bright eyed and excited about the daily new serving of vagina, he'd looked like a man who had lost the mystery and magic of the world.

Maybe that was some sort of lesson about being careful what you wish for?

Whatever the reasoning, I sure hadn't seen this as my future, but at least I understood it.

"Is that it?" the vampire asked, hardly restrained distaste saturating the sharp words.

"That's it." I handed off the small envelope to them, long past worrying about what was inside it.

I delivered a multitude of things, after all. Sometimes they were personal letters, trade agreements, courting requests. I'd once delivered a live squirrel. That had been strange, and I'd nearly kept the thing because I rather liked it.

So long as it wasn't a murder weapon, I really didn't care, and I only cared about *that* if I got blamed for it.

The vampire turned on her heel and walked away as though I weren't of any interest any longer. I doubted I'd ever been that interesting, though.

At best, most of the Spirits saw me as a curiosity, something worthy of a side-show and little else.

Since gaining my seat on the council, of course, that had changed a bit. I got more side-eyes. They now saw me as a slightly more interesting freak, but little else.

It was weird, really. In some ways, I was on par with Kelvin, with Galen, with Porter. I was the head of a clan, after all, with my own lovely little seat at that weird-ass table. However, once you moved past the fancy title, the rest of it?

I had no power, wasn't super-strong, not scary, no army at my disposal. I still barely made rent most months, so what exactly did I have to show for any of it?

Without an answer, I could only sigh and glance down at my forearm. No more deliveries assigned to me for the day. It left me with the rest of the day free, something I could probably use. Fuck knew that all my time tended to get taken up by Kelvin or Galen or some other emergency.

In fact, I wondered if I'd had a real break since I'd almost gotten executed for murder.

My phone rang, earning me the immediate glares from others in the room. Vampires didn't tend to like cell phones that much—Kelvin being an obvious exception—and apparently one ringing in the center of their precious central space was just unacceptable.

I smiled as though I had no idea they were mad, then looked down to see who called.

The moment I did, I answered. It didn't matter what was going on in my life, how much it all went to shit—when my mom called, I fucking answered.

"Hey, Mom," I said as though I were in the library instead in the middle of a room full of vampires—glaring vampires.

"Hey, honey. Are you coming?"

"Of course I am! Where?"

She sighed—the universal sound of a mother so over their child's shit. She managed to do that still, after all these years, as though it were going to make a bit of difference.

It hadn't in high school, I doubted it would do anything now. This was when old dog and new tricks came into play.

Still, bless her heart for never giving up on me and always trying.

"Saturday, we're having dinner here."

"Right. Saturday. And today is…"

"Thursday."

I nodded as though all the pieces were falling into place finally. I was going to Galen's tomorrow, Friday, which meant I'd be dead or free come Saturday. "Right. Then yes, I'll be there."

"You should bring someone."

"Someone?" I paused and thought about my options.

Galen? He was probably the easiest to pass off as a respectable boyfriend, but if I let him get anywhere near my mom, he'd just join in with her to lecture me more. I didn't need that shit.

Kelvin had already met her, but I had somehow managed to survive that awkward evening. I didn't need another.

Porter would probably laugh at me if I invited him. I didn't see him as a real 'go with' who'd attend just because I asked.

What other options did I have? Harrison still didn't answer calls from me, so there went that one.

Ruben?

I choked on the very idea. I was pretty sure he hated me most of the time, and when he didn't? No thanks. If I brought him, he'd probably just tell me about how dangerous it was to expose humans to the Spirit world. No doubt he thought that cutting them off would be the best, safest option for all involved.

If we got past that, he'd just tell my mom what a horrible employee I was.

"We'll see," I answered, unwilling to outright tell her no but having absolutely no intention to just gather people who I hardly got along with at the best of times to join me at some family get together.

They didn't need my fuck buddies crashing the party.

My brother was still pissed about the whole *bringing a Mind into his urgent care* thing. I'd dodged his calls best I could, pretending I was just super busy instead of having to have any more talks with him. I imagined that hauling in any of those other folks would only make him worry all the more.

"Okay," she said, her tone one of thinking I'd still do as she wanted even if I fought it a bit. That was usually her way, though.

She told me what I should do then waited for me to learn the lesson all on my own. She was there to help me, don't get me wrong. She was there to support me when I inevitably fell on my face with the first attempt, but still, it was nice to know she'd at least help me up afterward.

I finished the call and hung up, only to find even more people glaring at me. It seemed taking a call in their lobby was something they absolutely couldn't accept.

In fact, I even got a look from a few thralls that seems to imply they struggled to believe I'd be that stupid — or still alive.

Then again, if they only knew how many stupid things I'd survived, I figured they'd be mighty impressed by it all.

Really, I was most of the time.

I slid my phone back into the pack of my jeans and went a step further than the smile to actually wave at all the disapproving glances.

I wondered if word of this would get to Kelvin. Maybe they'd call and complain to Ruben? Who knew? It felt like a win either way. Some pathetic little part of me that had never grown past being a kid who thought all attention was good attention reveled in the idea of being a problem.

And my passenger — that crow spirit that was full of mischief and chaos — enjoyed it far too much as well.

I strolled out of the lobby of the ground floor, the place where I'd waited for the receiver of the letter to meet me, and onto the street. The sun had just started to dip behind the mountains, and I had no more deliveries for the day, which meant it sounded like a fantastic night to take myself out for a good meal.

* * * *

Chalk this up as one of the few good choices I'd made in my life. The large platter of nachos — piled high with cheese, carne asada and more toppings than I could count — smelled beyond fantastic.

I'd nursed it — along with what could have passed as a fishbowl of margarita — for an hour and it hardly looked as though I'd made a dent in either.

Music poured through the restaurant, a bit too loud to allow for much conversation, but seeing as I was flying solo, I didn't mind that a bit. It overshadowed everything else — the sizzle of foods in the kitchen, the laughter from the drunk college girls a few tables away, the fighting from the old married couple behind me. Those things drifted away so I could only hear the music, like some ambient noise that drowned out the rest of the room.

I popped another chip into my mouth, a thick piece of carne asada on top, and held back a moan at the taste. There was something about Mexican food that just soothed the soul, that made me think everything would turn out okay.

The server stopped by and replaced the small empty bowl with another full of salsa without a word. He kept a close eye on the table, quick to grab anything I needed.

Then again, I came here pretty often. It wasn't on the strip, and tourists usually didn't venture quite this far outside of the happening areas. That meant the prices were lower, the building less busy and rideshares didn't have to fight with valets in order to pick me up at the end of the night.

All in all?

It was a favorite of mine, and the servers knew me well enough that they were always nice to me.

Well, almost always. The time I got into a fight with a guy at his bachelor party had ended with them banning me for a week.

Fuck, had I missed their food...I could have starved!

"A pretty girl like you shouldn't eat alone." The cheesy pickup line might have made me roll my eyes, but when I peered across the table to find a man who was hot enough for me to pretend it had been a *good* pickup line, I lifted an eyebrow.

"How do you know I'm not waiting for someone?"

"Because I can tell. If you were waiting for someone, you'd be looking at the door every time it opened. You just keep staring at your food or drink, so you don't expect anyone to show up." He sat across from me in the booth without asking.

"Maybe I just like eating alone."

"Again, you'd look happier if that was true." He sat back in the seat, his gaze unnerving.

He was tall, but narrower than many of the men I dealt with. He wore a polo shirt, the buttons undone at the collar to show off a little bit of chest. His eyes were dark, intense, and they made me uneasy. It felt like he clearly was hiding something, something I didn't want anything to do with.

Yet, for a reason I couldn't understand, I struggled to tell him to get the fuck away.

Why?

Maybe it was because everything else in my life was such a mess, why not add a little more?

It was like having your phone fall to the floor, then deciding to pick it up and throw it against the wall. It made no sense, but people still did it.

And I still sat here across from this asshole. "What's your name?"

He smirked as though he'd just won something. Maybe he had — who fucking knew? "Ergon."

"That's a weird fucking name."

"What's yours?"

"Grey." As soon as it came out of my mouth, I winced. Maybe Grey wasn't that usual, either. Who was I to talk crap about anyone's name? "What are you doing here? Other than picking up girls who aren't interested?"

He chuckled. "You're feisty, aren't you? I tend to like that, personally. It's so much more fun than women who are dull. There's nothing worse than a woman who is as entertaining as drying paint. I get bored easily, you see, but I could tell with one look at you that you weren't boring."

"Right, because a girl stuffing her face with nachos is exactly what any man is looking for." As soon as I uttered that, it made me stop.

If that was what he was looking for, he had to be a freak, right? What was he, someone with a feeder fetish? Because while every woman dreamed at some point of getting fed grapes by some super-hot shirtless man, it had been a long time since my fantasies had gone in that direction.

I tended to have more weird fantasies now. Like getting abducted and the kidnapper ending up being super attractive, or my tax accountant having to deduct my pants one year. Maybe it was a sign of my damaged psyche. My point was that I certainly wasn't into someone who liked to watch me eat.

That was too freaky for even me.

I went to stand, but realized the ground was moving around me. A glance at the margarita revealed I'd drunk much more of it than I'd thought, with the drink almost entirely gone. That accounted for the spinning room.

Except, Ergon didn't spin. He stayed right there, staring at me the whole time, like reality twisted around him.

Be careful, little crow.

The words echoed around in my skull, and I scratched my ear as though to dislodge it. Knot had been missing in action for a while now, so I didn't need echoes of his words, especially as a drunken hallucination. I'd prefer that if he had something to say, he'd come right out and say it. That would have been the polite thing to do.

"You don't know your own limits, do you?" Ergon said and somehow was beside me so fast, it was like he didn't even move. He slid an arm around my side, holding me up, keeping me from collapsing to the floor.

He was larger than me, and he held my body easily, trapping me against his side.

"I need to pay." The words came out slurred, unclear. How had the alcohol hit me so fast?

It wasn't that I wouldn't get drunk—my many *many* antics before proved that to be a lie. It was just that I usually saw it coming. I'd eaten, too, so why the hell was I this out of it?

He reached into his pocket and took out a stack of bills. Anyone keeping that much cash on them was bad news, and as a former drug dealer to school children, I knew bad news. He tossed a few hundreds onto the table, more than enough for the cost of the meal and a good tip.

At least the servers wouldn't get mad at me.

I leaned over for my bag, and only his hand on my waist kept me on my feet.

"Let's go," he said, guiding me toward the front door.

I shouldn't go.

It wasn't just Knot's voice in my head, but also my mother's, and every true crime video I'd ever watched. This was an absolutely horrible idea. I should not head out to fuck knew where with some asshole who I'd just met.

However, no matter how good that advice seemed, it couldn't gain any footing. I couldn't stop myself from following his lead, from heading out into the cool evening.

I should have called a rideshare — that had been my original plan. Doing so didn't occur to me as he guided me toward a waiting sports car, the sort that sat so low to the ground it was like an acrobatic trick to get me inside of it.

Getting in was the last thing I remembered, too. I didn't even recall the door shutting, the car starting, none of that.

It was like the world had grown fuzzier and fuzzier up to that moment, then disappeared to nothing right afterward.

When I opened my eyes again, when my brain jumpstarted back to working — at least as much as it ever did — I found myself... in my bed?

I patted to the side, looking for Ergon.

Nothing.

I forced myself to sit up despite the pounding headache, my dry throat. While I hurt quite a bit, I didn't ache in those specific spots that implied anything had happened.

I wore the same clothes from the night before, none of them askew. I didn't feel sore anywhere, no signs of hickies or evidence that he'd done anything.

So he'd just taken me home?

That didn't sit right at all. I was too smart to believe in there being people who were kind just to be kind, who looked out for others just because it was the right thing to do. That was like a fairy tale, and I didn't put stock in those anymore.

I looked around, the sun having risen to midday, telling me I'd slept in late, and I couldn't work out exactly what had happened.

If I was fine now, though, it couldn't have been that bad...right?

Except, no matter how much I told myself that, how much I wanted to believe it, some little part of me just refused.

I had a feeling that Ergon would come back to bite me in the ass, even if he hadn't done that last night.

Chapter Four

Galen's house felt as it always did, something that reassured me. This had been the first place I'd gone when I'd really known what I was, after I'd changed, when everything had been so difficult and confusing. Back then, I hadn't understood what about me was different—besides the fact I could turn into a crow—but the entire world had turned scary and larger and much more dangerous than it had been before.

And life had never been safe for me. That was for sure...

Galen had brought me here, assuming that the whole turning into a bird thing had pegged me as a were. He'd protected me, letting me rest in this home.

It still gave me some of those warm, fuzzy feelings, even after five years.

I didn't bother to knock—I never had with him—and instead strolled into the house.

"You're late." The unhappy voice came from Galen, who stood, tapping his foot like an angry wife, while

Porter ran his finger across the spines of the books on a large shelf against the wall.

"Looks like you did just fine on your own." And, to be honest, I hadn't wanted to come at all.

I'd seen a stray that first night, when it had attacked, when only Galen's intervention had saved me. I saw no good reason to purposely get close to another one.

However, it seemed these two felt that any third party — *even me* — would ease the tension.

The things I did to avoid an all-out war...

"Basement, I'm guessing?"

Galen nodded. "We have three different subjects, all of them scheduled for execution. One is a wolf — newly changed. They were picked up only two days ago and had to have been changed only a week or less before that. We have a panther who had good control for a few years before this happened. They seemed unable to control their beast one morning. Lastly, we have a raven who is at least three hundred years old. Again, they've never struggled with control before, with resisting urges. I chose these three cases as they are all so different. All came from the California/Nevada/Arizona region, so we could get them here sooner. No connections that I could find between them."

The raven caught my attention.

There were no werecrows, that much I knew. I'd asked Galen about it before, wishing that I could find others even a little like me. It might not be perfect, might not be exact, but a black bird was a black bird, right?

I tried to hold off on my excitement, to not let it show. I didn't need them to realize how much that meant to me. For one, they'd only make fun of me.

Neither of them understood just how isolating and lonely it really was to not have others of my kind, to not have anyone who understood me.

I had Knot, but he wasn't any help. He disappeared whenever he wanted—as he'd done since that last cryptic meeting we'd had—and he never made me feel less lonely. If anything, he annoyed me, since I was desperate for answers and connection where he seemed to hate both.

Galen lifted one of his eyebrows, telling me he'd caught my excitement. He'd explained to me before, after realizing I was from an entirely different clan, that I'd have nothing more in common with any were bird than I would with any bird from nature. I'd never cared to listen to good advice, though, so I smiled at him as though to tell him I'd be happy if I fucking wanted to be.

He let out an audible sigh before walking toward the basement. I let him go first because I wasn't anywhere close to equipped to deal with strays. If they'd broken out or were feeling especially hungry, I'd much rather they run into Galen first.

We headed down the stairs, a slight anxiety eating at me from the last time I'd been here. I'd had a crazed werebear threaten me—and not just a little, 'hey, maybe I'd like to kill you' sort of threat, but the kind where he'd grabbed me and could have done exactly that.

So I wasn't a fan of what we might find down here— black bird or not.

"You know," I said, the words escaping me faster than my brain could keep up just to break those nerves inside of me. "You bring a lot of people to your dungeon basement. I never figured you were a kinky type. A basement dungeon would be something I'd expect from Kelvin, not you."

"Do I really have to listen to kink talk?" The rough voice came from the dimness just past the light that spilled in from the stairwell. It sounded like a dry throat, one that hadn't had their thirst quenched in days.

Which made me wonder if Galen was starving these Weres? He didn't seem unnecessarily cruel type, but it was hard to be sure about anything anymore.

People constantly surprised me, and rarely in a good way.

We reached the bottom of the stairs and the person who spoke became clear. Thankfully, the cell looked less horrible than it had when Trey was here, back when he'd been so crazed that no furniture would survive. Instead, all the cells had blankets, mattresses on platform stands—probably so they couldn't pick them up and throw them. It wasn't that cold down here, either, which suggested that Galen had it heated.

A bottle of water sat inside the cell, beside the woman who had spoken. She had a pixie cut and oddly wide eyes, with freckles that spanned her cheeks. She was pretty in a strange, ethereal way. "Since I don't think I get to participate, I'd rather you didn't talk about such things," she added, seated on the mattress, her legs stretched out.

"Is she not drinking water?"

Galen rubbed the back of his neck. "She is, but she roars so much that it strains her vocal cords." Galen stopped in the center of the room, then pointed to each cell.

The pixie cut was the panther it seemed—I wasn't sure if that was any more fitting—an older woman was the wolf, and that made the raven the young man who sat cross-legged on his bed, eyes closed.

It was strange to be reminded again that the age people appeared had nothing to do with their actual age. It was a lesson I struggled to learn time and time again. I still found myself surprised each time I spoke to some who looked young enough to possibly still need to ride in the back seat of a car only to discover they were hundreds of years old.

I doubted it would ever feel quite natural.

And, given they were Weres, all of them were significantly stronger than me.

Annoying.

Porter walked first to the older woman, suggesting he probably wanted to check on them in order. He said nothing, as though they were beneath him or not worth his time.

Or, more likely, he only spoke to people whom he deemed he had something to say to. It was less about respect and more about efficiency.

He set a hand out, palm flat and toward the woman. Nothing shot from hand—no cool colors or flames—but a strange sensation moved through the air, as though sparks of electricity ran through it. I shivered.

Porter had used little power in front of me. He'd freed the wolves Kelvin kept at his property, but that was it. Other than that, a part of me wondered why he was head of their clan. It didn't make a lot of sense, all things considered. He didn't seem anywhere near as powerful as the others.

Then again, neither did I.

This reminded me yet again not to judge people by what little they chose to show me.

The woman didn't react with more than a low growl, a warning as though she felt the intrusion and didn't care for it, but neither did she find it overtly threatening.

Porter shook his had, like clearing something from it, then moved onto the panther woman with the pixie cut. He repeated the action, though she snarled a bit louder. Why? Was she more sensitive to it, or did it hurt in a way it hadn't with the first?

We all stayed silent as he finished and moved to the last—the wereraven. The boy didn't so much as open his eyes or acknowledge the strange probe, but his body did tighten, like tension held it that he didn't want to admit.

When Porter finished there, his hand dropped, less controlled than the others. Had it taken more out of him this time?

He shook both hands, the action almost cute. "I've gotten when I can from them."

"Any ideas?"

"It is the same energy I found in the animals."

"I thought you already knew that?" I pointed out.

"All energy feels different. It's how Spirits are made, after all, from energy derived from those clans. However, this energy is Were but feels...wrong. It's thicker, like it's coagulated. It doesn't flow easily as it should. It has a scent to it that's almost like rotting."

"So something is wrong with their Spirit energy?" Galen asked.

"That is all that makes sense to me. I can't explain why it is like that, what has caused it to become so, but I can only say what it feels like. I have never experienced something like this before."

The raven in the cell laughed, the first time he'd broken the silence. "The young always forget too soon."

Talk about freaky...

The words in a thick Louisianan accent took me off guard, reminded me that he wasn't anything like what he seemed. It felt as though it had come straight out of some old Cajun swamp somewhere. He was at least a few hundred years old, and when beings got that old, it became difficult to tell for sure.

Just like humans, they liked to lie about their ages.

"What do you mean?" I asked, coming closer to his cell.

He opened his eyes, then narrowed them. "You smell wrong."

"Rude to say, but okay."

"She isn't a were," Galen explained.

"Obviously. Only a fool would confuse her for a were."

"You know, you're not great at making new friends. Or keeping old ones, I bet." I crouched down to look him in the eye, hoping that might make the conversation a little easier. The way he stared back at me didn't suggest it would, however.

"What did you mean about what we've forgotten?"

"Thick energy isn't new."

"I've never felt it," Porter said, not like an argument but rather as though he needed to understand.

Again, the raven laughed, the sound lacking kindness. "Because the young always think what they see now is how it has always been. Their memories are too short. I recall, a very long time ago, that same thick energy. It coursed through the bodies of Spirits who fell sick, who struggled to survive day by day. They were dragons."

"Dragons don't exist," I pointed out. "I know this because I wanted one, but Galen told me they weren't real."

A sharp look from Galen suggested I hadn't helped our cause at all with that one.

"They don't exist — now. They did, however, and for a long time they held power. There were never many of them, so they were rare, but they still existed, still had a place in our world."

"Had? So what happened?" Porter asked, keeping us on track.

"The same thing that happens to all Spirits who have that illness. They died."

"There's no cure?" Galen broke in. "No way to save those who catch it? How does it infect others? How do we keep it from spreading?"

The raven shook his head, an unnerving smile on his lips. "You don't understand. This isn't an infection of the body, of the individual. You can't stop it because it doesn't spread, at least not the way you expect. It is an infection of the source energy, the Spirit energy that makes you a were. I've seen three clans fall to this in the past, and each time, it wiped out the entire clan until there was nothing left of them."

I struggled to remain crouched, to not lose my balance as his words hit me, as the reality and gravity of what he'd said became clear.

Worse, he didn't look all that upset over it. "You know that includes you, too," I pointed out. Perhaps that was cruel, but the way he so easily accepted death pissed me off.

"Of course I know. I've been alive long enough to see exactly what happens to Spirits, what we do to others, to each other. I remember a dragon I took care of in his last days, the way he writhed in pain, consumed by it. He asked if this was a punishment, if it was the gods telling us we'd committed some unforgivable sin. I assured him no, that wasn't it. We weren't forsaken — that was unthinkable. Now that I feel it, though, now that I can't grasp the control I used to have, now that the energy churns through me so slowly, sloshing around like milk left out to curdle, I wonder if he wasn't right. Did we anger the gods? Did they turn their backs on us? All I know for sure is that I have seen this happen before, and I have never seen it solved or stopped. You should ready yourselves, because soon the council will lose another clan."

Chapter Five

I wanted to kill him.

Sure, I had that feeling a lot, a general desire to rid myself of annoyances that bothered me, but it was usually less intense.

With Knot, though, I had no question, especially after he'd yet again pulled me through my dream to somewhere.

I wanted him gone. Out of my life, out of my head, out of this entire universe.

"You shouldn't frown like that," he said.

"Why, wrinkles?"

"No. I have a thing for wrinkles, actually. What can I say? Older women are hot. It just scrunches up your eyes and makes it harder to see dangers."

Just as he told me that, my foot caught an uneven piece of sidewalk and I pitched forward. I'd have hit the ground if not for Knot grabbing me in an easy grip, pulling me against him to save me.

Fine, that was impressive.

He smirked, telling me he knew it, damn it. If anyone didn't need their ego stroked, it was this asshole.

"Last time I saw you, you were running like something was after you."

"Something's always after me. If I stopped living just because of that, I'd never get anything done."

"You get things done?" I pulled away from him to stand on my own.

"Of course, important things." He tucked his hands into his pockets as we walked side by side.

Where were we? Everyone spoke English around us, which made it a rare visit. Knot tended to pick other counties, but the accents told me it was somewhere in America. A long street was in the center of the town, and people wore cowboy hats. That gave me some suspicions.

Then I spotted the thing that nailed in where we were. A large pen of longhorns sat at the end of the street, and I recalled the cattle drives down in Texas. Where was it?

"Dallas Forth Worth," Knot said. "I like to eat barbecue here."

"That seems a bit rude, don't you think? I mean, you sit here and eat cow in front of cows?"

Knot bumped his arm against mine. "You know, I find it so charming how naïve you can be. It's cute and rare, especially after everything you've been through. Come on, let's go to this place I know. They put the food on a huge tray and you'll have never tasted anything so good."

As twisted as it might have been, I had to admit, the food *was* good. I wasn't sure how I could even taste it, given I wasn't actually here.

Not that that mattered to Knot. He'd asked for a table for two, despite the way the server had given him a strange look and asked if the other person was coming.

Knot had smiled and not addressed the question, as though it hadn't mattered. He'd ordered two meals, two drinks, all of it. I'd been able to interact with the items, but no one seemed to notice, which made me suspect the food wasn't floating in the air.

In short?

I was again made aware of the fact that while I still wasn't sure who or what Knot actually was, he sure as fuck was powerful.

Is he a god?

The idea hit me from time to time, but I just couldn't accept it. It didn't seem possible. The idea of gods walking among us was strange enough, but this was Knot we were talking about. He hardly seemed competent enough to be considered one.

And I still hadn't accepted the idea that gods were a thing. People made their own stories up, promoted powerful creatures to godhood in their myths to make sense of the world.

People had done it with vampires and werewolves, in fact, had elevated them and worshipped them. I could only assume Knot—and anything else someone called a god—was the same sort of thing.

"You were right," I admitted about halfway through the quiet meal. "It is good. I don't love eating it while we watch all the steers walk by, but still. It's good."

He smiled and popped one of the delicious little deep fried cheese curds into his mouth. "You seem stressed. I'd ask if you were having more problems, but you're *always* having problems."

"Thanks to you, I'm always having problems."

"You like to pout and blame me, but you were chaotic well before I ever interacted with you. If you weren't, I wouldn't be that interested in you. So, tell me, what's going on this time?"

I blew out a long breath and sat back. "Have you heard about the issues with the Weres?"

"Weres? No. I try to avoid Spirits whenever possible. Are they peeing on the floor or something?"

His joke would have amused me at another time—I might have even made it myself—but I didn't feel all that joking after what the wereraven had said. "Their energy is thickening. That's what Porter said."

"Porter?" He frowned, then groans. "Oh, that's the Nature, right? With the horns? Yeah, I wouldn't trust him normally, but he's probably right."

"So you do know what's going on?" I sat up straighter, hopeful. Knot was clearly well connected, so if he had an idea of what had happened, what was going on, maybe he knew how to stop it?

"It's not your problem," he hedged and waved his hand. "Why do you keep sticking your nose into things that don't affect you?"

"Um, the first incident was when I was framed for murder and the second was after I got attacked by a drugged-up mind. I am pretty sure they both affected me."

He sighed—loudly. "No, they might have affected you for a moment, but that didn't mean you needed to dive into them or fix them. You risked your life both times, nearly got yourself killed. That was all unnecessary. You did those things because you couldn't help it, because you have an affliction I have never been able to cure you of."

"And what exactly is that?"

"Empathy." He screwed up his face and shuddered as he said it, like he was diagnosing me with leprosy or something.

"Oh the horror," I deadpanned.

"It really is. You have no idea, because you're still young and stupid."

"Someone else just called me young and naïve. I think I like that one better."

"That's probably because *they* were young and stupid. If they weren't, they know that all young people are stupid. That all young people think the world is whatever they want to think it is instead of the truth. That's just reality. That's how it works. As you get older, you recognize how little anyone else cares about you, about what you're doing, so trying to do shit for them will only destroy you." His little tirade might have seemed convincing, at least at first, but the reality was that I could *hear* the way it bothered him, the way he seemed to break slightly near the end, with what could almost be considered an emotion leaking through.

"I can't just ignore this," I told him, choosing honesty for a rare time. Besides, I had a feeling he already suspected as much.

"You *can.* You just don't want to."

"Fine, I refuse to."

"Is it because you love that wolf or something?" He asked as if it weren't possible, like the very idea were entirely absurd. Made sense, though. If he didn't think much about caring for people, he would really be put off by love.

I wanted to say no, to tell him that there was no chance that I actually loved Galen. He was frustrating and he lectured me and he was a constant thorn for me.

The desire to say that he was just comfortable, that he felt safe just because he introduced me to this world, because he'd been an ally from the start tempted me.

I doubted the truth of those words, though.

I thought about my draw to Galen, about the way we orbited each other, how he watched out for me, risked himself even when he had no logical reason to do so.

Fuck. Was that love?

I dropped my gaze, unwilling to admit or deny the allegation, unsure of the answer myself. "Just tell me what you know," I said.

"What I know is that this has happened before and it'll happen again. It's the natural life cycle of Spirits. Clans come into existence and they disappear. There's no reason to fight against it—you won't win."

"So it's *never* been stopped before?"

He shifted in his seat, his expression telling despite his smile. It seemed I'd gotten to know him well enough to read even his subtle changes. "It has, but always at a cost most regret paying. And it's failed far more than it's ever succeeded."

And that was *exactly* what I needed. Just a little hope, just a little direction, anything to give me a push of what I needed to do. "How did they do it?"

He shook his head. "I'm not about to tell you that. You get into trouble all on your own, but don't think that means I'm going to just hand you to loaded gun so you can shoot yourself with it. Drop this one, Little Crow, it isn't worth it."

"You don't get to decide if it's worth it or not."

"Of course I do, since I'm the one with the information. This is a suicide mission and I won't let it go, won't just accept that you're going to do it. I worry that I've spoiled you too much over the years, that I've given you too much leash. I've had to watch you strangle yourself more than enough already."

Was he...mad? It was a strange sight, something I rarely saw from him. He seemed as though he didn't care about anything, yet cracks had been forming in that façade for a while, tiny glimpses that implied he might feel more than he let on.

"I understand you're worried," I told him, trying to appeal to his logical side—if he had one. "I get that you don't think it's a good idea, but I still have to do this. I still have to try. You helped me at my trial, right? You showed up there and even if you haven't told me everything, I'm pretty sure you've been paying the price for that."

"You have no idea the price I've been paying for *that* little stunt."

"Then you should understand why I have to do this. Sometimes it's worth it to do something foolish, to help even if it makes no sense, even if it's risky. Some people are worth doing that for."

He let out a rather dramatic sigh more suited for a teenage girl than a grown ass man—or whatever he was. "You know, you really are a challenge. You test me constantly. I'm not going to give you permission— not like you'd care if I did or not. In fact, I *still* think this is a bad idea, but until you recognize that for yourself, you'll never believe me. So, I'm going to suggest you go talk to that serious Justice you know, the one who was at the trial."

"Ruben?"

"Maybe? I don't care about his name. He's a Justice, so ask him for access to the old archives and look up a book titled—" Knot tapped his finger against his bottom lip as though deep in thought. It made me wonder just how many years of memories were locked up in his head, were hidden there. How much did he have to sort through?

Just what *was* he?

He nodded as though he'd just worked it out. "It's a yellow book. I don't remember the name, but it's on the top of the far left, next to a book bound with human skin."

"Skin?"

"Yeah, I wouldn't touch that one if I were you. Even tanned human skin holds some nasty things on it."

I wasn't sure whether I should believe him or not— he tended to like to make jokes, after all. "And what will I find in that book?"

"A history that will explain why what you want to do isn't possible. If anything can make you realize that you have no chance, I'm hoping that does." He set his fork down and stared straight at me, the look giving me time to really notice his face.

It was strange how people became important to us, how they went from strangers to being a part of us, to being something we couldn't lose, something that we recognized anywhere.

Knot was one of those people to me. It was crazy given how things had gone for me over my lifetime to think I had people I could rely on, people who had my back. No matter what kept happening—and fuck knew it was a lot—I had people who didn't turn away from me no matter what.

It was priceless, really, and as fucking weird as he was, Knot was likely one of the best examples.

"Look at me like that and I'll blush," he said, though his words didn't show any actual embarrassment.

"Thank you. I know I don't say it much, that I'm more likely to curse at you than anything else, but thank you for making me into this, for staying with me through it all."

He lifted one of his eyebrows. "Getting the book isn't *that* dangerous. No need to give farewell thank-yous. Besides, is it even a thank-you if it doesn't come with a gift?"

"I'm not really here. How am I supposed to give you a gift?"

"Excuses, excuses. *Five* birthdays have passed and not one birthday gift!"

"Do you even have a birthday?"

"Of course I do. What a rude question. I picked it out after I saw someone else having a party. It's December twenty-fifth."

"Christmas?"

He smiled widely. "I like a little competition."

"Well, actually show up in person and I'll make sure to give you a gift this year."

"I'll hold you to that, Little Crow. Now, I think it's time you wake up or you're going to be late."

That same sensation as I returned to my body unnerved me, but sure enough, when I opened my eyes, the blaring of my alarm told me he was right.

I rolled over, hitting the button to silence it, trying to get the sound out of my head.

As always, I wasn't sure if things were better or worse after a conversation with Knot...

He really was an enigma.

* * * *

"Absolutely not." Ruben crossed his arms, his expression stern, as though the very fact I would ask annoyed him.

It seemed a little dramatic reaction to borrowing a book, but whatever…

At least he looked good, all closed off like that. Other people needed to smile to be attractive, but Ruben looked best like this.

Or maybe I just never saw him smile, so I couldn't compare it to anything?

"Come on. After everything I've done for you?"

"If you mean your courier work, we pay you well for that. Other than that, I can't recall anything positive you've done in my life."

Ouch. "Really? I baked you a cake!"

"It had laxatives in it."

Right. I'd forgotten about that part. "Well, you had taken away my day off when I was supposed to go on a date. What about the time I gave you dating advice?"

"Your advice was to lean into my 'Daddy Dom' look and try a sex dungeon."

"And that is amazing advice. Did you try it?"

His cheek didn't even twitch, making me suspect he probably hadn't. Pity, because he really could pull that off. He had that stern, disapproving, older man expression that would just make any brat or little fall in love.

It wasn't my fault if he refused to use his best assets.

"Come on—this is important."

"Tell me why and I'll consider it. Those archives are not open to the public, so I need a good reason to break protocol and show them to you."

"It's important. Can't you trust me?"

He didn't have to even cock an eyebrow for his expression to say that, fuck no, he didn't trust me.

Fair.

I hadn't done much to be trustworthy.

"You know the problem with the Weres? Well, I've gotten a lead on that."

"And it's in a book in the archive?"

"That's what my source says."

He paused, then tilted his head. "Knot told you, didn't he?"

"Does that help or hurt my odds of getting what I want?"

"Grey, I know you trust him for some reason I don't understand, but he's dangerous. We still don't understand what exactly he is."

"What I know is that he's helped me before, and there isn't any harm, is there?"

"How would he even know where the book is without knowing the name? No one is allowed in there—he can't have gotten access."

"That I can't answer, but why not check? If it's not there, then we're done. What if it is, though? What's the risk?"

"Those books have forbidden knowledge in them, things from well before the council was created. There are secrets that would best remain secret. It's something Justices are taught from the start, something impressed upon us. This idea that transparency is always good is faulty at best. Our job is to preserve the balance, the peace, and sometimes that requires secrets."

"Yeah, well, I feel the same way about secrets as I do about locks, which is to say, I'm not a fan." I crossed my arms, mirroring his stance as though that were going to prove to him just how serious I was. "You know the Were situation is getting worse. If we can't put a stop to it, if we can't figure out what's causing it, there's no way the other clans will just stand back and ignore it. They'll step in if the Weres keep causing problems."

"The Justices have kept peace for a long time now. There is no reason to think we won't be able to again."

"You've never had to face an entire clan. What if the whole clan goes feral? What if they all turn into this? How exactly is it you think you're going to deal with that situation? There aren't enough Justices, not nearly enough for a problem of that size. Add to it that if the Weres keep getting out of hand, the other clans *will* step in, and you've got a war—the very thing you were set up to prevent."

A line appeared between his eyebrows, proof that he knew this all and didn't care one bit for it.

Which made me wonder…

"This isn't about the Weres or the book, is it?"

He huffed, turning his gaze away. "You keep getting involved in things that nearly end you. Forgive me for not wanting you to have to deal with this one problem, for me not wanting you to have to take responsibility for this one thing. Even if all you say will come to pass does, *you* are not involved. You are a clan head, but a clan of one. No one is seeking you out, no one will attack you—they have no reason to. However, if you choose to insert yourself into this issue, if you choose to jump into this, you may very well find that you are out of options. You will end up drawn into a fight you don't want any part of, that you have no business in."

What was this? Try to save Grey day?

Still, at least he seemed honestly worried about me, not so much because of my skills — or lack thereof — but because he knew just how badly this could go.

So for the millionth time recently, I had to explain myself. "I can't just sit back and do nothing, not if I can help. This problem is my problem, because this is my world. Sure, I might be a clan of one, I might not have the power of other clan heads, but I'm still a part of this world and I'll be damned if I see it go to war when I might be able to help. So, please, let me look for that book."

He pressed his lips into a tight line, and for a moment, I thought I'd lost. His stern expression said he didn't like this one bit, and I'd bet he didn't want to help at all. My best hope was that he gave in for the same reason most people did — because he recognized that I was going to do it with or without him, and he'd have a lesser headache if he helped.

I hoped that by this point, he understood that well. Fuck knew I'd gone behind his back enough times that he should have learned it.

"Fine," he muttered. "The archive isn't in this building, though. It's hidden elsewhere. I will get it set up and we can go tomorrow. The trip will take all day, so prepare yourself for that. I will pick you up at seven a.m. — ensure you are ready to go."

The way he said that last part implied that he really doubted I'd manage it. It made me laugh, the way he didn't quite trust me.

Which, to be fair, seven in the morning was pretty fucking early.

My phone rang in my pocket, and when I pulled it out, my eyes widened.

"Shit."

He stood straighter. "What?"

"Um…look, this might seem weird, but could I get a ride?"

"A ride?"

I nodded, then answered the phone. "Hi, Mom. Yes, I'm on my way! I'm almost there." I tapped my fingers on the desk beside Ruben. "Yeah, hear that? It's my turning signal. I'll be there in like…five minutes. Hanging up now!" I slid the phone back into my pocket, then focused on Ruben. "See, I'm supposed to be somewhere like, thirty minutes ago, and if I don't hurry it up, someone might just kill me."

"You said 'Mom'."

"Exactly! She's the one person I really think could kill me."

"Didn't you drive here?"

"I did, but you know how the parking lot is for employees. It takes forever to get out of it!"

He narrowed his eyes.

I went on. "So because you're special, you get that snazzy reserved parking spot right in the front."

"I am not a chauffeur."

"I know, but listen. You didn't want to show me the book because you wanted to protect me, right? Well, here is a time when I actually *need* protection! My mom is terrifying, and I'll never live it down if I can't get there right away. Please, Ruben, be my knight in a very lovely fitted suit?"

He rubbed the bridge of his nose, as though he couldn't believe he had to deal with something like me this late in the day. Still, after a moment that was honestly shorter than I expected, he nodded. "Fine. However, you will owe me."

"Yep. Fair. Let's go already! She thinks I'm almost there." I waved him on as he followed, not moving nearly fast enough for what I needed.

He drove a large, king cab truck with an extended, covered bed. I wondered if it was so he could put bodies in the back?

I wouldn't put it past him. Ruben did some shady shit, all for the sake of the council and the Justices. It was amazing, really, because he barely seemed to care about anything beyond the rules and regulations.

And only the rules of the council. He didn't fuck about anyone else's.

I had to use the step and hoist myself into the truck, given the height it had and the height I didn't.

Despite the huge size of it, Ruben maneuvered it easily through the crowded streets. In fact, it amazed me that he drove so well. It didn't seem fitting, somehow. Probably because I imaged him as old and serious and not at all modern. Watching him drive a large modern truck didn't work well with the aesthetic I'd built up in my mind.

"Why are you late?" he asked.

"I just lost track of time."

"You do that a lot, don't you?"

"I mean, sometimes?"

"I believe you were cited six hundred and three times for lateness over the five years you've worked for the council."

"You know that offhand?"

"Well, it is a record."

I sighed and leaned back in the truck, watching the buildings and houses move past us. The city was strange in that there weren't as many defined commercial versus residential areas. It came from the constant expansion of the cities in the low desert, where one large road might have been the only commercial area, but expanded as more and more people moved here. It meant that everything mixed together, eventually, with individual houses dotted right beside restaurants and shops.

"Why are you always late?" His question pulled me from my distraction.

"I just have a lot of things in my mind, a lot that I deal with. I can't help it if I'm always going a mile a minute. Things like dealing with appointments or being exactly on time are just strange to me. I mean to be there, but other stuff just inevitably gets in the way." I thought about it, then frowned. "Plus, I'm pretty sure my crow hates being on time."

"You're really going to blame your bird for your actions?" He scoffed as though I were blaming elves or Santa.

"I'm serious! Just like she can unlock doors for me, I swear there are times that she creates chaos. One time, I set my alarm an hour early, got everything set up the night before so there was no way I'd be late to a meeting with you at eight in the morning. I did *everything* that you're supposed to do. It was the one where we were talking about the cake incident."

"I recall you were an hour late to that one." Talk about annoyed — his tone said he didn't at all appreciate the reminder, and I could almost picture him stewing over it all.

"That's the thing, I did all of that to get ready, and do you know what happened? A power surge fried my phone so my alarm didn't go off. Then, when I did wake up — only a little late — I found a pipe in the bathroom had burst, ruining the clothes I'd set out. Add to those things a flat tire, three ride shares who canceled on me, and my badge not working at the front door. What I've found is that the more I try to be that organized, regimented person people want me to be, the less I manage it. The more chaos occurs around me that ruins it. The truth is, things run much more smoothly and it's less stress on me if I just go with the flow."

Ruben didn't answer at first, so I turned my head to see him staring forward, through the windshield. Not angry, just pensive, as though weighing my words. Finally, he responded, his voice soft. "I suppose I never realized it might be that much of a struggle for you."

"Most people don't. They don't know what I am, don't understand what it means. We all know about Minds, about the risks and problems that go along with them, so we accept the limitations. We know they might need time away, that they might get upset, that they struggle to contain their powers when they are overwhelmed. No one knows about me—not even me, really—so people expect me to be...perfect." I sighed at that word, at the weight of it. The truth was that I'd never been perfect, even before turning into this. I didn't think I had a chance at it no matter what happened.

One of the things I'd learned was that some people were built for perfection and some were just built to survive—hopefully. I was the second type, even before Knot intervened and changed everything. Even back then, I'd been more focused on what I had to do, on just keeping up, on things getting away from me and me just trying to keep all the plates spinning.

It was like I lived in a constant state of disaster, and my only choice was to sit back and hope I could manage it all before it came crashing down.

And from time to time, boy fuck did it crash.

The truck slowed, making me glance around and frown.

We were at my mom's house.

"Um, I didn't give you directions," I pointed out.

"Did you notice that I didn't ask for them?"

"So you've known where my mom lived this whole time?"

"Of course. As if I'd ever not know everything about those who I hired, especially those who cause as many issues as you do. I like to keep a close eye on such people."

"Lucky me… And here I thought I managed to keep my secrets pretty well." I sat up straighter as I took a look at a number of cars in the driveway that certainly didn't belong.

What the hell?

The sports car was easily recognizable, of course, since Kelvin's flashy car stood out. The others, though, gave me a bad feeling.

"That's Galen's car," Ruben said, putting the truck into park after stopping it by the sidewalk. "Did you invite him?"

Something that could only be described as dread rushed through me at the implication. What exactly did this mean? Why would Kelvin and Galen be here?

I cursed softly as I saw my mother walk out of the house, her hair braided and tossed forward over one shoulder. She glared at me, probably because of my lateness, but just like always, an air of softness remained at the corners.

The truth was my mother was the one person who I could disappoint, who could tell me off and lecture me all day, but who I also knew with absolute certainty would still love me and all my mess.

I rolled down the window. "What the hell is this, Mom?"

"What do you mean?"

Right, like her tone wasn't suspicious as fuck. She'd never been a good liar, and it showed right then.

"Mom…"

"Come on in, the party's going."

"What party? I thought it was just a get together."

"It is a get together — for you."

"For me?" I eyed her on full alert. "It's not my birthday. I haven't done anything worth celebrating."

"Well, your brother mentioned something a while ago, that we don't see you as much as I would like, that maybe we don't pay you as much attention as we should. You sort of breeze in and out and none of us know what's going on in your life. I realized he was right."

"So you threw me a party?" I gestured at the sports car. "And why is *he* here?"

"Who? Kelvin? Oh, he stops by from time to time since you introduced us a while back. He's a lovely man. I told him I wanted to have this party and he seemed excited about it. He even gave me a list of numbers to call to invite your friends."

I cringed at the idea that my mother had actually thrown me some sort of weird surprise party, then also called my 'friends' to invite them over? My friends being powerful Spirits, most of whom I was currently fucking — or was soon to be, if the situation continued as it had.

"Oh, I'm so sorry. My name is Grace. You are?"

Ruben opened the door to his truck and I grabbed his arm.

"Not a chance. Come on, let's make a break for it. I've seen you drive—we can get away before anyone can give chase."

He shrugged off my grip. "And miss out on this? Never."

I stayed put in the truck as he went around, his size dwarfing my mother.

It still made me uneasy having her around these people, feeling as though the two parts of my life collided. I'd worked so hard to keep them separate, to protect my family by keeping Spirits away. The last thing I wanted was to be at fault for any harm coming to them.

He took her hand to shake. "My name is Ruben."

"Ruben? I'm so sorry for not inviting you. Kelvin didn't give me that name."

He smiled—*he knows how to do that?*—and shook his head. "No worries, ma'am. I'm actually Grey's boss, so it would be unusual for him to include me in a list of friends."

"Her boss? She's so secretive about what she does. Please, come in! Join us."

I eyed Ruben, hoping he understood my 'you have better fucking not' look. It was a warning that I'd make his life hell if he didn't listen—well, more so than I already had.

I wasn't sure if he didn't see the look or if he didn't care, but he smiled and nodded at my mother. "Of course, I'd love to."

And just like that, I fucking hated all the men who decided to screw my life over. They could enjoy each other, because they weren't getting into my pants again, not after this betrayal.

Chapter Six

The house wasn't crowded, but given the nice evening, I had a feeling that they'd all accumulated outside. Considering how large each of the men was, it wasn't a shock that they wouldn't want to be crammed inside.

I mean, that sounded like the start to a fantastic porn flick, but probably not best at a family gathering.

My mother had already taken Ruben, escorting him outside to meet the others. She'd slid her arm through the crook of his elbow with such ease, and he'd responded like any gentleman.

Funny, he sure as fuck didn't act that way to *me*. It made me roll my eyes, the fact that he could put on such a show for her benefit. I wanted to give him a flat tire, to step on the back of his shoe, then tell my mom that he wasn't nearly so nice when he was berating me at work.

Instead of that, I headed into the kitchen as they went out back, giving myself a moment to collect myself before facing off against the horde of problematic red flags outside.

There I found my dad, standing by the counter, arranging cheese on a platter. He took one look at me and laughed. "Sorry I couldn't tell you."

"You traitor. I told *you* when she bought you that stupid gift a few years back so you could school your features when she gave it to you."

"I know, but if I'd told you, you wouldn't have come. I don't like to see your mom sad. I figured you could probably survive one little party."

I grabbed a hard lemonade out of the fridge, then leaned my back against the counter beside him. "How could you let her invite my friends behind my back?"

"Well, Kelvin seemed to think it was a good idea, and to be honest, we've been curious. You never like to tell us anything. Can you blame your mom for going a little overboard to find out more about your life?"

I didn't tell them about my life because I didn't want them to get killed because of it. As much as I wanted to say that, I really doubted that he'd understand, that it would do anything to help calm their nerves.

That was the exact reason I'd been so secretive.

Besides, it wasn't like I was doing anything impressive.

I sighed, thinking about my siblings, about what amazing people they'd become. "I just didn't think there was much to say."

Sure, I was a Spirit, but what did that matter? Even my council seat wasn't actually important. At the end of the day, I was just a little mess of a girl who struggled to pay her bills and delivered things for a living. Nothing had really changed for me, no matter how much I wanted them to see me as something else.

Compared to a doctor and a CEO, I was the disappointment in the family.

Not that either my mom or dad would say such a thing to me, but they had to think it, right?

"You know, I think you worry too much. You think you need to catch up to someone else, but you're your own person."

"That's what we always tell stupid people so they don't feel so bad about themselves."

He handed me a piece of sharp cheddar as he worked at laying out the plate. "You know what I remember? When your brother got scammed out of his money when he was thirteen. He'd worked that side job over the summer, but some person offered to sell him a coupon to a spa, and he wanted to give it to your mom for her birthday. The coupon ended up a fake, of course."

"He's always been too nice."

"My point is that that would have been the end of it. He'd have lost out on all that money, on his gift, and he felt horrible. None of us knew what to do, even the police just said it was a lesson learned the hard way. *You* went out and found the scammer though, all on your own, and you got his money back."

I laughed softly, thinking back to when I'd been young and human. It hadn't actually been that hard. I'd gotten the description of the idiot who had scammed my brother, then waited out to find him trying his trick again. The truth was that conmen never stopped a good con. Since he'd gotten some money from it, he'd do it again.

Sure enough, I'd found the little twerp and followed him to his car. People like that always had enemies, always had people looking for them. I knew it, because I was like that.

The only difference was that he still worried about it.

It hadn't taken much prompting to make him realize I could be a very big problem. He'd given me the money back just so I'd leave him alone, and I'd used it to get an actual spa ticket — along with the bit of donation that he'd given me to keep my mouth shut — and handed both off to my brother to give to our mom.

"It wasn't that hard," I argued. "Anyone could have done that."

"Maybe, but anyone didn't. *You* did. That's the point, Grey. You like to compare yourself to others who you think are better, but the truth is that you're unique. You do things your own way. Maybe it isn't the same way others do it, but that doesn't mean it's bad. That doesn't mean it isn't important, that it doesn't matter. *You* matter, Grey, and you're a bigger part of this family than I think you always feel. That's why your mom did this, because she wanted to really show you that you're part of this family, that we love you and want you here."

I blew out a long breath. "You're really going to just guilt trip me like that? I can't just run away after you said that."

He snorted. "I know — why do you think I tried that? It might be tricky, but it's also true. Though..."

"What?"

"Well, you have an interesting group of friends. It wasn't what I expected."

"What did you expect?"

"Bikers and circus performers?" He smirked and gave me another piece of cheese like a peace offering.

"Well, you pretty much got that, didn't you?"

He picked up the tray and handed it to me. "No more avoiding it. Off with you. Take these out there for everyone." A push to my back got me moving, my drink in one hand and the tray balanced on the other.

Each step took longer than it needed to, my nerves slowing me down. It felt like if I went slow enough, maybe I could miss the whole thing?

I laughed at the stupidity of that plan.

If I didn't get going, I was pretty damned sure someone would come and drag me out. Who it was, that I didn't know, but it didn't matter, either. Someone would get me and I doubted I could argue with anyone of them.

The door to the backyard was open, with strings of lights illuminating the space. I paused at the doorway, as though surveying a battlefield instead of a party.

Sure enough, I spotted Galen and Kelvin—at opposite ends of the patio. I sure didn't expect to spot Porter, though, seated in the corner, my mom's cat in his lap. No doubt he'd rather be there instead of speaking to anyone else. The fact he was there at all amazed me. He wasn't exactly a party type.

I had a few options for where to go, but I knew the first person—the one at fault for this whole mess.

I stalked over to Kelvin, who was drinking a beer as he stood there, his gaze locked on me. It was unnerving, made it difficult to walk over to him with the confidence that I would have liked, but anger had a habit of being able to really dissolve nerves.

"You're late," he pointed out, as though I didn't know it.

"Yeah, well, seeing as you shouldn't be here at all, I don't think that's a big deal." I set the tray down on one of the bar-height tables set around the patio. "Why the hell would you do this? And I hear you've been stopping in to see my mother?"

"You know I'm not a man who fights fair. When I realized how close you were to your mother, it seemed only obvious that I should use that to my advantage. If your mother likes me, the odds of you accepting me go up as well. I will take every advantage I can because this isn't a battle I plan to lose."

"Only you would view romance as a battle."

"Does that mean you see what we have as romance?" He cocked a dark eyebrow, the expression taunting and far too sexy.

I released a sound of pure aggravation and considered punching him. It wouldn't hurt him, of course. He wouldn't give a damn about it, in fact. It might make me feel better, though.

"I wouldn't," he said as he leaned in, whispering the words to me. "If you hit me here, your mother would think awfully poorly of the behavior."

Which he was completely right about. "If I get kicked out of the party for it, it feels like a win-win for me," I answered, keeping my voice equally low.

"Grey." The unhappy response came from my brother, forcing me to step back and turn to face him. And, yep, there was that glare. He was not thrilled with this turn of events. "Could you excuse us?" he asked Kelvin.

"Certainly." Kelvin nodded, the action unbearably polite, before heading off to speak to my sister.

"What the hell?" my brother asked in an exasperated tone. "Last time you show up with a mind and now *this*?"

"To be entirely fair, I didn't do this. Mom did this. Go yell at her."

"Why would I do that? She has no idea who she invited over! You do, though. She might have invited them, but *you're* the one in contact with them all. You brought that vampire here to start with, and don't think I don't recognize a few of the others, either. You knew these Spirits well enough that they decided to attend after getting a call from your *mother*. That is very much a you problem."

Everything he said was true, though it didn't feel all that fair. It wasn't like I'd done anything specifically.

"In case you've forgotten—I'm a Spirit," I pointed out, hating that I had to say it.

"Technically."

"No, not technically. I turn into a crow. Trust me, I'm one. I might not be one of the kinds you're used to, but that doesn't mean I'm not one."

He sighed, his gaze darting away like he wanted to come up with a proper argument. No doubt his issue was that he didn't want to insult me while he really wanted to insult what I was.

Instead of forcing him to go through those acrobatics, I tried to let him off the hook. "I get it, okay? I didn't want them here, either. There's a reason I've never invited them over. There's a reason I've never brought them to a get-together. I've tried very hard to keep my life separate. I can't help it that Mom did this, though. You know that you all are important to me — that's why I've tried to keep you away from the Spirit world, why I talked Mom into moving here, to somewhere safer, why I never tried to let anyone find out about you all. I guess I didn't do a great job. All I can say for sure is that I will keep doing everything I can to keep everyone safe." I paused, then added on something I doubted he'd believe—I wasn't sure I did—but something that felt necessary. "And I know you might not trust the people here, but I can say that each of them has helped me, has saved me before. If I really thought you all were in danger from them, I wouldn't just let this happen, not even now."

My brother turned his gaze from me to the guests, roaming over each of the people I spoke about. I could almost see the disbelief in his eyes, the way he doubted anything I said about them.

He didn't know them, though. They were annoying and frustrating and no doubt dangerous, but they weren't evil. They weren't heartless. They'd proven again and again that at the end of the day, they had reasons for the things they did.

And I truly didn't think they'd use my family against me, that they'd do any harm to them.

I wasn't sure why I thought that, couldn't defend it with evidence, but it still felt true.

"I guess we'll see," he said, then sighed and walked away.

And fuck did that hurt. It felt like failing again, like not living up to what they thought I should do, what they hoped from me. It wasn't a new feeling, but I wasn't sure my brother had ever so openly displayed it.

"Are you all right?" Porter's voice from behind me forced me to suck it up, to not let the hurt show.

Was I all right? No, probably not, but was I ever?

Also no.

"Yeah." I turned to find Porter still holding Molly, my mom's cat. The cat hated me—cats usually did—but it seemed to adore Porter. Guess that was the benefit of being a Nature and all. "I'm surprised you came."

"The call surprised me."

"And you didn't let me know when I just saw you."

"Well, your mother said it was a surprise. I assumed that meant I wasn't supposed to say anything about it."

"Traitors everywhere, I swear. Why'd you come?"

He paused, his fingers rubbing Molly behind her ears. "I was curious."

"About?"

"Natures are born this way, so I didn't have a very traditional upbringing. I was curious what a normal family was like. Perhaps I was also curious to get to know another side of you."

"Well, I don't know about normal. What do you think so far?"

"It is interesting. Warm. Welcoming. I don't spend much time around humans when I can avoid it— they're always noisy and erratic."

"If you don't like noisy and erratic, you probably won't like me or my family."

He smiled, the expression strange as he always appeared so aloof. "I'm surprised to say I don't think I mind this form of noise. It is happy in a way I am unaccustomed to. In fact, I think I rather like it." The look on his face was so soft that it made me go still for a moment.

He always seemed so far away, so different. Yet I'd gotten to watch him in a few new circumstances recently, and it made me recognize just how little I really knew about him.

I wondered what his day to day was like?

I knew it for others, for Galen, for Kelvin, for Ruben. They spent their days working for the council, heading their own clans, taking care of all those problems.

But what about Porter? Part of me imagined he just spent it in the wilds, with the animals like some old-school hippie.

I had a feeling that probably wasn't entirely true, however, and judging from the strange longing in his eyes, I suspected he felt lonely — at least at times.

"You know," I said, trying to stop myself from speaking even as I said it. "My mom has an open-door policy. She'd probably love it if you showed up here anytime you wanted."

He peered over at her, then down at the cat. "Maybe just to visit Molly."

I laughed at the way he said that, the obvious deception. Still, I could save egos if I wanted. "Right, just for Molly."

There was no reason a man like Porter should be adorable, but he fucking was...

* * * *

Two hours later and I was exhausted from all the visiting and playing peacemaker.

The only good thing was that the men seemed willing to put their issues aside for the sake of me and my family. They jabbed, just a bit, but nothing that couldn't be laughed off as a joke between friends.

Even Kelvin and Galen, the worst of the offenders, seemed willing to hold off for at least tonight.

My mom had gone inside with my sister and brother to clean up, leaving Ruben, Galen, Porter, Kelvin, and myself outside.

"Well, this went better than I would have figured," Kelvin said with a knowing chuckle.

The asshole didn't even pretend to be sorry for being the person at fault for all of this.

"Oh, don't think I won't get you back for this."

"I look forward to it. Besides, what was I to say when your mom asked? You know me — I can't resist a pretty woman's request."

"First, don't call my mom a pretty woman like that — it's gross. Secondly, I'll skip over the fact that you were even talking to her, and go straight to very real option you had of saying no! You could have told her that I didn't want a party, or that you didn't know any of my friends. Why would you possibly think this was a good idea?"

"I figured if you had the inside track, you wouldn't give it up," Galen said, a beer in his hand. "You're not one to give up an advantage."

Kelvin waved off the suspicion. "I'm playing the long game here. It's better to know your enemies, to defeat them fully prepared. The biggest risk in any fight is to underestimate an enemy, to assume you've won before you have. That isn't a mistake I like to make."

"You didn't invite me," Ruben pointed out.

Kelvin grinned. "Did I hurt your feelings? Honestly, this" — he waved his hand between Ruben and me — "surprised me quite a bit. I'd seen tall and grumpy watching our little bird, but I hadn't thought he had it in him to actually make a move."

"You really are an asshole," I said to quiet Kelvin down. "And you don't know shit, by the way."

"Perhaps I'm simply not so shameless in my affections," Ruben said, his voice low but steady. "You show little loyalty, moving from person to person depending on what mood you find yourself in. That isn't the way I like to behave. Perhaps you would do well to learn a bit more restraint and it would serve you better."

Kelvin stared back, his expression the same placid one, though I knew him well enough to read the anger beneath.

He liked to make it seem as though nothing bothered him, enjoyed the anonymity and freedom it afforded him, like the way others couldn't predict what he felt if he never showed it.

However, I'd gotten to know him better, had this bond with him, and it all allowed me to read him more deeply than others could. He was still, no matter how much he tried to hide it, the sort of man who didn't like being challenged.

And while he treated Ruben as though he were the help, like he could dismiss him anytime he wished, he clearly didn't care for the way Ruben challenged him now.

Perhaps he reacted worse because it was a challenge he hadn't expected.

"I suppose I was just taken off guard, given how Justices have no feelings. I would have assumed that included romance or affections. Grey is a poor judge of character, of course, but I never figured her to be into someone without any sort of emotion."

Ruben didn't respond. Not a tic of his cheek, not a shift of his hand, nothing. Instead, he turned his gaze to me. "Your family is surprisingly friendly."

The dismissal of Kelvin broke some of the tension there, especially when the vampire only laughed in reaction.

"Yeah, well, don't get comfortable. This isn't some flop house for you all to show up at whenever you want." I made sure to glare at Kelvin a bit more than others, since he'd already been doing that.

"Not my fault your mom invites me over," Kelvin muttered without shame.

"She asked me to help her with her computer," Galen admitted.

"She needs me to trim Molly's nails," Porter said.

I groaned, looking toward Ruben for help, grateful that *someone* hadn't gotten drawn into this nonsense.

Except one look at him said he had.

"Out with it," I demanded.

"She needed someone to pick up a treadmill next week, and it seems she knows no one with a truck."

"You're a Justice," I reminded him as though he'd forgotten that important fact. "What the fuck are you doing running errands for some random woman?"

"Well, at first I said I was busy, but after a few minutes, she wore down all my reasons and it seemed to make perfect sense to help her."

I groaned—loudly—and took another big drink of the hard lemonade. It had to be my third of the night. Not enough to get me drunk but enough to get me comfortably buzzed. It made the conversation easier. "Yep, that's how she gets you. I wanted a Komodo dragon when I was a kid. I was completely determined to have one. I had my presentation all ready, I knew why I wanted one, where to get one, and how to keep it. I'd priced out everything, had it all planned. Well, two days later I stared down at the bearded dragon lizard I'd gotten instead and wondered just how the fuck she'd talked me into this? She's good at getting her way."

I peered out at the group and, before I could stop myself, started to laugh. Here they were, some of the most powerful Spirits in the world, the ones who led all others, the ones in charge of...everything. They were feared through our world, able to send others running with just a lifted eyebrow, but my five and a half foot, sixty-five-year-old mother had them running her errands like they were bellhops at a fancy hotel.

I ran a finger under my eyes, removing the tears that accumulated from the laughter.

We were always chasing after peace, always trying to save ourselves and our way of life, fighting against another enemy, another problem, when the answer was in front of us all along.

If my mother ran the spirit world, I was pretty sure it would all go just fine.

And lord fucking help us all if she did.

* * * *

By the time everyone left, I was ready for some calm and silence. Sure, we'd packed a lot of people into this house, but I wasn't sure if that really accounted for the amount of noise present. Not just any noise, either, but tense noise.

It felt like someone always had something to say, some snide little comment that could get taken one of six different ways — all of them bad — and it was my job to keep everyone calm and, preferably, alive.

And despite that, the night had ended pretty fucking well. No blood, no fistfights, no one discovering that all those people coming from me were definitely not human.

All in all, I really couldn't fault anyone for how it went. My brother and sister had gone home already, and my dad had jumped into the shower before bed, leaving just my mom and me still there on the back porch.

The wind rustled through the fronds of the palm trees, and it reminded me of how it had always amazed me when those long trunks would bend at the hard gusts. Palm trees were planted everywhere in this area, and it never seemed possible for them to withstand such force, but they did, year after year, no matter how little sense it made.

"How mad are you?" my mom asked.

"Medium."

"Well, I think I can handle medium. Still, thank you, I'm glad we did this."

I twisted to look at her. "Why did you, really? I mean, I know what you said, but seriously, what did you think you were going to get out of this?"

She released a soft breath and played with the tie at the end of her braid. "I'm not getting any younger, Grey. Your siblings, they have families, spouses. I know they won't be alone after I'm gone, but you? I haven't met any significant others of yours and I just kept picturing you all alone."

I could almost imagine what she'd thought, the pathetic sight of me all alone at a table for Thanksgiving, a microwave dinner in front of me.

Joke was on her—that sounded like a fantastic night to me!

"Well, I'm sorry to worry you so much."

"I'm not worried anymore."

"No?" I thought back to the night, to the clusterfuck it had been, and wasn't sure exactly who had won her over. I didn't think any of them were really *bring home to your mother* sort of men.

She shook her head. "Clearly, you have people who are willing to show up for you. I was afraid you were alone, but I saw tonight that you aren't, not at all. It makes me feel better to know that even if you don't like to mix your worlds together, that you might not always want to bring your friends around, I'm just happy to know you have them. You could tell they all care for you—I mean, they were willing to drop everything to come to a party thrown by your mother out of the blue. Even with your boss, it was obvious just how much he cares about you." She smiled softly, more to herself than me, I suspected.

Had she really been that worried about me?

It was funny, since part of the reason I'd tried to be so secretive about my life was to protect her, to keep her from worrying. If she knew what I really did, what my life was really like, I doubted she'd be too happy about any of it. No one slept well at night knowing about all the bullshit I got up to.

Not even me.

But here I found out it had all been in vain, since she'd worried anyway. Maybe mothers always did, though. I wasn't a mom, didn't plan on becoming one— didn't know if it was even possible anymore—so just how was I supposed to know what was normal for one?

"Yeah, I guess they're good friends," I said.

"Just friends?"

"Whoa, now, let's settle down. This isn't the sort of talk to have with my mother. I'm not fifteen anymore with my first crush."

"Your first crush was well before fifteen, young lady. Don't think I don't know what."

"Ah, Ryan." I smirked as I thought back at the cute little boy I'd fallen for when I was seven and he'd been ten. He hadn't liked me, of course, but I'd been smitten and followed him around all summer, determined to win him over.

"Tell me the truth about them, won't you?" she prodded gently.

She always got me like that, with the soft questions I found it impossible to ignore or deny.

"I don't know. They're just friends for now, I think."

"All of them?"

"Is that weird?" I nibbled at my bottom lip, preparing myself for the worst.

For her to call me a whore, to kick me out, to label me as a pervert who didn't get to come to dinners anymore.

It was a stupid fear, really. When had my mom ever turned her back on me like that? Still, knowing that she was disappointed would've hurt, even if she wasn't about to kick me out.

Some part of me still wanted to be her little girl, for her to see me as someone who could do no wrong. I guess we never really outgrew the feeling of wanting our mom's approval.

"Honey, you should know me well enough not to worry about something like that. If you date no one, if you date a hundred people, so long as you're all honest and they treat you well, I really don't care a bit." She paused, then chuckled. "Plus, the idea of a single partner tough enough to put up with a hundred percent of your craziness is a terrifying thought. I probably should have seen this coming."

Her words came as a surprise even if they shouldn't have. When had she ever not supported me?

Even when I did something insane, like the time I'd brought home a badger I had liberated from a zoo, she hadn't turned me away. Instead, she'd gotten out an old dog crate and looked up on the internet what badgers ate.

Something about that eased me in a way I hadn't realized I needed. I hadn't thought I was stressed about the idea of what sort of future I had with the men around me.

It had all come about slowly, over the years, until connections had formed naturally. It hadn't given me the time to consider what it meant beyond the day, beyond the moment.

Was I really wanting a future with all of them? Or at least without making a choice?

The answer was so obvious even if I'd avoided it before now. Yes, that was exactly what I wanted. My mom's easy acceptance made it not feel so weird, so unattainable. If even she could see that and think it fine, it no longer seemed like some far-off pipe dream.

"However," she said, her voice turning serious. "Let me make myself clear. If they hurt you — any of them — I've still got a back strong enough to dig a hole however large enough I need for as many bodies as need burying."

And fuck knew I didn't doubt she could manage just that.

Those Spirits better watch themselves.

Chapter Seven

The clock struck seven-forty as I climbed into Ruben's truck. I wasn't sure if it was the early morning or the conversation we'd had the night before, but he didn't balk at the lateness.

Instead, he tapped the lid of a to-go cup. "Mocha."

"Why, thank you." I picked up the cup and took my first sip, not bothering to hide my moan and the decedent chocolate taste, the way it warmed my mouth, my throat, my stomach. There was something about sugar and heat that just soothed any complaints a person had.

And my biggest one at the moment was the whole before eight in the morning thing.

"None for you?" I asked when I noted his empty cup holder.

"I had a cup when I first woke around five this morning. I don't like to have too much caffeine."

"Does it affect Justices?" I gave him a side-eye, curious. They could hold this alcohol and didn't seem to gain weight no matter what they ate—nor lose weight if starved. Honestly, it seemed as though no laws of physics bothered them in the least.

"It makes me anxious," he admitted in a quiet, sullen tone. "I don't like to drink more than a cup because I end up feeling unsettled."

"*You*, anxious?" I couldn't quite believe that.

Ruben was unfailingly solid. Even when everything went to shit around him, his heart rate didn't seem to raise in response. Instead, he simply went about the steps to resolve the problem with little to no emotion.

Suddenly, I wanted to see him jittery. I could *almost* picture him vibrating around, trying to fix things, talking fast.

"Whatever you're picturing—stop. I'm sure it isn't all that flattering given the way you're smiling." Even as he said that, I swore I saw his lips curl.

I knew he didn't want to admit to being amused by me, but that didn't mean he wasn't.

"There are also pain relievers in the glove box, if you need them."

"Why would I?"

"You had a few of those drinks last night."

I blew out a sharp, dismissive breath between my lips. "*Puhlease*. Like I'd get a hangover from that. Those were barely a pre-game."

"You were slurring your words by the time I left." He paused, then added, "I thought about staying to see if you needed a ride home, but your mother assured me it was handled."

Was he asking if anyone else had driven me back?

I had to admit, while I wasn't usually a fan of jealousy, a little of it looked good on him. "I slept at my mom's. She drove me back home around six this morning."

"And yet you were still forty minutes behind schedule?"

"I had to make her coffee when she got here, then shower after she left. It takes a while, okay?"

He huffed. "Well, settle in. The drive will take us at least six hours, then we will see how long it takes to locate the book."

I did rough math in my head. "What, are we going to spend all night driving back?"

"We could, but I had your deliveries for today and tomorrow rerouted to other couriers, so we don't need to. If we want, we can spend the night somewhere along the way."

"From anyone else, I'd think that was a cheesy pickup scheme."

"Do you think I wouldn't attempt to pick you up?"

"No, I just think you'd be more upfront about it. Instead of, 'oops, I ran out of gas and it's cold out, hurry and climb in my lap to keep my penis warm,' you're more the type to just tell me you want me to take my clothes off."

"You make me sound rather terrible and unromantic."

"Not really. See, I don't get romance. That stuff is all weird and confusing to me. I'd much prefer directness. I'd rather people just tell me what they want. Life is so much easier that way, isn't it?"

"Well then, rest assured I will simply tell you in the future."

Weren't those words a nice little promise? I shifted in my seat at the strange tension that sprang up between us, the way it made me wonder if he was serious, if he though there was something more between us. It was a nice idea, right?

And given the way he'd kissed me before, he saw me in that way, too. Especially after the comments he'd made at the party.

However, it was easy to think that and different to address it.

The thought of something more with him was the kind of thing that was best safely relegated to fantasies and badly written porn — not reality. In reality, he was my boss, and also a Justice.

Did Justices have sex?

I thought about the ones I knew, and the idea sent an unpleasant shudder through me. They seemed about as passionate as old wet dog food. I couldn't picture them getting all hot and sweaty with someone.

Though, a momentary flash of Ruben proved my brain was just fine thinking about him in that way. It didn't mind it one bit.

I thought about his broad frame, that intense expression, all directed right on me. He was too much, but what if he put all that drive to pleasing me?

Well, I could think of a lot worse ways to spend an evening.

He let out a soft groan, one so quiet I almost wondered if I'd imagined it. When I turned to look at him, he wasn't staring at me, his gaze locked on the road. To anyone else, he probably appeared entirely focused on driving, on the path ahead, but I knew better.

A twitch of his upper lip, the way he gripped the steering wheel just a bit too tight, the slight tremble in his arm, it all said something had gotten to him.

Justices had excellent senses, after all. Could he have been able to tell what I was thinking? Or at least guess it based on my reaction?

I pressed my thighs together to ignore the wetness there, between my legs, while repeating to myself that I was at *work*, for fuck's sake.

This was going to be one long-ass drive…

* * * *

We went to a very questionable drive-through to grab breakfast sandwiches. Still, I'd eaten at far shadier places through my life. When a person didn't have much money — which for the vast majority of my life I hadn't — they get used to eating whatever it was they could get.

For lunch, we actually stopped at a diner, the place quaint and small and in a little enough town that we got a few weird looks from being there and not local. Still, it was tasty.

Through it all, the conversation flowed with the smoothness of sandpaper. Ruben's every answer seemed to give as little information as possible, like he'd cultivated that skill.

Not like Kelvin, who would just lie, or Galen, who would simply refuse to answer.

Instead, Ruben liked to answer in as short a way as he could.

I had asked him about his hobbies and he said, "My job leaves me with little time for hobbies."

That didn't say anything! Little was still some, and I doubted he had absolutely none.

The worse part about it was that even with all those *almost* answers, I still wasn't sure if he did that to everyone or was it a just me thing?. Was it just a game to him? Was he so used to responding to people that way that he didn't know how annoying it was?

Maybe he was out of practice.

Whatever the reason, by the time we pulled into the driveway of a small house up a long, twisted path in the forest, I was so ready to be out of the confined quarters of a car with him. I deserved a small break from this torture.

I lifted my arms above my head and stretched to loosen my bunched muscles from the long drive as I looked around.

The trees were tall, breaking up the skyline, so all I could see were trees and the sinking sun above us. Birds squawked, the fluttering of their wings loud in the quiet, as though we'd personally offended them by intruding.

Porter would love this place.

I shook the thought away. I didn't need to think about him, especially not here, not when I was busy with other things.

"No guards?" I asked.

"It's protected well by Justice skills. No one but a Justice can enter. Anyone else would be repelled immediately."

"By what?" Just as the last word escaped me, I moved closer to the door and dread hit me, so strong it nearly made my knees buckle. It was thick and choking, threatening to collapse my lungs with its intensity.

It felt like the fear of suddenly being shoved from an airplane, where I gripped the edge holding on, clawing desperately for a way to survive.

It drove me back one step, then another, lessening as I did so. My brain screamed to get away from it, to escape no matter what it took.

Arms wrapped around me, tugging me forward, toward more of that. I fought, blinded by anything but the need to get the fuck away from this place.

How could Ruben not feel it? Not understand the danger we were in?

He pressed his palm against the door of the house and it swung open. No matter how much I struggled, wiggling in his grasp, clawing at his arms to escape, he didn't loosen his grip. It was steel against me, impossible to dislodge.

The fear crystalized in my mind.

Ruben is going to die. In my head, I saw a million ways it could happen, that if we went forward, if we didn't turn back, something was going to attack. It would run him through, it would tear out his throat, it would take his head. A million different ways it could happen played across my eyelids all at once, until I shook and sobbed and struggled to draw air into my lungs.

We crossed the threshold and that overwhelming terror disappeared all at once. It shed like water from me, falling to the ground, shaken off by the movement.

My brain worked again, stuttering forward, and I peered around, wondering what I had just been so afraid of…

"Sorry," he offered. "I knew what the defense was, but I didn't think it would affect you so badly."

"Could have warned a girl." My voice came out thin and less confident than I would have liked.

"Usually it causes anxiety, but not that much. It locks onto a deep-seated fear, something that rests at your core, and exploits that. So people with more trauma, or more deeply rooted ones, feel it worse." He paused, then added, "What was yours?"

I pressed my lips together, not about to admit that. It was far too humiliating to even think about showing that part of me to anyone.

Fuck that.

"Spiders," I said, not even trying to make the lie stick. It was fine that he heard it for the lie it was, that he knew I was bullshitting him because I didn't want to tell him the truth. I didn't mind that one bit.

So long as he didn't know the truth, nothing else mattered.

He tilted his head, then nodded. "Let's go check the archives."

I peered around the inside of the house and frowned. "You sure we're in the right place?" The place was built like a little studio apartment, with a bed, a kitchenet, a seating and eating area. The items were nice, though rather dust covered, implying that it wasn't used often.

"What did you expect? Rows after rows of books?"

"Something like that."

He headed back toward a door that opened to reveal a closet. "Our defense measures work well, but there are always some who are immune. We set this up to appear like a rarely used summer cabin in case anyone finds their way in." He reached in toward the back of the closet and pressed his palm against the wall. Much like the front door, it opened instantly to reveal a dark stairway.

"Creepy. Also, if you take your dates to scary murder rooms inside of closets, it's no wonder you're single."

"Are you saying you won't come?" He lifted an eyebrow as though calling my bluff.

"Well, no, I'm not saying that, but I'm not like normal girls. I'm a bit more twisted."

"Which is why I brought you and not anyone else." He headed down the stairs, into the darkness, as though our conversation had ended.

It sort of had, I guess.

I took a deep breath, not a huge fan of the dark, but what was I supposed to do but head that way? When I crossed the barrier, when I got down into the stairs rather than the closet, the door shut behind me.

It plunged everything into darkness, and I lost my footing for a moment.

A moment was all it took for me to tip forward. *Great, I die on some freaky stairs.*

The only benefit was that since they *were* stairs, I'd probably hit Ruben and take him down with me.

Except the bastard kept his balance, even when I struck him from behind, stopping my freefall.

A breath later, lights illuminated the space, soft and flickering as candles ignited along the walls, which I could now see were made of brick, appearing much older than the house had.

"Neat trick," I muttered as I found my footing again.

A chill got to me, one that hadn't been there before. Granted, in the mountains it had been cold, but not like *this*. This was a different chill, a deeper one. I wrapped my arms around myself. "What the hell is up with the weather?"

"We aren't where we were anymore."

"Um, what?"

He tapped his fingers against the bricks, making me recognize that, yeah, these appeared *much* older than the rest of the building, like they were made to connect with something entirely different. "The threshold of the stairs is a portal made to connect this place with that. This place is far older than we've been located there."

"So where are we now?"

"Somewhere in Northern Canada."

"Well, that explains the cold, I guess. You didn't warn me, so I didn't bring my passport."

He shrugged off his jacket and wrapped it around me without saying a word. "Well, we'll have to avoid any immigration officers, won't we?"

I stopped as he turned around. "Was that a joke?"

He didn't answer, instead continuing down the stairs.

"Wait, I'm serious. A joke, from *you?*"

The stairs went deeper than I would have expected, and by the end, by the time we reached the ground floor, my knees were complaining about the whole thing.

However, the sight of the massive space that could only be called a library astounded me. It had to be at least three stories high, with bookshelves that ran from floor to ceiling all along it and large ladders hooked in.

It made me want to have that princess moment where I rode the ladder across the space.

Except I was pretty sure if I broke Ruben's precious archives, I'd be in trouble.

Bastard.

"So where did he say it was?" Ruben asked, rolling up the sleeves of his white shirt.

It was freezing in here and he was getting *less* dressed? What the fuck was wrong with him?

Not that I minded the sight one bit. That could warm a girl up quite nicely on its own.

He turned to look at me, prompting me to recall his question.

"Yellow book, top shelf, left side, next to a book made of human skin that I shouldn't touch."

"That doesn't narrow it down much. We have a lot of yellow books and there is a left side to each of these rows and shelves."

"Okay, but do you know where the book made of human skin is? Because it's next to that one." At his look, I groaned. "You really have so many made of human skin that even that doesn't help? Great. Just fucking wonderful."

He shrugged. "If it makes you feel better, few of these were made by Justices. We collected them, stored them here, but we didn't craft them. They were made by humans and Spirits."

"Humans? But they don't have any magic…"

"That isn't wholly true. Think about the tales of old witches."

"But I figured those were some sort of Spirit, one that didn't exist anymore."

He shook his head. "Some people believe that, but most Justices don't. We know that there are things that exist out there that appear to be human in nature but still retain certain qualities of Spirits, but none of the energy. Besides, if this realm has none of its own power, how do you think the Justices were made?"

That drew me short.

I hadn't thought much about how Justices were created. I knew what they did, that they kept the peace, that they prevented war, that they were terrifyingly powerful—and shockingly boring. I hadn't really considered who made them or what power had crafted them.

"So you're telling me that humans — and Earth — have their own energy?"

"Of course. Think about it — why wouldn't they? We just don't often recognize it because it is the majority, because it is present in everything, including Spirits."

I wasn't sure what that meant, exactly, or how I felt about it. Did that make me happy? I wasn't human anymore, of course, but I still had more of an affinity for them than most of the other Spirits. Maybe it was because I'd never really vibed with the Spirits that I clung to those roots.

Instead of forcing me to talk about it, Ruben turned toward the first large shelf. "I think our only choice is to check the top left of first every shelf, then every bay within the shelf, since he wasn't clear."

I groaned at the sight of the ladder that just earlier had seemed like so much fun.

First the stairs, now the ladder.

What the fuck was today, cardio day?

Chapter Eight

Three hours later and I was ready to ring Knot's neck for sending me on this little errand. I sat on the floor, my back to a shelf, taking a break.

At least I had a nice view. I watched Ruben heading up the ladder, giving me a fantastic angle to see his ass.

He might have appeared older than the other men I knew, but he sure didn't let that stop him. His ass was faultless, and I wondered for a moment if he'd had those pants tailored just to showcase it like the piece of artwork it was.

I pictured him walking in and explaining to the tailor that he wanted his assets highlighted to their full glory, and fuck if that tailor didn't do the job perfectly.

Chef's kiss.

"You know, my senses are good enough to feel when I am being stared at," Ruben called down as he peered at the books on the top shelf.

"Not my fault your ass looks like that in those pants," I called back.

He turned his head, dangling on the ladder in a way that would have made me nervous if it were anyone else.

If anyone could keep themselves steady there — or be just fine after a fall — it would be Ruben.

It would *have* to be Ruben, because I sure as fuck couldn't drag him out of there. He was far too heavy.

"Do you always talk like that?" he asked, his tone more curious than scolding for once.

"Like what?"

"So forward? Are you like this with everyone? Do you actually mean any of the things you say, or is it merely a game to you?" He must have read my expression from that distance, because he added, "I'm not faulting you. I just want to know how to read the things you say, how to understand how seriously I should take them."

I blew out a breath, thankful to have him so far away for this conversation. It felt easier to talk to him when he wasn't quite as overwhelming.

And I could still see his ass, so that helped, too.

"I've never really seen a reason to be lady-like, okay? That whole play it coy thing, that never really was my thing. I never did it well. So, I prefer to just say what I think. If people don't like it, well, they don't really like me. I'd prefer to know that upfront."

"So it isn't just a joke?"

"I mean, I think I'm pretty funny a lot of the time, sure, but I'm not going to say things like that if I don't mean them."

He seemed to consider my words, to mull them over before descending the ladder and moving to the next without addressing it further.

I didn't know if I'd given the answer he'd been looking for or not. His expression gave away so little, I couldn't be sure. He at least didn't seem *less* happy than he'd been to start with, so that was a good thing, right?

My legs ached from the up and down, and I figured this was one of those times when people had to do according to their skills. If we were talking about squeezing into a tiny space, well, me and my crow were absolutely the right choice. If we were talking endurance and brute strength, well, that was Ruben's department.

However, after another twenty minutes, I figured I was as rested as I could hope for. Instead of climbing back up, though, I tried to take a general view of what was around us.

Left. Knot was always mysterious, rarely gave me exactly what I wanted, but usually gave me what I needed. He wouldn't have sent me here if he didn't think it would help.

Which meant he wouldn't tell me to come here unless he knew the item I needed was here. So...where was it?

I thought back to his answers, to the way he phrased things, never direct, always slightly skewed. I'd assumed that left and on top meant the top left of the shelf, but what if it didn't?

What if he'd intended something far less obvious?

"Do you have a section of books that are different from here?" I called up to Ruben.

"What do you mean?"

"Books that are either set to be destroyed or sent out or something. I don't know — anything that makes them put aside?"

He darted his gaze away for a moment, then widened his eyes. "We have a section for unsorted books, ones that need to be gone through and categorized. We call them the Left Behind, since they are often taken from the archives of others."

"Left," I said with a chuckle as Ruben came down.

Leave it to Knot to tell me everything I need and still do it the most annoying way possible.

I followed Ruben past the shelves to a back room, only to find stacks of books on tables, in boxes, all over with no real discernable order. Dust covered many of them. "Guess you don't go through these that much, huh?"

"We used to have a few Justices dedicated to this work, but over the years it fell out of fashion. I guess most decided that we didn't need to worry about that, that we knew everything we needed to know. This has become a much less supported position for the past fifty years or so."

Yellow. I peered around the space. Yellow and at the top meant it couldn't have been at the bottom of a pile, right? Not tucked inside a box somewhere, hidden away.

In the corner, I saw a bright yellow book on the top of a precarious pile, the sort of pile that seemed to defy gravity. Still, it was the only yellow I spotted.

I maneuvered through the crowded space, careful to *only* touch that book and not the beige, questionable, possibly human skin cover beside it.

It was in English, something that shocked me, and the cover of it read, *The Source.*

"I think I've found it." I held it up to show Ruben, the dust cascading off and making me cough.

Ruben made his way over and took the book from me. "This hasn't been touched in at least thirty years, given the state. How could he have known it was here?"

"Maybe he saw it in a vision? He seems to be able to communicate through visions, so maybe he can like…astral project?"

"No. I am fairly certain he was here."

Before I could ask Ruben why, he twisted the book to show a makeshift bookmark placed between two pages—a lollipop wrapper.

Yeah, that suggested he'd been here in person. I doubted few others would be able to—let alone *want* to—sneak into a place like this and have themselves a piece of candy.

That was pure Knot behavior right there.

I opened the book to the section marked—to find nothing but a rather well drawn cartoon of a dog urinating on what had to be the crystal in the main council chambers.

Yep, that was him.

It made me feel a little better, though. I laughed.

"What is so funny?"

"If we'd opened this book—that hasn't been touched in thirty years—and found exactly what we needed I would have been really concerned. That would have been like Knot could see into the future, that he knew what was going to happen. I don't like the idea that he's *that* powerful. I much prefer the idea that it was sheer chance that he could help, that he was breaking in and defacing precious ancient texts and had no idea it might prove useful later."

Ruben ran his finger across the drawing. "He did it in ink. I don't think this will ever come out. Do you have any idea how old this book is?"

"Well, I know that it's been sitting in a dusty room for half a century — at least. I don't think you're all that worried about it. Now, can we just take it with us? I don't really want to have to stay here to read it."

"Normally we don't allow the items here to be removed, but I can make an exception this time. It's almost midnight — let's get out of here."

And that sounded like the first good plan he'd had.

* * * *

I flopped down on the large bed, suddenly feeling every year of my age all at once. My back ached as though each vertebra in it ground against the one on top and the one below. It made it painful to sit, to stand, to exist.

Which meant getting to stop here for the night — even if it was already two in the morning — sounded like a fan-fucking-tastic idea to me.

We'd gotten a room at a little motel along the way. It seemed to be a honeymoon destination, because all the rooms had weird themes.

Jungle. Forest. Roman. Circus.

I hadn't cared if I had to sleep in a shoe, just so long as I could sleep.

They'd put us in Wild West, which meant the walls had cheesy western décor. A steer head above the bed — what said romance like a dead animal skull? — horseshoes everywhere, and wooden furniture that could have been out of the old prairie shows.

The only thing that made me think the room was actually perfect was the number of whips on the walls.

We could make use of those…

We got a single room, mostly because Ruben didn't sleep much. Given that, he said a separate room was pointless, and he'd simply work while I slept. I had a feeling part of it was that he wanted to keep an eye on me, but really, what trouble could I get into?

A lot…

I went to stand, to go brush my teeth, when my calves seized up. I hissed in a sharp breath through my teeth at the cramping pain.

Ruben was there in a heartbeat, leaning down to feel the muscle.

And when he pressed on it, when it hurt *more,* I kicked him right in his shin for the effort. "That hurts," I snapped.

"Why? Did you pull a muscle?"

"No, I'm just not used to exercise like that. I'm sore."

"You're sore from just that?"

"What, you don't get sore?"

He shook his head. "Most Spirits don't because we don't grow or lose muscle the same way as humans. Minds do, I believe. It seems you are not one of the more physically superior types."

"Physically superior," I muttered, mocking him by raising and lowering the intonation of the words.

He shook his head as though he weren't surprised by my little outburst. "You should take a hot bath, then rub out the knots in your muscles." He paused. "I could help you with that if you wish. When people do it themselves, they rarely do a good enough job since they tend to avoid pain."

"Yeah, I'm a big avoid pain person, so maybe not?"

"You will hurt far more tomorrow if you don't take care of it tonight. I assure you that you will sleep better if you just do as I say."

"Only if you talk dirty."

He snorted softly then rose. "I'll start the water. You don't need to soak long—I know you're tired—but some amount of hot water will help your muscles to relax and make the massage more effective." He didn't wait for my opinion, instead walking toward the bathroom.

The splashing of water in what sounded like a hella-deep tub came from the room, along with a delicate floral scent. Had he added some sort of bubble bath?

A place like this would probably have all sorts of goodies like that, wouldn't it?

He came back about five minutes later. "I set out a towel for you and one of the robes the hotel had. The water is still filling, but it is deep enough to get in now."

I got up without help—mostly because I refused to ask for it—and limped my way in.

That would have been far too shameful to let Ruben see it, especially as he strolled around the place like he was one hundred percent fine.

I closed the door behind me, then got a look at the bathroom for the first time. The tub was deep, but made of metal, like an old trough to feed horses. Other than that weirdness, the bathroom was actually pretty nice. It had a large window that opened to a private outdoor space, meaning I got to bathe *and* look at nature.

And for anyone with an exhibitionist kink, this was the sort of thing that would make their entire trip.

I never thought I had such a kink, but I felt like I kept discovering things about myself I never knew before. I'd say I was kink-suggestible. Even if I didn't think I was into something, it didn't take much for me to change my mind and decide I might just be.

I thought about the way Kelvin had watched Harrison and me, the lust in his eyes, the desire there as he'd held back and not touched.

Yeah, I guess I could understand the appeal of such a thing.

However, that was for a not sore and exhausted person. For me, I only wanted the water, maybe the massage, then hours of sleep.

Ruben had booked the room for two nights so I could sleep as late as I wanted and we wouldn't have to worry about a checkout time.

I stripped off my clothes — it took more work than it should have — and lowered myself into the water. It was extremely hot, but Ruben was right. The moment I submerged my legs, the pain started to subside. I turned off the faucet, the tub already almost full with me in it at as well.

There were no bubbles, but the water was oddly cloudy.

"What did you put in here?" I called out.

The door opened, and I put an arm over my chest to hide my tits, but leave it to Ruben to be gentlemanly even now. He didn't actually step into the bathroom, nor around the clouded divider, not where he could see me.

What a far cry from Kelvin, who would have been *in* the water with me if he had his way.

"What?" he asked.

"The water's cloudy and smells good, but there's no bubbles."

"Epsom salt. It helps with sore muscles. It was scented with lavender."

"Ah, that makes sense." I let out a nervous laugh with no fucking idea why I felt nervous. This was Ruben, after all. There was no reason to get all shy around him. Still, somehow, this conversation felt a lot weirder while I was naked and he was fully dressed.

It reminded me of just how vulnerable I felt, and how low my defenses were. The reality was that if he took a few steps into the space, I wouldn't have turned him away, that was for sure.

Maybe that was the real reason for my nerves, but I knew my actions only rested on what he actually tried. If he didn't push, if he didn't make that move, I wasn't about to, but if he did?

Yeah, I was going for it. Not a question in my mind.

I'd let him get away with just about anything.

However, he behaved himself like the responsible bastard he was. "Tell me if you need anything. I'll be looking through the book." The door clicked closed when he left, and I sank deeper into the tub, until my mouth was just above the waterline.

I could always get myself off if I wanted. There was something to that idea.

I was a strong, independent woman and I could get my own orgasms, after all.

However, the memory of his reaction after I'd gotten turned on made me wonder if he'd be able to tell if I did. He wouldn't say a word about it—that wasn't his way—but I didn't know if I could deal with the embarrassment if he knew what I'd been up to in here.

So I kept my hands to myself—from myself?—and finished my quick soak. The process of getting out turned out to be more daunting than getting in, however. Sure, my legs didn't hurt so bad, but they did feel a bit like that jellied cranberry sauce that came in the cans and I pictured them just collapsing into a puddle beneath me.

To my amazement, they didn't, and I pulled the robe around me. My hair remained up, since I wasn't about to waste my precious time trying to dry it. I could wash it tomorrow back at home, in my own space, and when I could sit in the shower.

I walked slowly as I emerged from the bathroom. Slipping on the tile floor was probably an all-time low I didn't know if I could come back from.

Ruben sat at the desk, his attention on the open book before him. He read it intently, so distracted he didn't even turn to notice me.

It gave me a moment to stare at him and wonder...when had this happened?

He'd been an annoyance for so long, just my boss who got on my nerves and caused me problems—nothing more. So why exactly did I view him differently, now? When had he gone from a pain in my ass to me really wanting him to be a pain in my ass?

I couldn't pinpoint the moment it had shifted, or even a trend. It was like dislike somehow transformed to like without me ever noticing it.

He turned his head, as though he'd just noticed my presence. A heat in his eyes caught my breath, held it there so I couldn't move.

Is this it?

I felt strangely nervous. I wasn't a virgin—no, I'd graduated to orgies, after all—so I had no reason to feel this sort of anxiety, but that didn't stop it from affecting me, from rooting me in place.

His gaze moved down my body, though I knew there wasn't much to see. I wore one of the fluffy white robes left by the hotel, which wasn't slinky or form fitting. My legs were bare, of course, and he sure looked a lot slower when he got there.

He swallowed hard, an honest-to-god gulp, before shutting the book and rising.

"Come on," he said, his voice tense. "I'll help with your legs."

Right. That was the plan. Leave it to me to completely forget about everything beyond my pussy. I wasn't just easy, I was eager.

I went over, trying to not let it show how much my legs hurt. Not just my calves, but my thighs and even my ass. All the muscles ached, and I had a feeling they weren't going to feel that much better for a day or two.

Still, I wasn't about to turn down a massage.

I paused on the bed, unsure how to lie.

"Whatever makes you comfortable."

I considered on my back, spread-eagled, but then wondered if something like that was too much for Ruben. In fact, part of me wondered if he'd go running if I tried such a blatant come-on.

Well, it was my calves mostly, right?

I lay on my front, shimmying to ensure the robe covered everything. I wore nothing beneath it, since I hadn't packed anything. Ruben had brought a bag that included a set of clothes for tomorrow for me—no idea where he'd gotten them, and I shuddered to think what he might have picked out—but he hadn't mentioned pajamas so I wasn't sure there were any.

The mattress dipped down beneath his weight when he sat on the edge, beside me. He'd undone a few of the buttons of his shirt and the sleeves were still rolled up, his jacket tossed over the back of the desk chair. He'd removed his shoes, leaving him in a pair of black socks.

It made him appear far more casual than I was used to seeing him.

I wondered for a moment if he ever wore casual clothing. What would that look like? I couldn't picture it.

Did I actually like him? The idea seemed strange to me.

Then he touched my calf for the first time, digging his thumbs into the aching muscles there, and I knew it—

No, I don't fucking like this sadistic asshole!

Despite a quick kick that I'd wanted to hit him in the face with, he caught my ankle with his other hand and held it down. "I know it hurts, but it'll feel better soon."

"Like hell it will. I know that people guess a lot about my proclivities, but I can assure you, I'm not that much of a masochist."

"Trust me."

"Why should I? I remember when you made me do that lube delivery to the nymph orgy. Anyone who does that does *not* deserve any sort of trust. Lube deliveries are not a trust-building activity."

"I sent you there because I knew you could handle it. Believe it or not, I don't coddle you like Galen or Kelvin. They both try to protect you from everything, to keep you away from the world. I knew from the start that you would need to have the skills to survive it on your own, so everything I've done as been to ensure you are strong enough to make it here, that you have the ability to protect yourself and not need me anymore."

His words stilled my struggles as though they'd disconnected my pain receptors for a moment. I thought back to all the times he'd put me in situations that I wasn't a huge fan of, the times he hadn't rushed in when it would have been nice.

And…all the times I'd grown because of it. When I'd stood on my own and gone home—tired and hurting, at times, but on my own.

"Even those times, I never was too far. If I was worried you might not manage something, I never failed to have other things in play, to ensure that you were not entirely on your own. I know I can be difficult, that I can seem uncaring, but that isn't how it is."

The words were nice, but when he started working the muscle again, I had trouble believing him. Maybe he just got off on this.

Then again, who was I to fault anyone's kinks?

So I bit my lip—though pained groans still left me—and tried to just accept the touch. Before I knew it, his words proved correct, as impossible as that seemed. It really did feel better.

The pain lessened each time he dug in, the knots looser.

"Roll over." His voice came out husky and deep.

I froze.

"Your quads will be sore as well, and I can't reach them like this."

Oh. I shifted, rolling, feeling the aching through my thighs and ass—even up to my ribs from where I'd balanced on the ladders.

Maybe he had a point.

The robe remained tied securely around my front and fell low enough to not let anything show.

I could handle this, right? I wasn't going to melt like some silly little virgin at a simple massage.

He dragged his fingertips over my knees, then down the sides to stroke the outer edge of my thigh.

And the moan I let out told me that was bullshit.
I sure as fuck wasn't going to manage to resist shit.

Chapter Nine

Ruben

How could a person be this *soft*? Grey's skin was beyond anything I'd ever felt before, reaching deeper than I thought possible.

It was as though she had a direct connection to something inside me, something I could no longer reach myself.

People said that Justices had no feelings, and they were neither completely right nor completely wrong. It rested somewhere in between those two things.

We had feelings, somewhere, but remained so detached from them that we rarely noticed them. They certainly didn't affect us.

Even sex was something we didn't crave, hardly engaged in.

On occasion a Justice would choose to, but it was rare. We simply didn't feel that need, so disconnected with lust to fall prey to such petty, primal experiences.

So why had my cock hardened? Why did my heart pound faster than it had during countless battles before?

And why did the tiny trembles of her thighs excite me this much?

It made no sense. That was the reason I'd found an interest in her from the start, because I couldn't believe that I had a reaction to her like that, that I wanted her in a way I never had wanted anyone before.

I'd assumed it a fluke, something caused by her unknown designation. At times, over the years, I'd even thought she was a test or a punishment, something crafted to yank me down into my own personal hell.

Now I wondered if she wasn't the opposite — perhaps my only chance at real salvation.

I tried to focus on the massage — I truly did.

That was the entire purpose of this, after all, to help since I knew she hurt. I didn't enjoy seeing her in pain, and I wanted to ease her as much as I could.

However, after I had seen her standing there in the robe, I struggled to recall any of that. It no longer was just helping her to feel better.

I wanted to touch her for reasons that had nothing to do with her aching. I wanted to tug the tie at her waist, to part the terrycloth that hid her, to see every inch of her displayed for me.

It was a strange desire.

That wasn't to say I hadn't thought about such things with her before. She had plagued my dreams and fantasies in the time since she had trampled into my life, disrupting everything I previously thought solid.

The difference was that this was the first time the need to act on such thoughts took such a firm hold. I couldn't ignore it as I usually did, couldn't relegate it to some dark crevice of my fragmented mind. Instead, it took over, returning time and time again with each movement she made.

I tried to focus on the massage as I worked out knots in her thighs, up to the edge of the robe. It fell just above mid-thigh, so enough to cover everything and keep much of the needed work area inaccessible.

"I'm going to need to go under the robe," I said, wondering if that was really my voice. It was deeper, darker than usual. It had this animalistic quality to it that startled me, that I didn't recognize at all.

The whites of her teeth appeared as she took her bottom lip between them and nodded.

Was she nervous?

I hesitated for a moment, worrying I might have scared her. A deep inhalation said no—what she felt wasn't fear at all. A spice wafted in the air, and I knew enough to identify it as her arousal.

Clearly, she didn't oppose this after all.

I took her agreement—along with her excitement— as consent and slipped my fingers beneath the edges of her robe. I forced myself to stay on task, working at the quad muscles on each leg.

It felt different, though, lewd in a strange way, since I had to reach beneath her clothing to touch her. It felt as though we were doing something forbidden, and it made my cock ache all the more.

She parted her legs when I reached toward the inside, the movement subtle but something I noticed instantly. It was a welcome, a trust I'd never expected, one I hadn't expected to ever earn or deserve.

She swallowed hard but again did that same movement, shifting her legs just enough to tease me, to offer me something that I still didn't feel fully ready to accept.

Memories of my past life, before I turned into this, were there, locked away, like something detached, like a play I had once seen but felt nothing about. I'd had sex then, of course, had enjoyed it, but I struggled to connect that with me now. I didn't know what it any of it meant.

I slipped my hands around one of her thighs, grasping her on both sides of it, then massaged the muscle. It felt intimate, to have one of my hands between her legs. I focused on the back of the muscle, moving until I reached the curve of her ass.

Again, I slowed to a crawl to see if she would tell me to stop, if she'd object.

If she did, I would, of course.

Nothing. In fact, she shifted her other leg, bending at the knee and letting it fall open in a clear invitation.

I pressed the knee of the leg I held and pushed it outward as well, to splay her legs wide. It caused the robe to ride up, to open just enough for me to see…everything.

Pinkness sat on her cheeks, and she'd closed her eyes. This was *such* a Grey thing to do, to know damn well that I could see her pussy but pretend I couldn't, to leave me with the torturous decision between telling her the truth and covering her up or letting it go and seeing where it led.

I for sure planned on the second of those options.

I ran my fingers softly up her inner thigh, savoring the way her muscles reacted with tiny twitches from the stimulation. I traced the inner crease of her leg, digging in slightly to the hip joint there, the back of my hand coming close enough to her cunt that the warmth teased me.

Fuck, this was a dangerous game we played.

I massaged her ass, the large muscles there, and each stroke of my hands caused her pussy to part slightly, to twitch.

I, who had faced off against countless Spirits over my years as a Justice, struggled not to allow my hands to shake. It was almost humiliating, yet a part of me didn't mind being brought low if it were by this person.

I had a feeling that nearly anything she did would be just fine by me, that I'd accept it, even revel in it.

And the sensation of feeling something new, something unexpected after so many years of feeling nothing intoxicated me.

Her eyes remained shut tight, her head tipped backward to expose her throat. Her tie had loosened enough to cause the robe to gap farther, so I didn't have to reach below it anymore. It didn't show her breasts, but exposed a valley of flawless skin between them, a space that ran down to show her belly button, her soft stomach, like a runway for me to drag my tongue.

But that would require moving from where I was, and I doubted I had the control to do that.

I shifted my hands in more, dancing dangerously close to her pussy as I massaged her ass, as I rubbed the inner creases of her thighs. Each pass let me inch closer to the goal that called to me, to that glistening slit that I wanted so badly to touch.

Yet we played this stupid game. Neither of us thought this was just a massage any longer, but that lie allowed us as to pretend and made it easier.

My fingers ghosted over her cunt, and she jerked from the contact. It was so slight that I hardly felt her at all, but her reaction said *she'd* felt it.

I paused, wondering if she'd tell me off, if she'd tell me to stop touching her.

Nothing.

If anything, she spread her legs wider.

That was an invitation, right?

I suddenly wished I were better with women, that I had something more to offer her than strange, old instincts that I couldn't fully understand or explain.

However, those fears and doubts couldn't stand against the need inside me, so I let myself go. I stopped trying to control this, to control myself, to do the logical thing.

Instead, I scooted back and bent forward, lifting her body just a little, to bring her cunt and my lips together. It felt like an obvious thing to do, as though some part of me still existed that could feel these things, these wants.

I ran my tongue up her cunt, and my first true taste of her lingered like rapture.

As it turned out, heaven or hell, I didn't give a damn. I wanted this woman no matter where she led me.

Grey

The stroke of Ruben's tongue against my cunt was all together unexpected. I didn't know how much experience he had—I was guessing not a lot—and given how tentative he'd been, I figured he'd be more a fumbling asshat when trying this sort of thing. In my experience, those who didn't know what they were doing tended to go right for the action, to satisfy their own desires.

To be fair, I was okay with that. A little rough, inexperienced sex had its benefit some of the time, after all, and if it was Ruben, I was pretty sure I could forgive most things.

Instead, he decides to eat me out? It was almost enough to make me laugh—if it wasn't for the movements of his tongue against my folds.

Again, men often had no fucking idea what they were doing and treated eating a girl out like it was just a quick kindness—with lots of drool—hoping that was enough. Not Ruben, though. Instead, his every touch seemed centered on discovering my entire pussy, of ensuring no tiny piece of me went unmapped with his tongue and his lips.

I made no sounds—I was sure of that—but he must have paid attention to my breathing or any other way my body betrayed my true feelings, because anything that felt exceptionally good, he repeated as though to make sure he'd gotten it right.

It meant it didn't take long, between the massage and his skilled lips, that he brought me so close to release that I wondered if I could hold out.

I didn't normally hold back much. That wasn't my style. I much preferred letting myself go. It wasn't like coming once was going to end a night, after all, and there was *nothing* worse than trying to hold back and never finding that place again, than going to bed wound up and horny all because I'd tried to resist.

It was like refusing dinner because you thought you were getting something better later, than that thing getting canceled, so you had to go to sleep hungry.

I didn't like sleeping hungry or horny, so I rarely resisted.

However, something about this moment felt so fragile, I feared interrupting it. Funny to think about Ruben as innocent, but a part of me worried that if I came, he might get scared off, that he'd skitter back to the friend zone we'd been in before if I dared break this little game we played.

His lips left my body for a moment though his breath still warmed me. "Go ahead," he whispered, the words absolutely sinful in the small, silent room. "This will help you sleep, too."

That shook apart any fantasies, and I wondered if I'd be able to come at all after it.

Sleep?

Sure, I knew the game we were playing, that we were pretending this was just a massage, but it loosened my grip on everything. Surely, with his lips literally on my clit, he didn't want to act as though he were still just doing me a favor, did he?

Is that what he thought this was? Just something he did because I'd walked up and down those ladders? Because I was sore and he wanted me to sleep?

I wasn't sure I really believed that, that he'd go this far, but Ruben was difficult to understand. Maybe it was. Maybe he'd started this and realized he didn't feel the way he thought?

Maybe I'd just hit that point where people usually decided I was too much.

He erased the fear that I wouldn't get off, however, when he focused his attention on my clit, when he dove back in as though my orgasm were his own personal trophy.

And I came despite everything, despite the questions, the uncertainty. I came apart beneath him, unable to hold myself together, to keep that part of me hidden.

As I trembled afterward, my body overly sensitive, I knew that was it. He wasn't going to keep going. Sure enough, he pulled a blanket over me and returned to the book at the desk, leaving me there.

This fucking sucks.

Chapter Ten

Morning-afters were inevitably awkward. It was like some unwritten rule that everyone had to follow, the idea that we wouldn't be able to act friendly, that we had to feel weird and uncomfortable.

And this morning sure did fucking follow that trend.

Ruben hadn't said anything about the night before. I'd woken up to find him gone, and had thought for a moment he'd dined and dashed on me.

However, he'd shown back up, surprised I'd woken so early, and with food. I could forgive most people if they bought me food, as it turned out.

We'd eaten in the room in painful silence before checking out and heading back toward home around ten in the morning. It meant I hadn't gotten enough sleep to feel well rested, but I wouldn't pass out, either.

The truck turned out to be just as uncomfortable as the hotel room, telling me that our awkwardness was hardly location related.

"About last night," Ruben started, his gaze locked forward.

Nope.

He had that flat tone and I wasn't sure I could handle him telling me that it was all a misunderstanding, that he'd done it to help me relax, because he knew I'd needed the sleep. What if he said it was some reward for me having gone on the trip and us finding the book?

So as I found was usually the better path than just waiting to get hit, I struck first. "It didn't mean anything. I know—it's okay."

He furrowed his brow. What, did he not like me saying it first? He didn't enjoy losing out on being the one who won?

Too fucking bad.

I went on, nerves causing my words to rattle out. "It was just a spur-of-the-moment thing because I was sore and needed a good night's sleep. Don't worry about it—I get it. I mean, you and me?" I forced out a laugh that probably didn't come across as all that honest. "Ridiculous. We're good. This is for the best, anyway. It's good for us to know where we stand. What's a little oral sex between coworkers?"

Even I winced at that last one.

He said nothing, his gaze still locked on the road out front. The silence carried on for so long that I worried we wouldn't speak again for the entire six-hour ride home.

Part of me wondered if that wouldn't be less painful, all things considered. Sure, silence sucked, but did we have anything to say worth saying?

After four minutes—according to the infotainment screen in the center of the truck's dashboard, because I watched—Ruben finally answered. "Okay."

It was a simple answer, yet it seemed to shatter something inside me.

Okay?

What the fuck was up with this disappointment I felt?

Why would I actually be upset over him accepting what I'd said? What, did I want him to fight with me over it? To tell me no, there was something more between us? That it was different than I thought?

Instead of risking opening my mouth again, I reached forward and hit the radio button on the screen, then cranked up the dial, letting music fill the cab.

It was country, which I didn't normally love, but which seemed to set the depressing mood perfectly right now. Some man sang about losing his woman, about how it destroyed his life, and if nothing else, it made me think that yeah — this was for the best.

Orgasms were one thing — giving away hearts was the thing that really hurt a person.

* * * *

Let sleeping dogs lie.

I wondered if the saying also went for wolves. Not that it mattered — I planned to do what I wanted no matter what old idiom told me otherwise.

Sure, Galen was cute as fuck in his sleep. He didn't have his glasses on, of course, and it made him appear less like a computer nerd. He also seemed oddly relaxed in a way he rarely was when awake.

It made it clear the weight on his shoulders, the worries he carried all the time. As alpha for all the wolves, as leader for all the Weres, he had so many things to deal with.

Looking at him like this, I could understand why girls so often fell for him.

Except *that* wasn't what was on the agenda for today. If I wanted to molest him while he was sleeping, that would have to wait.

"I found it," I said, lowering my voice to a whisper.

He jerked upright, his lips peeled back, his teeth already shifted into fangs. He looked around, his eyes bright, searching for whatever had dared woken him.

If I had any brains or self-preservation, I probably would have worried. Most people who saw that didn't see much past it—ever.

Me, though?

It was just Galen. No matter how he growled or snarled, I never found it in me to be truly afraid of him.

He twisted his gaze toward me, and I expected the fangs to recede, for him to recognize me and lecture me as he usually did.

That didn't happen.

Those bright eyes locked on me, and if anything, brightened…

That is not good.

A tense heartbeat later, he shook his head, then dropped it into his hands. A shudder ran through his body, and when he lifted his face toward mine again, he was back to fully human.

Not that that erased the memory of what had just happened.

"Why would you wake me up like that?"

"Well, I thought about waking you with a blow job or something, but figured you might object to that. Besides, I whispered."

He didn't react to my joke. Was he still groggy? All I knew for sure was that he didn't appear amused by it, or even that annoyed.

"Would you meet me downstairs?"

"But I've got stuff to say," I whined, then held up the yellow book. "It's all in here."

He slid out of the bed, on the other side, giving me a perfect view of his ass.

And this one could hold its own against Ruben's. Maybe it was because I saw Galen's in all its naked glory or something, but damn.

He glanced over his shoulder, a dangerous glint to his eyes, a warning and a dare.

It all seemed so unlike him. "Downstairs."

"Right," I said, his tone getting me moving.

After what had happened with Ruben, I sure didn't need to get rejected yet again. Once in a twenty-four hour period was quite enough humiliation for me.

I didn't turn to walk out, though. Nope. Even if I were conceding ground here, I wasn't going to waste the retreat.

So I walked backward toward the door, not willing to tear my eyes away from his broad, toned back, the way his waist tucked in toward his hips, the perfect curve of his ass.

Fuck me.

And I meant that in a pretty literal way. I didn't think I'd mind it one bit if he decided to go that way.

Of course, he wanted me to be his mate, so he'd probably start bothering me about that, wanting a commitment.

Just let me have that dick.

I caught myself just when I reached the stairs before I went toppling down them, when he bent forward slightly to pull on a pair of jeans.

Please leave them undone.

I sent that final plea into the universe before giving in and turning around to wait downstairs.

The clock above the kitchen table read four in the morning. I was exhausted, of course, since after getting home rather late from Ruben's and my little trip, I had immediately gone to work reading the book.

Ruben had complained, telling me that he should keep it, but it seemed his heart was less in the battle than usual as he gave up rather quickly.

That was fine with me. All I really wanted was the chance to go through it. I figured I was a better option, since Knot had told me about it. Besides, I was the one working on this, helping Galen with it.

Ruben couldn't get too directly involved without risking it becoming an official Justice problem and no one wanted that.

The Justices solved a lot of problems, sure, but they usually did it in a way no one liked. It was like when Mom came in and grounded everyone.

Sure, the fighting stopped, but we were all paying the price for it.

I'd rather not get scolded by Mother Dearest, so it was better the kids dealt with it ourselves.

I made myself a snack while I waited, since I'd missed dinner. The sandwich looked amazing, not because of my skill but rather because Galen always had the best food on hand.

It probably came from a fear that hungry werewolves could eat people, which meant they liked to keep good food around.

Just as I cut it down the center, Galen came around the corner, his bare feet soft and silent against the hardwood floors. His hair was messy, as though he'd simply finger combed the strands, and more tension than usual sat in his shoulders.

Was that because of me waking him up or was he stressed about the issue with the Weres?

He didn't address me at first, instead going over the coffee maker and setting it up to brew a pot.

I'd hit the point where I knew I'd just miss sleep for today, so bring on the coffee.

The scent filled the room, but the liquid percolating and spilling into the carafe was darker than usual. That seemed a sure sign that he wasn't doing that great, and probably not just because of the whole four in the morning thing.

We didn't speak as he made two cups of coffee. He made mine just the way I liked it and set it before me, then sat across the table.

He took a sip, closed his eyes as he savored it, then finally looked at me. "All right. Now, what was so important that you woke me up at four in the morning?"

"To be fair, I've snuck in here lots of times. You normally hear me before I ever get to your room." Saying it out loud made me realize just how weird that really was. Why hadn't he heard me?

"I've been dealing with a lot and not sleeping well. I suggest you don't try that again. If you ring the doorbell, I'll hear no matter what."

I pursed my lips at the idea of ringing the doorbell. I hated that, probably because I feared somewhere inside of me that if I asked for permission to enter, I wouldn't get it. I'd seen too many closed and locked doors in my face to want to put myself willingly into that situation.

"Do you want to hear what I found or not?"

He nodded. "You came all this way—you might as well tell me."

I tapped the book and explained how Knot had told me about it and how Ruben had helped me get it from the archives. He said nothing, just listened the way he often did.

I'd give him credit for that—Galen had always been exceptional at just letting me get the story out first.

"I stayed up reading it last night. See, Knot didn't tell me what exactly I was looking for, as usual. It took a while. The book is written about Spirits, about how they come into being or disappear. It's a book of stories, of fables, but this one here, the stagnant river, *this* is our answer."

"A book of fables is our answer?" His question came out dry.

"It's about a clan of Spirits who traveled too far away from their source. They wanted to find new grounds, always wanting to expand, to have more. So the clan picks up and relocates, over and over again. Each new generation spreads farther, moves farther away, and they start to forget where they lived before. They start to forget the river that had given them life, that had fed them and helped them to survive. They eventually don't tell those stories anymore, and the river forgets about them. See, the water has to flow much farther now to reach them, and the rivers fork off and because they've traveled so far, the water doesn't flow right anymore. It grows thick and is full of algae and illness. The entire clan ends up dying because they are too far away from the water source."

Galen took another drink of his coffee, and I couldn't read his expression. Did he understand my point? Did he read into the story? He set his cup down. "So you think that story has something to do with what is happening now?"

"Knot wouldn't have sent me there if it didn't. Look, we know that energy flows from central places, right? That's what creates the clans. Those central places of power are the waterfalls. What if because we've forgotten about those, we aren't doing something we're supposed to anymore?"

Galen sat back in his seat. "A long time ago, long before I became a Were, I've heard stories that the heads of the different types would make pilgrimages to somewhere in the forest. Every Were would when they first became one, and the elders at other times to honor the old god."

"I thought you didn't believe in the old gods."

"I don't. I think people—Spirit or human—are fantastic at turning things they can't understand into gods. They've done it forever. However, there might be something to what you're saying. Perhaps there is something that has to be done for the energy to flow correctly."

"Why would it only affect the Weres, though?"

"There are more Weres than other groups, so that could be why. Or maybe whatever has to be done, the other clans are still doing some of? Or it might still hit the other clans, but the Weres showed the symptoms fastest?" He shook his head, as though frustrated by the lack of clear answers.

"So what now?"

"There is a very old Were who might remember such times. He isn't really sane anymore."

"Is he locked up then?"

"No. He isolated himself a long time ago, so we leave him alone for the most part."

"Wolf?"

"Tiger."

I frowned. "I've never heard of those."

"They're rare, even more so because he is a white tiger. However, if anyone remembers the old rituals, he would."

"Maybe we should talk to the other clans about any rituals they might still do? See if there's anything useful there?" I suggested.

"I doubt they would tell me anything, but you are welcome to try."

I got the sense he didn't like saying that, as though he had a distaste for sending me off to do work like that — especially with the other clans.

"I would start with the Natures."

"Yeah, Kelvin doesn't seem very *ritual* to me, and the Minds…" I trailed off when I couldn't bring myself to admit that Harrison had still not reached out. How long had it been since everything had happened, since I'd killed his brother to save him and myself?

"Still no word?" Galen asked, his voice gentle.

I shook my head, then let out a hollow laugh. "I guess he's as good at holding grudges as I am."

Galen lifted his hand, as though to reach across the table and hold mine, but paused before he did so. He closed his hand into a fist and pulled back.

What the hell is that about?

"I'll make the arrangements to go see the tiger."

"When are we leaving?"

"We aren't. I am."

I let out an exasperated breath. "Come on, Galen, haven't I proven myself yet? I'm the one who found this." I tapped the book. "I want to know what he says."

"You don't need to get any more involved in this than you are."

"You're the one who's always talking about mates, but you won't even accept my help?" I knew that was a dirty card to play, but I couldn't help it. I'd come this far, helped this much, I couldn't stop now.

And whether Galen wanted to admit it or not, I *was* helpful. I didn't see the world as he did, as most of the Spirits did, because I wasn't one of them. So the things they took for granted, the truths they just assumed, I questioned.

"Given the situation with the strays, I don't know if the tiger will be safe or not," Galen admitted.

"So? I've seen you take on a werebear."

"I don't think you understand. This weretiger is thousands of years old, maybe more. I don't know how strong he is, or whether or not I could protect you."

"Well, good thing I can protect myself." I moved my hand to open my personal bay, the portal shimmering into sight where I could put my things—one of the rare advantages to my job as a courier—and pulled out a small black device that fit into my hand. "See? Stun gun. I'm good!" I tossed it back in when he looked less impressed than I'd hoped, and closed the portal.

"Grey…"

"Look, I'm going whether you want me there or not. If you try to leave without me, I'll just follow you. If you try to trap me, I'll escape. If you make it really difficult to go with you, then I'll find him and go myself. So, your options are to take me with you or let me go on my own, but make no mistake—I am going to go meet him." I picked up my coffee to drink it like a badass.

Only I had forgotten just how hot it was, so the large gulp I took burned my mouth and tongue, and I spit it back into the cup with a pained hiss.

So much for looking like a badass, huh?

Still, even with that little display, Galen sighed. "Fine. If those are my options, I guess taking you with me is the safer of the two. We'll leave in three days."

"How far is it?"

"He lives in a forest in South America."

"So I'll need a passport? Because I don't have one."

Galen shook his head. "I have access to a private plane and we can make it over the borders without notice."

Even with that worked out, however, I noticed Galen didn't exactly look happier. In fact, I'd venture the opposite. He appeared tenser than he had when I'd arrived, as though every little bit of time here, with me, had only caused him more uneasiness.

Why?

He'd never been a super-chill dude, but he'd never been like this.

The memory of how he'd pulled his hand back stuck with me. I chalked it all up to stress, to the frustration of what was happening, the fear that his entire clan might be in danger and that he might not have a way to save them.

Galen always took those things on himself, felt responsible for it all, for everything.

So I finished the coffee—more slowly this time—and didn't address it, didn't risk making it worse by pointing out the way he was acting.

I could only hope that when we fixed this, when we found a way to save them, he'd relax.

Because the thought of him snapping scared even me.

Chapter Eleven

"Rituals?" Kelvin gave me the exact response I expected from him. Good to know he wouldn't disappoint me, even if I didn't like it. The word came out on a laugh, as though I were asking him about Santa.

"Yes, rituals. Do you know of any?"

"Graves aren't the superstitious type."

"You are literally brought back from the dead—let's not act like you're somehow immune to crazy beliefs."

"Be that as it may, no, I'm not aware of any vampire rituals."

"What about other Graves?"

"Necromancers might, mediums might, but anything else? I don't know."

I blew out a disappointed breath before adding, "Maybe not now, but can you think of hearing about anyone ever doing such a thing?"

He tapped his finger against the top of his knee as he stared out of the large window.

He'd moved into the penthouse — and boy fuck did I not feel comfortable there. I couldn't quite get the memory of the last leader of the Grave Clan, William, whose body I'd seen in here.

And whose murder I was framed for.

Sort of framed by Kelvin, no less, even if not on purpose.

Sure, Kelvin had gutted the place, redone every wall, all the flooring, moved in furniture that was more fitting to his style, but the layout remained the same. It was why I preferred to meet at hotels for our time, but sometimes coming here was my only choice.

I had access to the penthouse now, not just for deliveries. The records showed me as his thrall, even if there were some questions about how the bond worked. It gave me the ability to come and go as I pleased, and vampires tended to give me a pretty large margin of space now.

Even after all that mess, however, after knowing that Kelvin was involved in some shady shit, in the vampire extremist group Blackstone, we'd never really addressed it. I had a feeling that anything I asked wouldn't get a straight answer anyway.

"There are stories of things vampires used to do, yes. I don't know if I'd call them rituals."

"What things?"

"Human sacrifice, for one. Blood sacrifices. Who doesn't love to sacrifice a virgin?"

"Well thank fuck for my promiscuity, because that hasn't been a risk with me for a long time."

"Are you certain?" He tugged me over until I moved into his lap, my knees parted around his hips. "I feel as though we could be extra careful, that I could ensure there's no chance of such a fate befalling you." He leaned in and whispered the words into my ear, his tongue flicking against my lobe in a blatant tease.

I shoved his chest as I sat up straight. "It's good to know a man whore like yourself is safe as well. Now, back to the rituals."

He let his head fall back to the couch, his arms flopping down beside him as though I were just far too exhausting for his liking. "Are you that concerned about the Weres?"

"You should be, too. Didn't you threaten Galen over this?"

"I threaten everyone over everything. It's not personal. Besides, if the Weres continue to go mad, it just means we'll get the okay to hunt them down and…" He paused, as though rethinking his word choice. "*Handle* the situation. If anything, any attempts by you might make the problem worse. You are known for that sort of thing."

"That isn't true." I thought back and fought the desire to frown as I considered the many times I'd made things significantly worse.

Like when instead of just looking for drugs I'd started selling them to kids, or the time I hid from the vampires by staying *in* their stronghold.

Okay, so maybe I had a slight history of escalating situations beyond where they started, but that didn't mean I did it every time. Plus, even when it happened, I typically solved them at the end, didn't I?

It felt slanted to only remember the hiccups along the way.

"Besides," I said, so perhaps he didn't think back on my many fuckups, "for all we know, what's happening to them could happen to you."

"We don't turn into strays."

"No, but it sounds as though other clans have gotten sick from this, died off from many different causes. Isn't it better to find a cure while there are more people searching for it?"

He lifted his head again to look at me. "You really push my buttons, you know that? I would never even think about doing something to help another clan, not without a direct benefit to my own, yet you bat those lashes and spread those legs of yours and I act entirely unlike myself."

"I haven't spread my legs."

He glanced down at my position and lifted his eyebrow.

"Tell me about the sacrifices."

"Then I can feed?"

We were a few days early from our normal schedule, but it seemed a fair trade. Besides, it wasn't like I didn't enjoy it, even if I'd never directly admit that.

"Fine. Deal."

He smiled, as though finally interested in our conversation. It amused me how quickly he went from bored and sullen to a boy reciting a book report he'd worked really hard on. "The sacrifices were done in the past to appease the royal blood. It was believed that we were vampire because we held sparks of royal blood, from a queen, and that she had to be fed and appeased or she would come to reclaim the blood we had taken from her."

"How did you do that?"

"They haven't done this in centuries, at least not that I'm aware of. There could still be small cults in places that practice it, but I don't know of any. I believe I heard it that the elders would draw lines in the sand beneath the bound victim, then slice them open and allow the blood to soak into the ground. They were not allowed to feast on these sacrifices, as it was a gift to the queen."

I shivered hard as I thought about such a terrible fate for a person. To be helpless, to lose their life in such a way just to old superstition? It was truly terrible.

I didn't blame the vampires, not entirely, since countless human faiths had committed similar atrocities. It seemed people of any type enjoyed the suffering of others, would do horrible things just because they imagined some being told them to.

I didn't know if I believed in some old queen, but perhaps there was something to be said about that ritual, something that let that energy flow freshly when they did it. It was hard to believe it mattered, that it would make a difference, but that didn't mean it wouldn't.

Before I knew about this world, about the vampires, the idea that a being could be dead, that they could feed off the blood of the living as their only source of sustenance, that made no sense to me. I would have disregarded it as a pipe dream, as a nightmare from someone who had too much time on their hands.

It meant I didn't write off stories as quickly as I used to. Besides, just because they used to do it that way didn't mean they *had* to do it that way. It was like when I thought that getting into fist fights made me skinny, and it turned out it was the fact it hurt too much to eat afterward that I skipped meals.

So the ritual might have given them something, but that didn't mean we couldn't change it to something that didn't require slicing people open and allowing them to bleed out.

Maybe some sort of vegan option?

Lips found mine, pulling me from my thoughts. Kelvin sure was good at doing that, though, at forcing me to think only about him, about what was going on, to wipe away everything else. I had to admit, it was one of the things I enjoyed about him.

He held the rest of the world at bay, letting me live in just one blissful moment when I got to experience just a little bit of pleasure.

Plus, he might be a sneaky asshole, he might lie to me about most things, but I never doubted his devotion to me. He proved that time and time again. Sure, if a body showed up, there was a good ninety percent chance that he had something to do with it, but that didn't change that I could trust how he felt about me.

So when he kissed me, when he pulled me tighter against his body, I lost myself. I stopped worrying about the Weres, about the meetings, about the book, about it all. I existed only in this moment.

He paused and stared at me, a question there, the same one he always asked me at this point.

Now?

Was I going to ask him to go further, to cross that line? If I didn't tell him yes now, before he bit me, before I lost my mind and *begged* him, then he wouldn't actually fuck me.

And boy, did I beg when we got to that point. The cloudy memories of it, of the times I almost cried pleading with him to take me, to fill me up, to fuck me, they woke me from sleep at times from filthy dreams that repeated over and over again in my head.

Yeah, I knew I wanted that, but I still held back.

It felt like the last bit of control I had, the last bit of self-respect, of safety. I could blame this all on the bond, on us needing each other, but if told him yes before the bite?

I had to admit, this was real. I had to accept whatever it was, to take personal responsibility for it, and I just wasn't ready for that. Wasn't sure I ever would be, really. It was too scary, too large, too real.

So I didn't answer. I didn't say no, but neither did I say yes.

Kelvin, despite this all, had never made me feel bad about the choice. In fact, he smiled, no anger or frustration in the expression. "That's the nice thing about being immortal — I can wait."

He tilted my head, pressed a kiss to my pulse, then struck with a familiar pain.

Yeah, this isn't so bad a way to ignore the rest of the world.

* * * *

Kelvin

Grey cuddled beneath my black silk sheets, her shoulder bare, her neck showing the marks I'd left on her.

I would have sworn my heart had stopped long ago but fuck if it didn't seem to pound at the sight of her.

Mine.

I knew it. Sure, she was my thrall, connected to me, bound to me in a way that was instinctual and primal and unbreakable. That was a part of it, but I suspected it went far deeper. She was something new, something unexpected in a long and hard life.

Even if I had never bound her to me, even if I had never attempted that, I would feel exactly the same way. Something about her shocked me to my core, made me uneasy and certain and confused all at the same time. She was perhaps the only thing in me that caused such conflicting feelings.

And yet she'd denied me again.

I never wanted her to know how deeply it wounded each time it happened. I deserved to carry that pain—not her. And I would keep taking blow after blow until she finally accepted my feelings, until we rebuilt whatever we had between us, until she learned to trust me again.

She frowned, her lips moving as though she were talking. Judging from the pinched expression, whatever dream she experienced wasn't good.

I leaned in closer, hoping to catch this tiny piece of her inner life, the part of her she hid from everyone, the part I desperately wanted to own. Was she having a nightmare? I knew little about her in many ways, but what I'd gleaned from both her words and background checks said many parts of her past hadn't been great.

She had a loving family now—I'd spent time with them at this point, gotten to know them—but that hadn't always been the case. No one gained the dark sense of humor she had if they lived a perfect life, after all.

I listened intently, hoping to catch something from her, to understand what she dreamed of as though that would unlock everything from her.

She whispered, her voice so low I had to strain to pick up the words.

"No."

No?

The stress in that word put me on edge, as though I could fight shadows for her.

I was fairly certain I would try, that I would find a way to enter her dreams, her memories, and rid her of whatever plagued her. I knew better than most that life was hard, that it hurt no matter how blessed a person seemed, that it didn't exist without pain, yet knowing that, I still felt determined to do away with what I could for her.

I wanted her to have the perfect life without strife.

"I want to pet the snake. Don't care if it rattles. It'll like me." She whispered those pleading words, taking away the unease inside me, making me smile.

Of course, she dreamed of being told she shouldn't pet a rattlesnake, and no doubt she'd still attempt to pet it—dream or not. It was so on brand for the chaotic woman that I had to restrain myself from reaching out and gathering her in my arms, to kiss her for the perfectly ridiculous person she was.

I held back. One of the benefits of our bond being I could tell how run down she was, how much she needed this sleep. I wouldn't dare disrupt it, no matter how adorable I found her.

Instead, I moved to the office to complete work while she slept. I didn't like to leave before she woke, mostly because the opposite would bother me. Rising to find she'd left never sat well, and I didn't want her to ever feel that same nagging doubt.

I threw myself into my work, sighing at the problems that constantly sprang up. I had hoped that I would take over and resolve it all. Perhaps that was the ignorance that always came with ambition, the confidence that one would gain power and make things better.

If people knew how little they could truly affect things, how much would still go wrong, they would never choose to still try to climb the ladder.

Blackstone had turned more unruly as well. I'd used them to my benefit when I'd needed them, riding them to my place here, figuring that our ideals were aligned, at least well enough to use to my advantage.

Now I wondered if they weren't like alligators in a moat. Yes, they had benefited me, but they would turn on me just as quickly if given the ability.

I certainly didn't want to lose a hand — or anything else — to those snapping teeth.

I moved one file away, choosing to consider dealing with that later.

The truth was that ignoring Blackstone had done little good. They'd chirped in my ear, then lifted their voices when they failed to get what they wanted.

If I didn't find a way to put them down soon, I had a feeling they would pose a larger issue. They had helped take down one head of clan—I was not so foolish as to think myself immune from them taking another swing at that nonsense.

My gaze found the wall, where Grey slept on the other side.

For the first time since becoming a vampire, I had others to worry about as well. I couldn't simply keep clawing on my own, couldn't cut and run and try to come back later. Instead, I had a weakness, a person for Blackstone to target if they felt I wouldn't play ball.

Which meant, for now, I had to placate them.

I signed an order that I never expected to, one they had presented, an antithesis to anything I thought would better the clan's future. I moved my hand faster than usual, as though that would make me not have to think about what it was I signed. The faster getting this done, the better.

I could deal with the problems later, could try to rein in this beast, but it was more important not to get bitten, first.

I was the sort of man to always play the long game.

Soft steps drew my attention, making me realize I'd worked for hours. Time often got away from me, since there were never enough hours in the day. Grey peeked around the corner, wearing her clothes from before.

I missed her naked, to be honest. Not just because it was nice to see her bare form, but because she somehow felt more mine when nothing obscured my sight of her.

"Sleep well?" I asked.

She pressed her lips together as though searching for an answer. "I had a weird dream."

"Oh yeah? Do tell."

She came in and sat in one of the chairs across the desk from me, bringing her knees up so her heels pressed into the edge of the chair, curling into the side of it. "You were in it," she said.

"Dreaming about me, hmm? How scandalous."

"You were snake," she snapped.

And just like that, even though she'd said it like an insult, I thought back to those whispered words and smiled.

There were worse things than her seeing me as a snake.

Chapter Twelve

"I can't believe you actually showed up."

Porter peered at me as though he had no idea what I meant. "Why wouldn't I?"

"Don't you have better things to do than make sure my mom's cat takes her medicine?"

"I find your family oddly calming. It was a small thing, and Molly does require the medication." He offered a rare, slight smile. "Also, I got to run into you here."

"Don't try for charm. It doesn't fit you. Besides, I'm not here to flirt. I needed to ask you something."

"Last I checked, we have phones."

"Yeah, but it wasn't the kind of thing I wanted to ask on the phone."

"No? Well then, I'm certainly curious."

I rolled my eyes, even though I doubted he meant it the way Kelvin would, saying the same thing. "Why don't you come with me? I know a great vegan place.

Well, I mean, great for vegan food. It's vegan, so there's only so much you can do."

He huffed softly at my rambling, but nodded. "Sure."

Twenty minutes later, we were seated at the little place that my mom had told me about when she'd gone on a vegan stint. The smells were delicious, and they tended toward a fusion of Thai and Indian food, with lots of curry. I figured that was on purpose.

Make a sauce tasty enough and no one cared if you filled the rest of the plate with rice and veggies.

We ordered before Porter looked expectantly across the table. "What was it that you wanted to ask?"

I tried to consider how to phrase it. "Well, we have a little bit of a lead with the whole Were thing, but I need to know about any rituals the Natures might do or used to do?"

"Rituals?"

"Yeah. Like, I don't know, dancing naked under the moonlight."

And boy did mentioning that get me thinking of Porter doing exactly that. He was lithe and cute, so I imagined he would look quite good like that. He'd appear almost ethereal out there, like he didn't quite belong in the forest, too delicate, but the moonlight would shine off him, reflected again outward.

Oh, fuck, I could get behind that sort of ritual.

"We don't do that," he said.

"Could you maybe try it?"

His expression didn't break or change, as though he had no idea what I meant or that I was blatantly coming on to him.

It made me again realize he was frustratingly naïve. Which was weird, as sex was totally a part of nature.

I'd seen wildlife documentaries, I saw what the animals did in them! They were freaky and they did it anywhere they damned well wanted. Sex was probably one of the most natural things a person could do.

Of course, saying that out loud made me feel like my mom that time she found porn on my brother's computer after he'd fallen asleep with the videos still going.

Guess he was rather content afterward…

She'd sat there and told him how natural it was as his age, and I could have died from the second-hand embarrassment.

In fact, I'm pretty sure I knocked over a glass of water just to help him escape it.

"I'm talking about things you did as a clan, maybe that you used to do. A certain ritual, or prayer, or offering?"

He had a while to think, since the server walked out with our bowls of food, setting them before us. It took him all that time—and a few bites—before he answered.

"I'm not sure."

"*Really?* I figured you all would be ritual-ed out."

"What I mean is that while other clans turned their backs on the idea of old gods, while they distanced themselves from who they once were, we are different. We have always clung to those old ways, to understanding our place in the world. Many things that we do might be considered ritualistic. We are most closely bound to the energy that runs through the earth, after all."

I took another bite of my food—and yeah, it was good enough I didn't miss the meat a bit, though they could have gone a lot lighter on the carrots—as I considered his point.

It was true. While the other clans had struggled with each other, always trying to gain more, to climb higher, to move away from whatever primitiveness they'd had before, the Natures had reveled in that side of themselves. They'd never wanted to change it, to be different, to distance themselves from their roots.

Did that mean that this would never befall them?

It might also explain why Porter could so easily sense the corrupted energy, because he had none of his own?

"So you believe that this is the reason for the strays that have appeared in the Were clan? That they have somehow moved away from the source of their energy, and that has caused the energy to grow ill?"

"It's my best guess. I found an old book that explained when it happened to others—well, I mean, to be fair it was a fable—but given when that wereraven said, it makes sense, right? We know that it's happened before, to other clans, and it seems to be affected the Weres all over the place, so it *has* to be something other than a normal sickness or we'd be able to track it."

"Do you have any idea about what ritual the Weres used to do?"

"Galen said that a long time ago, like centuries, they used to go on pilgrimages to somewhere special. It was to appease the old gold. It fell out of fashion, though, and they don't do it anymore."

"So you'll try that?"

"That's the plan, if we can figure out where it is. There's a very old weretiger who might know, so we're going to question him in a couple days."

Porter nodded, his hands folded together, his gaze distant. "Some of those places..." he said softly, then paused.

"What?"

His gaze moved to me. "I don't know exactly where the Weres went, mind you, but I have my suspicions. You see, Natures understand there are places that are not *fully* here, in this realm. We understand the ties between the different energies better than many others. We are, in many ways, the most closely connected to this place. If the Weres went to commune with the old gods, with the source of the old powers, then they would have gone to one of those old places, the ones that are not fully here but not fully elsewhere, either. They're dangerous, and even we don't venture there without purpose and without a guide."

"We don't know where it was, though. Maybe it was just down the street, in like, Billy's basement?" I pictured Weres making some long pilgrimage just to find themselves waved toward the basements steps by some guy in a white tank top, holding a beer.

I wasn't sure how I'd react to that, personally. It'd probably be pretty disappointing.

Porter shook his head. "Those ancient places are few and far between. Or perhaps they are all one place with different doors? It's hard to say. I would say don't venture there if you can avoid it, however."

"Why? It's just energy."

"We are all just energy."

"Are you telling me you believe in the old gods stuff?"

He had the decency to think about it for a long moment, as though considering it. Finally, he answered. "I don't know. I've never seen one, but I also don't believe myself so great that I think it impossible, that I think we are the most powerful beings around. I can tell you that *something* lives in those old places, perhaps things we are not yet wise enough to fully comprehend. If you go there, Grey, tread lightly. What dwells there is like nothing you have faced so far."

Talk about ominous…

* * * *

Private planes aren't that bad.

I, like most people, had bitched and moaned about others' use of such frivolous travel. I mean, a private plane? What the fuck was that? It was pretentious nonsense.

But fuck was it comfortable pretentious nonsense…

Only Galen, the pilot and myself were on the plane, so no service, but that was fine. We'd gotten to the small, private airport that flew out of Yucca Valley early in the morning, and the process to get off the ground was easy and quick.

A hell of a lot more convenient than when I'd flow commercially, when they'd packed me into that plane like a can of those cocktail weenies, bumped my seat each time the attendant rolled the cart around and lost my luggage.

Sure, private planes weren't good for the environment, but I could finally see the appeal.

Galen had been tense, still, less like himself than usual. He'd said little, bringing his laptop to work on during the long flight. We had a few layovers for refueling, but the Spirits seemed to know how to get around government interference because we had no problem slipping past the borders and going where we wanted.

"Have you heard from the Mind Clan?" I asked, keeping my voice casual, as though that were a totally normal question that made perfect sense and was not in the least bit telling or suspicious.

Yet Galen took that opportunity to shut his laptop, as though settling in for a long talk.

So not that subtle, huh?

"Not much."

"Are we sure that the Clan Head is good? Like, he didn't get kidnapped by a nymph or something, right?" I laughed as though this didn't matter at all.

"I've gotten word that people have seen him out and about, so no, nothing terrible has happened to him."

Which meant he still just didn't want to see or hear from *me*.

I'd figured as much, but actually hearing it hurt more than I wanted to admit. I hated the idea that he was so angry with me that he would ignore me like that, that he'd completely fall out of my life.

I'd thought we were closer than that, had started to really rely on him.

Funny how things turned out.

"Sometimes it just takes time," Galen offered, his voice gentle. It took away most of that unease he'd carried, like if he focused on my problems his didn't seem so bad.

Good to know I'm useful for something.

"Are you sure? Come on, be honest. There are lines I could cross that you couldn't forgive me for. Things I could do that you'd never be able to look at me the same way again." When it looked as though he'd argue, I interrupted him. "*Really* think about it. What about if

I betrayed your pack? If you really have no limits, then you're not in love — you're just a doormat who doesn't mind getting walked all over. I don't want that, either."

He gave himself time to think. "How about we say that I know you well enough that if you did something — even something that felt unforgivable — you likely had a good reason. I believe I wouldn't feel the way I do about you if you were the kind of person to do something that terrible."

I slumped back in the comfortable leather seat. "That feels a bit naïve, doesn't it? How do you think people end up in abusive relationships?"

Galen shrugged. "Maybe you won't ever understand Weres, really, but we are fairly simple. I believe that instinct wouldn't pair me with you if you were so terrible as to do something like that."

I blew out a long breath. "But what if I *did?* What if I killed someone you loved?" I spat the question out so fast that I slapped my hand over my mouth, as though that could keep it in.

It didn't, of course.

Galen's expression held pity, and I regretted my words immediately. He knew what had happened — I'd told him that night, after all, when I'd still been out of my mind from the fear and anxiety and everything else.

I hadn't breathed a word of it since, however. Hadn't told him how it kept me up at night, how I had nightmares about what I'd had to do to Harrison's brother, how I feared he'd never forgive me for it.

I hated how pathetic I felt about it all, how logically I *knew* I'd made the only logical choice. No matter how much he loved his brother, I couldn't allow him to kill us both. It wasn't just saving my own life — it was saving Harrison's.

Given the silence from him, however, and the clearly intentional avoidance of me, I had to think it wasn't something he could get over quite so easily.

"You did what you had to do, Grey." Galen using my name went to show just how serious he was about it. "You made the right choice."

"Is it the right choice if it hurts someone else like this? If I lose someone I care about, was it really the right choice?"

"It was the only choice."

"I'm not so sure. Harrison held off for so long because he thought he could save him. What if he was right? What if I had given Harrison the time and he could have talked sense into his brother? What if I robbed him of that?"

Galen set his computer aside and moved to the seat next to mine. He slung his arm over my shoulder, only a slight hesitation before crossing the barrier. It seemed me being upset was worth him overcoming whatever was getting to him. "You can drive yourself mad with what-ifs, but you know that you did what you needed to. No, don't interrupt me, just listen for once."

"Don't get all 'do what I say' with me," I argued weakly. "I only follow directions in bed."

"Well, try here for something new. The reality is that you had to make a choice, and you made the right one. You picked two lives over one. You would have backed down if he'd given you the option, but he didn't, so you had to respond. I know it wasn't what you wanted. If you were some monster, it wouldn't bother you this much, still. That proves that you did it because you had to."

His words were like cool water on a burn. It helped ease the sting, at least for a moment, but I knew the moment I turned it off, as soon as I moved away, that burn would start hurting again. It would heal—all things did—but it was going to take a while longer and hurt like hell in the meantime.

"What if he never forgives me?" I whispered, leaning into Galen, feeling an odd sense of safety here. He really had that responsible, I'll take care of it vibe going, didn't he?

"Then it's his loss. I won't tell you that he will, because unlike him, I'm no mind reader. He might decide to hold onto this grudge forever because blaming you is easier than blaming himself, or accepting that some things can't be changed." Galen paused, then spoke softly. "I know a little something about that. See, back when I'd first turned into a werewolf, I had struggled with letting go of my human life, my human family. There is this difficult transition that happens, where because we don't age, we have to distance ourselves from those who would recognize the fact. It doesn't happen the day we change, but it does eventually need to occur. I held on longer than most, however, trying to hide the fact I didn't change while my siblings and friends all grew old. Well, I ended up having my little sister stop by unexpectantly one night—a full moon. She caught sight of a few Weres changing into their wolf forms." He sighed, as though the weight of the memory was incredibly heavy. "She was never quite right again. She didn't mention what happened, didn't tell anyone, but she only made it another three years before she took her own life. At first, I blamed the pack, blamed anyone I could find. It was easier to do that than recognize that I should have cut ties well before, and that not everything is within our control. I hope that Harrison realizes it too, but if he doesn't?" Galen squeezed me tighter against his side. "You'll be fine."

I wasn't sure I agreed, but it was nice to hear.

Chapter Thirteen

"I need to ask Kelvin if my blood is just exceptionally good because these fucking mosquitos seem to think so." I swatted my arm but just missed the sneaky little bastard using me as its own personal buffet.

"That question and image are incredibly disturbing," Galen pointed out as he walked in front of me.

"So is being feasted on, so it's better we both suffer."

"Yes, well, seeing as I don't choose to be a meal to a vampire, I suspect this is a you problem."

I mouthed his words back sullenly as I kept pace with him. The path was narrow, barely a single person wide, and he used a machete to clear bits of leaves from our way.

I'd never been to a jungle like this, having only had experience with the north American forest type of trees.

This was a whole different beast, as it turned out. I wouldn't have dared stepped foot in a place like this if it weren't for Galen keeping an eye on it all. In fact, I suspected most of the peskier critters recognized him as an apex predator because I noticed a distinct lack of wildlife.

Except bugs.

Whether they were too stupid to fear him or just didn't care, they didn't keep their distance.

At this point I'd almost rather deal with a snake or panther rather than these fucking mosquitos — or the huge spider I'd spotted on a tree then promptly ignored because my psyche could not handle that shit. I'd been through enough, dealt with enough horrors, that an eight-legged arachnid the size of a dinner plate was so *not* something I was ready to accept as real and in this world.

Nope.

I would live in my happy little fantasy life where spiders were tiny and not furry.

"How much further?" I asked in a whine.

"You've asked me that six times."

"Well, it's a new answer now, isn't it? We weren't there yet ten minutes ago, but we might be now." I knew I sounded like a kid complaining from the back of a car, but that was fine with me. I just really, really wanted to be *done* with this whole trip.

I knew I'd never been a huge outdoorsy sort of person, but this really solidified the fact. It was muggy and gross and I wanted a cold shower and a bug-free sleep.

Galen took out the tablet from his backpack and studied the map on it, giving me the chance to sit on a large, overturned log. Thank fuck he was guiding us, because I was pretty sure I would have gotten us entirely lost.

Then again, it would have been *much* easier if I could fly.

I imagined soaring over the canopy, getting that sort of view. It would have been pretty nice, right?

Except, each time I tried, it failed miserably. At the very least, I'd gotten better at small flutters that slowed my descent.

I thought back to when Kelvin and Galen had attempted to get me to fly, back in my first year of being a crow shifter. Galen had been sweet, but Kelvin had been convinced that a tough love approach would get me where I needed to go.

Which meant he'd taken the role of a mama bird and *thrown* me off the side of a building. I had promptly crashed and broken my wing — which translated to breaking my arm when I turned human again.

I could flutter now, so if the same thing happened, I suspected there'd be less damage.

To me, at least. There would be far more damage to Kelvin if he ever threw me off a building again.

That was the sort of thing I only allowed once per a customer limit.

"I think it's just a few minutes," Galen said, tucking the tablet back into the bag. "Just ahead there should be a rocky area to the left, and a slight path up that. We follow it and we should find the hut."

I picked myself up and off the log, the idea of almost being to our destination given me a little extra energy.

His directions seemed on point, because we managed it to the rocks he mentioned, and after a few minutes on that path — which was more upward than I would have liked — a clearing in the dense trees revealed a small hut. It had a roof made of leaves, all tightly packed, and walls of roughly cut wood. The door was slightly ajar, and the windows had no covers on them.

Outside was a pit with ash inside it and a few rocks in a circle around, along with a stick that balanced above it—for roasting meat?

It wasn't a bad set up, if you liked the rustic sort of life.

I didn't, of course, suddenly grateful that we hadn't decided to spend the night here. Despite my complaining, the walk from the town was only about an hour and a half, which meant we could easily head back. Galen had packed flashlights in case we had to return in the dark.

I was *not* going to sleep here—that was for sure.

"Stay here," Galen said, his steps changing as he approached. They turned lighter, and he cocked his head as though listening.

It reminded me that he was alpha, that he wasn't delicate as he might seem when he wore his glasses and worked on his computer.

He was a killer even if he didn't act like it all the time.

He approached the hut, making a low noise. It wasn't a growl, not exactly, but there was no doubt it was an animalistic sound. A warning? A greeting?

Fuck knew I didn't speak dog.

And, come to think of it, I doubted the tiger did? Perhaps they all had some level of understanding, like different dialects of the same language.

He pushed open the door and stepped inside.

After a long, silent moment, he returned, still walking softly. "Not here, but he didn't leave that long ago." He peered out at the tree line. "This isn't set up with much in the way of supplies, so I'd guess he hunts and gathers water and other food. He probably went to do that."

"So we just wait?"

He shook his head. "Hunting for a tiger could take all day, and if he shifts into his animal form, he could choose to simply sleep in the forest and wait for tomorrow to try again."

"So we're going to go track the scary ancient tiger in the jungle? Yeah, that sounds good."

"Not we—me. You won't be able to move fast enough and you're far too noisy. I'll track his scent and find him, then get him to come back here."

"And I get to sit here and wait all by myself?" I peered around. The idea sounded absolutely terrible. I didn't want to get left behind while the muscle went traipsing through a jungle.

This was the *exact* moment when someone got killed off for being stupid in movies.

"We don't have another option. I can tell that he's been here a while, so nothing else is going to come anywhere near this place. It smells like tiger. So you're safe from anything else, and I'm going to be tracking him, so you don't need to worry."

I sat down on one of the rocks with a huff. "Yeah, well, if I die, let me assure you that I have every intention of haunting you forever. I'm going to disrupt you every last time you masturbate, so be ready for an eternity of blue balls if your wrong!"

He let out a soft laugh. "I guess that's a fair deal. Just stay put and wait for me. I'll be back soon." He paused just before he turned away, then shrugged his backpack off and left it beside me. "If I'm *not* back in two hours, follow the path back through the jungle to the town."

He didn't wait for me to agree, instead turning around and heading off at a full jog.

It went to show how much he'd been holding himself back during our little hike. I'd figured we'd moved pretty fucking fast, given how out of breath I was.

It was *nothing* compared to the way that Galen traversed the small space before disappearing into the trees, hopping a log and moving between the trunks with an agility that was fucking impressive.

It seemed he really had been slowing down to accommodate me. No matter how much I hated the idea of waiting here, there was no possible way I could keep up, not like that.

So I twisted my hand, opening the portal to my personal bay, and retrieved my stun gun.

Ready or not, here I was…

Galen

The tiger moved fast. The way his scent wound through the trees showed his comfort with this area. I was in his home turf, and I couldn't let myself forget that.

Still, a part of me had to admit—I enjoyed the hunt.

When was the last time I'd gotten to really track anything? To let go of my control just a bit and use my instincts?

Being an alpha meant problem after problem. It meant dealing with issues, solving conflicts, and doing so many mundane tasks that, at times, I felt more like a politician than a werewolf.

Leaving Grey hadn't been my favorite of ideas, even if it were the best, but at least it meant I got to release the pent-up frustrations inside of me, that growing discomfort, the aggression, and point it all in a singular direction.

Part of me hoped the tiger *was* feral in some way. I wanted a fight, wanted to find a way to get rid of these feelings inside me. The tracking helped, but the anticipation was for a fight, for the way I could deal with it when we found it.

So I moved through the jungle, giving up control, letting myself run based on the sensations running through me, trusting myself to my wolf rather than my human brain. I inhaled deep, pulling all the conflicting scents into my lungs to let my wolf sort them out, categorize them. I didn't even know which way to turn immediately, but my body did, grasping a tree trunk to help catapult me in that direction. I didn't need the blade tied at my waist to clear a path—I made my own, leaping rocks, vaulting over debris, a sense of freedom I had long forgotten rushing through me.

I almost wondered if *this* wasn't some sort of forgotten ritual of its own. Too often we Weres tried so hard to give everything to our human sides, to ignore the animal inside of us, to tame it until it was no longer what it once had been.

We did that to exist in a society, to civilize ourselves, but we rarely let go like this.

I twisted around another corner, time having passed strangely in this state. I wasn't sure how long it had been, what had happened, but I only knew that I was chasing something I desperately wanted to catch.

I jumped a large clump of fallen trees, but the ground didn't catch me as it should have. Instead, it gave way, sending me plummeting down into a deep, dark pit.

I struck the ground hard on my back, pain shooting through my shoulder, my gaze cast up to the space above.

Where I spotted a white tiger, peering down into the pit, the eyes far too clear to be only animal.

It tilted its head, then took off, leaping over the open pit and toward the camp.

I let out a roar as I realized just how badly I'd screwed up, especially when I turned my head to see a bloody spike through my shoulder.

Chapter Fourteen

Grey

I clutched the stun gun in my hands as though that was going to make this all better. It had been about an hour so far, and I'd had to admit, Galen had been right.

Much like when we'd walked, I saw no signs of critters around the hut. They must have smelled the tiger, knew they wanted no part of that mess, and kept their distance.

If only I could make that same choice.

To be fair, I wondered if it might not be safer out there. If rabbits and deer and other cute creatures stayed away, I had a feeling I should probably follow their lead. In fact, I noticed I hadn't even heard the flutter of wings anywhere around here.

They must have recognized that the tiger was one hell of a threat.

And here I was, sitting at his house, waiting, as though I had an invitation.

Yep, dumb plan all the way around.

At least this had been Galen's dumb plan rather than my own. It was nice not to be at fault for once. Not to be the one causing the issues this time. If I got mauled, I could blame Galen for his stupid ideas.

It was sort of a nice and rare position for me.

For once, Galen could be the bad guy. That's right! If he got me killed here, not only could I haunt him, but I was pretty damn sure that at least Kelvin would be pissed.

Knot might make his life a living hell—maybe. I never knew exactly where I stood with Knot, after all.

The crunch of dead underbrush had me turning toward it. "Took you long—" My snide comment cut off when it was not Galen walking into the clearing but rather a massive tiger.

Yep, Galen's getting the whole poltergeist treatment for this one.

"Hey there," I said as I tucked the stun gun into my pocket and stood, my hands forward as though to prove I didn't have anything they might consider a weapon. "I'm friendly, see." I smiled widely.

The tiger bared its teeth and snarled.

Me being friendly wasn't the issue here, was it? It was all well and good if I was friendly, but the real problem was whether *it* was.

And it did not seem to be.

"Look, I came here to talk to you."

It came forward, step by step, head down. It reminded me of when a house cat stalked something—the slow, methodical movement, the focus, the twitching of its tail.

I tried to imagine this tiger as just a really big house cat.

Nothing to worry about, right?

Right?

My little pep talk did little for my mood, to be honest, but I still tried it.

"We're not there to hurt you or bother you. Well, a little to bother you, I guess. I need to ask you a question."

The tiger pounced forward, and only my reflexes — honed by years of near-disaster events occurring — allowed me to leap out of the way, just avoiding its massive, outstretched paws.

Murder mittens indeed...

I hit hard ground but rolled, getting back to my feet, trying to keep at least a little distance between us.

I got the sense that it played with me, of course, because I doubted I stood much of a chance against a fucking tiger. There was a reason it never went well when idiots climbed the fences in the zoo to pet the kitty.

"It's about the Weres. Their getting sick, losing control. We think you might know something that could help us stop it." I paused, then added with a nervous laugh, "Do tigers actually live in this jungle? It just occurred to me that I could be an idiot talking to an actual tiger. Boy, wouldn't that be embarrassing? Huh, guess you don't really see the humor in that. That's okay, my humor is a sort of learned torture," I rambled, my gaze skirting the peripheral just look for anything I could use.

A stick? A rock? I had the stun gun still tucked in my pocket, but that required getting *far* too close to the bitey bits for my comfort. It had seemed like a great idea before, like I were invincible, but now?

Now I got why Galen had given me such a chiding look when I'd shown it off like a get out of death free card.

"You don't want to eat me," I assured him. "I eat crap *all the time*. I also pet random animals, so who knows what sort of weird diseases I might have. It's much better to just let me go."

The tiger rushed me again, this time giving me much less room to maneuver. It pinned me, but he didn't appear to use his claws, since there wasn't any tearing pain. Nothing but a crushing weight against my leg.

I yanked but to no avail. I couldn't get free, couldn't pull away from him.

Fuck.

The tiger stared down at me, its massive weight trapping my leg. I was entirely at its mercy, which was *not* a place I wanted to be.

I had no idea what else to do, so tried something that was likely *not* pleasant for either of us—I shifted.

A flightless bird wasn't that useful against a tiger, but that wasn't the reason I did it.

Instead, it was that rush of fire that licked across my skin. It was enough to burn off my clothes.

I felt like the tiger had earned a little singed fur for its behavior. In fact, maybe it would teach them some manners, because they sure as fuck didn't seem to have any of their own.

I didn't know how much damage it would do—if any—but it couldn't feel good, right? Unless the asshole one was hardcore masochist, but I'd take *that* over getting mauled to death any day.

I wasn't a sadist at heart, but to get out of this? He could call me Mommy for all I cared.

My body twisted, that fire destroying my very nice outfit — including the fancy boots Galen had bought me — but it seemed to do what I needed.

The tiger let out a pained sound, one that was at least a little angry, as it leapt away, hissing.

I took the chance to stretch my wings, reacquainting myself with this form. I didn't use it often enough to really understand it, which meant each time I did it, I had to get used to it again.

Of course, the time to get used to it wasn't when a fucking tiger wanted to eat me, so I'd have to find my wings, and fast. Instead, I fluttered, the closest to flying I could manage, which allowed me to get atop the hut. There weren't any trees around for me to get to, and even if I could, I was pretty sure tigers could climb. I looked around, searching for a rock cliff, for *anything* that would give me some much-needed distance.

Nothing.

A howl came from the distance, one pained and furious. *Galen?* Well, at least that implied he hadn't gotten killed.

Good, I wanted to kill him myself. No one else deserved the chance. I'd earned that shit.

I hopped around on the top of the hut, searching for a way out, an escape route. The tiger was faster than me — no doubt about that. I didn't see a path that I could take that it couldn't, or one that would slow it down enough. Maybe going tree to tree? Of course, if I missed a hop, I was fucked.

The hut shuddered, and I swiveled my head to find the tiger perched at the side, having leaped up from ground level.

Nice kitty...

I doubted it could decipher that from the squawk I'd just let out, like a language that it didn't speak, as I backed away.

My feet reached the end of the hut, my nails curling slightly as I realized I had no more room. I sure didn't want it to land on me from above, so jumping down seemed a bad choice.

Of course, bad choices went out the window when the tiger pounced at me.

Instinct took over, and I fluttered, trying to avoid the strike. I didn't make it high enough to fully escape, but at least the tiger didn't grab me between its paws like a toy. Instead, it batted me on the side as it stretched, fucking up my amazing fluttering and sending me careering down.

I hit the ground hard, the air and most of my thoughts flying from me at the impact.

Ouch.

I normally would have said I'd never shake that off, but fear of dying did amazing things to a person's stamina. As I rolled, getting my feet beneath me, I spotted something black beside me.

The stun gun.

I'd dropped it before I'd taken my crow form, so it hadn't gotten ruined.

I shifted again, that familiar flame licking across my body. Dirt clung to my skin as I reached over, grasping the stun gun, not giving a damn that I was naked in the middle of the fucking jungle.

This felt totally on point for my life.

I grasped the stun gun, placing my finger on the trigger, praying it still worked. I'd get *one* shot at this.

The tiger looked pretty mad, so I doubted it was all that willing to listen to me.

What exactly happened to a Were when hit with this sort of voltage, I didn't know. Maybe I should have tested it out on one of the pack that I didn't like first. For all I knew, the Were would shake it off as though nothing had happened.

It was still my only option, so I told myself it would work.

I crouched slightly, trying to gain the best balance I could. I curled my toes into the dirt, reorienting myself in place, ignoring the aches of my body from the fight already. This was it. One shot. It call came down to this.

"I didn't want to do this," I told the tiger. "All I wanted was a little question answered, so don't blame this on me. This is your people problem. You should take a class or something—they have them online—" My tirade was cut short by the tiger moving forward in a rush.

It didn't pounce this time, didn't leap, instead coming at me in a full run. At the last moment, it lifted from the ground, paws out, and I twisted to the side. Not enough to avoid it entirely, but enough to hopefully get its flank.

I hooked an arm around it, dug the stun gun into its side, then pressed the button.

An absolutely horrid sound left it—high pitched and frantic—as we hit the ground. Its massive weight pinned me, but as quickly as it happened, it lessened.

The tiger hadn't gotten off me, and it took a moment to realize what had happened as I shoved the no-longer-furry form off me.

Had the stun gun forced a change? It was like the tiger couldn't hold that shape anymore, having been thrown back into a human body.

A moaning, incoherent, barely conscious human body.

Which made me recognize that this human was actually pretty damn good-looking…

He had long, black hair, braided back, and sharp features. His eyes opened and closed at random intervals — and not together — like he was still trying to work them out, but when they *did* open, I got the thrill of enjoying some of the darkest brown eyes I'd ever seen.

Wait, no, don't ogle the dangerous tiger-man.

I patted to the side for a rock and held it up, above him. I heard Kelvin in my head telling me to swing. This tiger might have been feral, unable to help us, if he could have ever done so, but I knew he seemed to want me dead.

Except… I couldn't. As I saw him shaking his head, I felt too terrible.

Instead, I held the rock like a threat. "Are you done yet? I told you this wasn't what I wanted."

He blinked slowly, his gaze seeming to lock on me. "You're not going to kill me?" The words were heavily accented, though I couldn't tell where the accent came from. Maybe something Mediterranean?

"I told you already — I'm not here to hurt or kill you. You need listening skills, too."

He stared at me for a long, tense moment. The truth was that I didn't know how long a stun gun would affect him. It meant he might just manage one good swipe that took me out before I could do a damn thing, but this was too important.

The answers he gave us could mean the difference between saving the Weres or losing them all — including Galen. That was worth this risk.

Instead of lashing out, however, the man started to laugh. It was a deep, full belly sort of laugh, the kind that makes it impossible not to laugh at least a little right along with them.

And sure enough, after a moment of staring at him like he was a fucking nut job, I joined in.

Maybe we were *both* nut jobs.

We laughed so hard it was nearly a hysterical cackle at the end and I dropped the rock to the side. What the fuck was this?

Another roar—closer this time—echoed through the tree line just before a huge, hulking beast.

Yeah, Galen sure knew how to make an entrance, didn't he? I wasn't sure if it was that he saw I was safe or if the entire sight forced him to skid to a halt, but at least it made him take pause.

Here I was, naked, straddling another naked man, both of us laughing as though we'd just heard the funniest joke in the world while being high off nitrous.

He paused, then shifted back to human—and fuck, did he look good like that—then crossed his arms. "What the fuck is going on here?"

He didn't curse much, but this was probably a pretty fair time to whip one out...

"Long story," I said, then looked down at tiger boy and collapsed to the side, laughing again.

Fuck, was life weird.

Chapter Fifteen

I ate a bite of the cooked meat — though I didn't ask what sort of meat it was — as we all sat around the firepit.

The tiger — named Alpho, as it turned out — had started the fire and left before returning with something that looked vaguely like an animal but without the fur, skin or head, I couldn't tell what kind. He'd put it on the spit and roasted it.

Galen remained in his human form, and the wound at his shoulder had mostly healed. It had been a gaping hole — a sharpened stick in a pit, from what Galen said — but he didn't seem to hold a grudge against Alpho.

Galen had packed an extra set of clothing in his bag which meant we had something to wear. I hadn't replaced the last set I'd taken from my personal bay, which meant I had to share what he had. He'd put on the pants and given me the shirt and boxers. Wearing his underwear felt oddly intimate.

Was I some sort of perverted freak who got off on stuff like that? Fuck if I knew, but I felt all too on display in them, despite the fact they didn't show much.

And Galen and Alpho had both just seen me entirely naked.

"It's good," I admitted as I ate the falling-apart, delicious meat from the plate Alpho had given me. "I'm surprised you can make such good food out here."

"I do go into town now and then for spices, and meat is easy to make well no matter what. You came a rather long way just to ask me a question," Alpho said, the first time we'd actually gotten back to the conversation at hand, the one interrupted by him trying to murder me.

Galen sighed. "I'm the head of the Were Clan and the wolf alpha."

"I thought you smelled of dog," Alpho muttered, his tone lacking any sense of respect.

I rarely heard people speak *that* rudely to Galen. His own pack never would, and even Kelvin tended to avoid outright insults.

I sort of liked Alpho better because of that. Someone with a mouth they couldn't control was always one of my favorite parts of friendship.

"You try," Galen said to me, then pouted as he stared at his food and ate.

Men...

I rolled my eyes, because this wasn't even my problem! So I had to fight the deadly tiger and have the conversation, too.

Figures.

"I said before, you know, during the whole you trying to eat me thing, that there are Weres getting sick."

He nodded. "I've felt it. The energy is souring."

I sat up straight. This was the first real spark of hope I'd found in a while. He not only knew about the issue but seemed to identify what it was. That had to be a good thing, right?

"That's right. Well, I have a working theory that it's because the Weres have stopped doing ancient rituals. I heard about a trip that all Weres had to make, to the old places. You're the oldest were that we know of, so I was hoping you might know where that was."

He nodded, leaning forward and resting his elbows on his knees. "Yes. I made the trip, a very long time ago, as all Weres used to do." Shadows danced in his eyes, something that told me the trip wasn't a pleasant one.

Then again, hadn't Porter warned me of the same? That wherever this energy came from, it wasn't the kind of place that anyone should want to go willingly.

Maybe it was like the gynecologist — no matter how much it sucked, you still had to go.

"So you can tell us where it is?" I pressed.

He nodded. "Yes, I can, but it isn't so much a where. It's a how."

"You know I'm not that smart, right? Let's not play games, because I'll never catch up."

He huffed softly as though amused. "You know, it's been a long time since I've shared a meal with anyone, since I've spent time with someone like this. It's not as bad as I remember. What I meant by that is that the place isn't a real place, at least not one you can walk to or find. A pathway is opened by an old prayer that a Were has to invoke. When it does, a shimmering golden doorway appears. On the other side of that doorway is a different world, one that does not follow the rules of this one. It is wild, soaked in Spirit energy. There are many paths, but finding your way is not so difficult because there is a pull. I saw other clans there, other Spirits who were not Weres, all pulled in their own ways. I believe that all the old energy exists there, in that place, but we can each feel it. It's instinctual." He had a strange expression, one somewhere between awe and fear.

"What did you do after you followed that path?"

He shook his head. "I'm not sure. That was a very long time ago, but I did talk to others, and none seemed able to recall what happened when they reached the end of that path beyond walking into a cave with a shimmering amber lake. I remember the huge cave filled with crystals imbedded into the walls and a body of water in the center, but it wasn't clear. It was the same color our eyes change to, and it called to me. The next thing I remembered was waking up back where I had left from, back where the doorway had first opened."

I didn't respond right away, letting the information soak in, trying to mull it over.

It fit, didn't it? Everything I'd found, to everything I'd heard. Porter had said that another place existed, that it was dangerous — it sounded like the same place. The story had mentioned a lake, so it sounded as though it might not be as metaphorical as I had thought. Maybe the source of the Spirit energy was there, in that place. If we went there, we had a direction, a way to at least work out what had happened.

If the water was trapped in some way, no longer flowing to the Weres, we could figure out why. We could see what the Weres were supposed to do and hopefully fix the problem.

"What's the invocation?" Galen asked.

"By tradition, it must be done under the full moon, and the Were must speak as they shift. That is the way to call the attention to open to doorway. Then the Were must say 'I seek an audience with the one I came from.' I've seen other invocations used by other types over the years, so I am not sure that the specific words even matter so much as the action and attempt."

I glanced over at Galen, who stared into the fire instead of at me. I wondered what went through his head, what he thought about that made him that serious.

After so long feeling like we were close, like we had so much in common, there was this strange distance between us now. I could tell he had something on his mind, but he didn't tell me what it was.

Sure, he'd never been the kind to complain much, but he'd never had something bother him this much, either.

Maybe it was just stress over what was to come, over how difficult the job was really going to be.

Whatever it was, no matter how much I wanted to make it all better, I knew I couldn't. This wasn't a problem I could fix for him, but fuck, I just hoped we could fix it at all.

* * * *

"Absolutely not." Kelvin sat up straight in his chair, his eyes already edging toward red. Funny how difficult he was to read at the best of times, but right now?

Right now it wasn't hard to figure out what exactly he had on his mind.

It came tumbling out from his mouth, after all.

"It's not that bad."

"Not that bad? You're telling me you plan to go to some dangerous other realm to work out the doggy problem? Like hell I'm going to just allow that."

My crow bristled at those words, as though he had any say over anything I did.

I kept that in because it would only send us all down a bad path and the one we were on wasn't great to start with.

We were all in the council meeting room — though, as usual, Harrison had sent a representative in his stead, one who never fucking said a thing. They just sat there, listened, and abstained from any votes when they came up.

Galen had gathered the meeting because if we didn't do something, the issue with the Weres could result in even larger casualties. We had two weeks before the next full moon, which meant we had time to plan.

"I'm going to have to agree with Kelvin," Ruben said, his tone more controlled. "This is a problem that affects the entire Spirit world. We aren't talking about a few Spirits becoming dangerous — we're talking about of clan of millions. The repercussions are too great to just send the two of you."

"This isn't a field trip," Galen snarled. "Weres have done this ritual for a long time all on our own."

"Yes, and back then, it worked. We have no idea if what you expect to find, if what they used to find, is what is there anymore. What if the problem requires more than just a wolf and a crow?" Ruben pointed out.

Even as he spoke what seemed like entirely reasonable words on the surface, I couldn't fail to notice the way his gaze moved to me between the statements. I had a feeling that all that logical sense he was spewing was only *part* of the reason he didn't want us going alone.

"It could be dangerous," I pointed out.

"It will be," Porter interrupted, the first time he'd spoken since Galen had told the council our plan. "That place is extremely dangerous normally. With what is happening now, there is no way to say it won't be worse. Many Natures have died there, even very strong ones."

"You are not helping," I muttered, not surprised when he didn't appear all that chastised over it.

"This has to get done. The dangers don't matter," Galen finally said, his voice holding a tinge of despair.

"The dangers would be mitigated if we worked together. I suggest each clan sends a representative to go with you for protection. This has to succeed—for all our goods. The damage the Weres would do if they went mad, the power vacuum if they disappeared, it can't be allowed to happen. Besides, from what Porter found, it is possible this sickness could infect wildlife or even other clans. Choose someone capable, strong and loyal. Have them meet Galen at the designated place the night of the full moon," Ruben said.

No one spoke, not to argue, because who could? We all understood what could happen if the Weres truly went mad. They were extremely powerful and with so many of them around, it was a disaster waiting to happen. In fact, they could end up turning far too many humans on top of every other risk.

This might have started out as a Were problem, but it was clearly an all of us problem, now, and we were going to have to work it out together.

The rest of the meeting went quickly. The other problems seemed so petty in comparison, with most of the little complaints and treaties set aside until after the full moon.

It was like worrying about paying a speeding ticket as a comet sailed toward Earth.

Not our biggest problem.

I went to follow Galen as we all rose, but when I reached his side, he shook his head, not looking at me. "I'm going home alone."

The words took me back, made me hesitate. He'd threatened to leave me or kick me out a lot of times, but he'd never actually done it.

He swallowed hard, and I thought for a moment he'd take it back. He rarely stayed mad long. Except, he didn't. He shook his head slowly. "I'll meet you at my house on the night of the full moon. Until then, I think it's best you don't come over."

He didn't wait for me to respond before he walked out, never looking back, never meeting my gaze.

And the asshole had done that in the middle of a room full of people. Yep, private humiliation wasn't good enough for him. He wanted everyone to see him turn me down, to see him push me away so hard I was lucky I stayed on my feet.

"You want somewhere to stay for the night, Birdy?" Kelvin asked in that come-hither voice he used, the one that probably worked on anyone with a heartbeat.

I knew him, though. He did it not so much because he wanted me over — though he did — but to help take my mind off what had just happened.

I smiled brightly and shook my head. "Thanks, but I should probably get a good night's sleep, too. Besides, if we're going on a big trip, it'll be good to get things settled at home. No one seems to know how long this ritual takes so I've gotta get things in order.

The idea of sleeping alone sounded horrible, but that didn't stop me refusing a pity fuck just because it might feel sort of nice for a moment. I was better than that.

Or so I told myself. I didn't know if I actually was, or even if I felt better, but I'd rather not appear as pathetic as I might be.

He narrowed his eyes just a bit, a sure sign that he knew I was bluffing. Still, he didn't call me on it, didn't tell me I should do as he said. He nodded. "Fine, but if you get lonely, just call."

"Thanks." And, for once, I actually meant it.

I never would have thought I'd rely on Kelvin as I did. When I'd first met him, when he liked to haul me in for petty shit, I'd thought I'd hate him forever. I'd figured I'd never find common ground with him.

To think we'd somehow ended up here, with the two of us actually close, never failed to surprise me.

He nodded, then walked out.

Porter came over, his gaze following Kelvin. "This mission might end up being a bad idea. You realize that you could get hurt, right?"

"I always could get hurt. At least this time's for a good reason."

Porter snorted softly, the sound a sure sign he didn't agree. "Make sure you rest plenty. There is little of that once you cross that barrier. It is unlike anything you have faced before." He left on that cryptic message, though I was pretty used to that from him. Porter was a weird-ass guy, at the end of the day. He seemed so connected to things in one way, but like he was from a totally different world at other times.

It left only Ruben and me, Harrison's representative already skirting out of there the moment she could, as usual. She never spoke to me, as though I were somehow off limits.

It made me wonder what horrible things Harrison might have told her about me. I hated that idea, but it made sense. He probably said I'd killed his brother, that I was dangerous, and she treated me the way friends treat a person's horrible ex.

Which sucked, because people liked me, damn it!

Well, some people.

Not that many, if I really thought about it.

I shifted and sat on the edge of the table, letting my legs swing.

"You know, sitting on the council table is considered a breach of protocol," Ruben said, as though we were playing 'fun fact of the day.'

"Well, what are you going to do? Throw me in a cell? *Again?*"

"What would be the point? You always escape."

"On of the rare benefits of what I am. Sure, I'm always in trouble and always getting myself fucked over, but hey, at least I can't get stuck anywhere!" I paused, then snickered. "Though even that isn't *always* a good thing. One time, I went on one of those trips where you take the elevator up to an observatory. Well, it got stuck halfway up. I was trapped. What do you think happened? That's right, the doors opened for me, however, given that we weren't actually at a *floor* I got to just see the freefall I could have taken down while the others screamed. It wasn't as helpful as my crow probably thought."

Ruben huffed a soft laugh before leaning his hip against the table. "That seems quite on brand for you. You have a habit of turning things that seem rather straightforward into far more complicated and messy versions."

"It's not like I mean to."

"I know, and to be honest, I don't mean it as an insult. Yes, there are times it is frustrating, times when I wish I could predict or control you in some way, but most of the time it is unexpectedly fun. It is something that I have never really experienced before, a sensation that it surprising to me. I don't feel much, for the most part, but you cause me to actually remember what it is like to have fun." His gaze seemed far away, like he thought about all those years that came before.

"What do you remember of your human life?"

"Most of it, but it's like remembering the plot to a movie. It doesn't matter to me. I don't feel anything about it. It simply happened."

"Do you miss it?"

"Being human? No, not at all." He paused for a moment, then added on. "Perhaps that isn't entirely true. Sometimes I see how you react with others, how some things come so easily to you all, and I feel envious of that. I wish I knew what to say, how to act. Perhaps I do miss that."

I bumped his shoulder with my own. "You don't do so badly."

"No?" He lifted his dark eyebrow as though to call me either a liar or an idiot. Worse, when I thought back, I saw his point. He was impossible to read, to understand, and how many times had I wanted to punch him in his face when he stared back with complete confusion over my annoyance?

Far too many times.

"Fine," I said. "There might be times it's a bit of a nuisance. Still, I don't think I'd want you any other way."

"You wouldn't prefer me human? Or from another of the clans? It wouldn't be easier?"

"Nope, not a bit. Trust me, I've dealt with all the Spirits and they're all annoying in their own way. I think that's what really binds us all together at the end of the day—it isn't that we're alike exactly, it isn't common ground, it's that we're all really fucking annoying in totally different yet equal ways." I shook my head. "Except for Knot. He is annoying in an entirely unhinged and extreme way no one else comes close to."

Ruben didn't laugh, but asked softly, "Are you sure you have to go? Can't the others handle the Were problem on their own?"

I swung my feet some more, like burning off that little bit of energy helped me to settle. "No, I can't. You know me better than that, don't you? There's a problem for people I care about—not just Galen, but you all. I can't just sit back and do nothing when I know I could help. This is too important."

"But you're more fragile than the others."

"Hey, you knock that off. In case you've forgotten, I fought an ancient weretiger—"

"You *what?*" His sharp tone cut off my bragging and made me realize that, yeah, Galen had sort of skimmed over that part, hadn't he? He hadn't fully explained what had happened with the tiger, only what he'd said.

Which I totally understood the reason for. No one really needed to know that I'd done that or how close it had been to going very bad.

And yet I'd managed to out myself — as I usually did.

"Yes, fine, I fought a weretiger, and guess *what*? I won! So you really have no good reason to worry about anything. I'm tougher than I look. I mean, I survived getting framed for murder by vampires and I survived a crazed druggie who wanted to dig around in my skull. I can survive this, too. I think surviving might be one of my few really useful traits. No matter what happens, I tend to survive, somehow."

"Until you don't. That's the thing people don't realize until too late, that all trends end. You survive until one time you don't. Until it's all over and everyone else is left behind to realize that things are never as solid as they seem." His voice was so soft, I had to strain to hear him, each word pained.

I got the sense it wasn't just about me, however.

"Well, you don't have to worry this time, at least. I'm sure it'll all work out great. I'll have Galen there and then whoever the other clans send. It'll be one great big party and we'll get it all taken care of fast."

I didn't believe that one bit, of course, and neither did he. When had things *ever* worked out well? When had they gone my way? When had they not spiraled out of control into one big fucking mess where I had no idea how to get through it all?

However, I hadn't been lying. No matter how back they got, no matter how difficult, I always came out on top at the end.

Well, maybe on top, but at least alive. That was the only one that really mattered at the end of the day. Alive meant I could keep trying, that I could make things better afterward, that I could continue.

On top? Winning? Those weren't things I really knew much about, but scraping by to fuck up another day?

Well, that was one thing I was really damned good at.

Chapter Sixteen

"You don't even want to try it?" my mom asked, a spoonful of something I could only identify as a fuck nope held out to me.

"No, I don't." I narrowed my eyes as though the food were the worst thing I'd faced recently. "I really, really don't."

She sighed and set the spoon back into the bowl. "You *never* want to try anything. How do you know you won't like it if you don't try?"

"Because that exact thought process is how I got myself roped into both BDSM and essential oils, neither of which were a good idea!"

She rolled her eyes, a sure sign that she was used to my nonsense and not all that bothered by it anymore. The truth was that I hadn't eaten her cold salads in years and I sure as fuck wasn't going to start now.

I was happy she liked them. The weird textures, the quinoa — I still wasn't sure what that was exactly — and the random veggies all mixed together to make one big fat nope from me. I'd support her all the way with her eating them, but it was like doing one of those mud races.

I would cheer from the sidelines, but I was *not* jumping into the mud myself.

"Did you come over just to insult my food?"

"That was just a happy side effect. Besides, didn't you tell me I could always come over?"

"You can, but that doesn't mean I like it when you won't try the things I make."

I plopped down in one of her chairs, the act of sitting reminding me just how little sleep I'd been getting.

One week to go.

Seven days until the full moon, until I ventured to fuck only knew where, until I was going to have to put everything aside and had no idea if I was going to make it back.

Well, no wonder I'm not sleeping that great…

The truth was that I would have much rather headed out immediately. Having to wait like this was so much worse. I just dwelled on it all, on the future. Even my get together with Kelvin hadn't helped that much. The second I'd left him, the worries had all come swarming back.

What if we fail? What if I can't stop this? What if I never make it back and there's no one to say no to my mom's gross recipes?

It all mixed together until my chest tightened and I worried I might just fall headlong into a panic attack.

I'd never done that before, mostly because I wasn't smart enough to really think about things enough to get a panic attack.

My mom tilted her head as she stared at me, and I wondered what she saw.

Her disaster of a daughter? Her oldest who was never as good as the later, newer models? The black sheep of the family who was always the topic of conversation when she wasn't around?

I sighed because I knew they were all true. On way or another, I never lived up to anything, did I?

"Why don't I make you a cup of coffee," she said. "Meet me out back."

I followed her order without thinking, too used to doing what my mom said to even consider not doing it. A few minutes later, she walked out with a cup held between her hands, steam dancing from the top and escaping into the cool air. It was cold for California, but anyone from any place that had *real* cold would call the fifty degrees outside good weather.

She handed me the cup, and I smiled at the light color. She took her coffee black—when she drank coffee at all—but I couldn't stand it that way. She'd always complained about how much cream and sugar I put in, but judging from the way this looked, she must have figured I'd needed it.

I wouldn't bitch. I took a sip, thankful that she was willing to help me like this, to do for me when I didn't seem up to myself.

She took a seat beside me on the outdoor sofa. "Is everything okay?"

I considered her question, not answering right away, mostly because I really wasn't sure what the answer was.

No, everything wasn't okay. That was obvious. I was stressed out, afraid I couldn't solve this problem.

The worst part about it was that it wasn't just my problem. So far, the things that had thrown me, the things I'd suffered through, they'd been all about me. If I failed, I paid the price.

Maybe it was what happened to Trey, but I couldn't just ignore things like I used to. I couldn't pretend they had nothing to do with anyone else. That wasn't true at all. If I failed, if I didn't get shit done right, *everyone* could pay the price.

I thought about Galen potentially losing his mind, or him having to watch all of his pack go mad, him having to put them down. I thought about Porter watching so much of the nature get destroyed in a war. Kelvin wouldn't likely care much about vampires dying off, but he'd worked hard to get where he was, and despite the way he acted, I knew he didn't want to see the violence that would spread from this. Harrison worried so much for his clan, and they were hardly equipped for a war like this, for this sort of thing to happen, for them to have to try to survive it all.

Even Ruben would suffer if we couldn't get this to work. He would be on the front lines, the one expected to make sense of it all, to figure out how to fix it. There would be no peace to be had, only destruction, as he tried to keep the Weres from wiping out everyone else.

That was just the Spirits, but I knew better than to think for a moment that this would stick with the Spirit world. It would spill over into the humans, who were not even close to equipped to deal with it. My mom...

My brain refused to go there, like a huge 'do not cross' sign sat in the way and prevented me from traveling any further down that line of thought. I couldn't imagine how I would make it without her. Even if I didn't die in this stupid mission, even if the upcoming war didn't get me, I didn't think I could make it without her. She'd taught me how to live, how to be strong, and she was my backbone each time my own failed. Even through the hardships we suffered, the years when we struggled to get by, she always gave me her all.

No, there was no chance that I could deal with any of this fucked-up life on my own.

"I don't know," I admitted.

"You know, you often say that. You often don't think you're ready for anything that is coming, but you always manage it."

"Someone told me the other day that always is a lie, that trends are only trends until they stop."

"For other people, maybe, but not for you. If there was anyone in the world I would trust with figuring out how to do the impossible, it'd be you."

"Yeah, well, as much I normally love the mom support, you thinking that doesn't make it true. Just because you want to think that I can do anything doesn't mean I can. If I told you I was going to start a cult that lived in a cave and was going to make the ocean cover the land you'd support me and cheer me on. It doesn't mean it's realistic."

She smiled, the expression so unfailingly loving that I just about needed to look away from it. "If anyone else said it, I'd tell them good luck. If you said it? I'd make sure we had floaties around. The fact is that you've always done things I didn't think possible. You've always managed to get yourself out of hassles that I thought would take you down. I learned a long time ago no to doubt you. It'd be nice if you learned it, too."

I sat back on the couch, against her side. She put her arm up, then ran her fingers through my hair. The touch was oddly calming, like I was a little kid again and had nothing to worry about, no thoughts, only vibes. I missed that old life, when things were hard but they were simple.

Paying the rent wasn't *easy* but it was basic. I knew what I had to do no matter how difficult. Now problems were so large that I struggled to really wrap my hands around them, to grip them, to make sense of all the details. It wasn't as easy as just doing something, but rather knowing *what* to do. That was the worst part of any of it.

I sighed and looked out at the yard, wishing I could look ahead a few weeks, that I could see how it was all going to work out. I wanted the confidence to know that this was what I should do, but life didn't work that way.

"I'm going on a trip next week," I said.

"Oh really? Again?"

"This one might be a bit longer — I'm not sure yet."

"Where are you going?"

I figured telling her it was some weird otherly realm was probably not an ideal way to start this conversation, so I hedged the truth. Lying to my mom wasn't exactly new for me, after all. "Florida." I liked to pick Florida because it felt like the land of extremes and weird shit. Basically, no matter what *really* happened, if I told them it had happened in Florida, there was a good chance they'd believe me.

I was chased by a tiger in Florida. I was in Florida when someone person bit me! This one time, someone turned into a smoke creature and I had to banish it with magic.

That doesn't sound like something that happened.

I was in Florida.

Oh, okay then! Makes sense!

Sometimes I think I belong in Florida. That probably why I'd never actually gone, because I was pretty sure I could give Florida man a run for his money, and if I found my people there, I didn't think I'd ever want to leave.

So instead, Florida remained my *someday* vacation spot that I liked to use as an excuse until then.

"Are you going with anyone?" The way she raised her eyebrow had me laughing. Yeah, that was one hell of a suspicious face, wasn't it? She wanted to know if any of those men who came to the party—and it seemed stayed in contact afterward—were going with me.

It was safest to offer the truth. "Galen."

"Oh, he was nice. A little stuffy, maybe, compared to who I'd imagined for you, but sometimes opposites are good. They can help each other stay level. I think that works well. If you found someone as wild as you, I'm not sure this world could survive it."

I laughed as I thought about exactly who she meant—even if she didn't realize it.

Knot. He was every bit as crazy as me, every bit as unpredictable and prone to disaster. I couldn't argue that, yeah, I wasn't sure how well that would work if we ever tried something more than...whatever we were.

In fact, the very idea of us trying that nearly had me laughing at the absurdity. Not only of the relationship itself, but at the idea of us acting like love-struck puppies.

Nope, not happening.

"That's fair," I pointed out. "And he is responsible. Sometimes too responsible, I think, too worried about everyone else, but he's good."

"You seemed like you've known him for a long time."

"Five years or so."

She nodded slowly. "Five years? That makes sense."

"What do you mean?"

"It was around five years ago that something changed about you. I didn't know what it was—I still don't—but it was like you'd drifted before then and you suddenly found some focus. You seemed to make better choices, or at least make choices at all. You're still always you, but you seemed more grounded. I wonder if that was his influence."

Nope.

Well, I mean, he could have played a part. That was the time I'd changed, when I'd gotten thrown into an entire world I hadn't known existed. Sure, Galen had come into my life then as well, and he was important to me, but he hadn't been the main reason for that change. Instead, he'd been a helpful rock in an all-new river that threatened to drown me.

But I couldn't explain that to my mom, so I shrugged. "Maybe. Five years ago I think I realized the world was bigger than I thought. I figured out that things were more than I'd known before. It was like living my whole life in this tiny studio apartment then having someone throw the door open and seeing that there's way more to it."

My mother nodded as though she had any idea what that meant.

Fuck, I wasn't sure I even knew what it meant, not really. It sounded good, but without going through it, no one could really understand.

"Well, I'm glad you had a friend like him. I've always wanted you to rely on your family more, but I understand that you can't always, that there are lots of other things for you to do and think about and deal with. It was good to realize you had so many people who care about you. So, when are you leaving?"

"Night of the full moon."

"Can't you just say Monday like normal people do? Must you make it sound so dramatic?"

I chuckled at the annoyance in her voice. "Sorry. Monday evening."

"Okay. Make sure you call me when you land."

"We're going to be road-tripping it. Cell phone free, you know, off the grid."

"No phones?" And there went that old mom-suspicion that never failed to catch the shady shit. "Why would you not have phones?"

"Digital detox?"

She narrowed her eyes, and I wasn't sure if she bought my story or if she just recognized that I wasn't about to give her a better answer. "Fine, but be careful."

"You know me — I'm always careful!"

She rolled her eyes and ran her fingers through my hair again, the action taking me back to being a little kid. I didn't get to be a kid much, not before she remarried. She'd always done her best to protect me, to give me a childhood, but reality got in the way a lot. I didn't blame her for that, knew she'd worked harder than most people could, but that didn't mean it had been a good time.

But even at the worst times, there had been good moments. I had always loved when she'd run her fingers through my hair like this, the action making me feel as though all the bad things in the world were held at bay just by this. It had tugged at my scalp but in the best way, this reassurance that nothing could get to me.

I knew I'd have to leave this safety — I always did. That was part of life. I couldn't just stay here, and I also had grown up enough to know that no matter how safe and comfortable this felt, it wasn't. The bad things in the world wouldn't stay away just because I liked the way this felt.

But knowing that something would end didn't change the happiness in the moment. It was one of the rare lessons I think I'd actually taken to heart. I knew better than most how quickly things could get snatched away, how fast they could go from great to shit. My crow had taught me that, especially since she rather liked causing things to go to shit. For that reason, I'd figured out that enjoying what we had, what I'd found, was vital, no matter how temporary it might be.

Which meant I snuggled against my mom and pretended I was five again, that I didn't have these worries on my shoulders, that I didn't have to think about all of this. Sure, I'd go back to the real world in an hour or so, but I'd still be in the same place then whether I stressed about it now or whether I took a little break, put my feet up, drank my coffee and acted like a kid again.

Tomorrow was a bitch, and she showed up no matter if we were ready for her or not. No reason to wear myself out trying to avoid her.

* * * *

I'd stashed items in my personal bay for safe keeping. I had no idea if I'd be able to get to them wherever we were going. It wasn't like there were many couriers around, so they rarely got to test out such things. In addition to that, however, I'd packed a bag that I had slung over my back.

It felt like camping, but my last attempt at that hadn't been a great one.

Maybe this time I wouldn't get nearly eaten by a tiger.

The moon had risen, full and bright enough to make it easy to see. We were in the space behind Galen's house, the acres of desert landscape the perfect place to ensure no one saw us. He'd told his pack to stay away for tonight, and while a few had no doubt grumbled, none had shown up.

"Where is everyone?" I asked. "I'm usually the late one. I don't think I like being early."

Galen seemed just as tense as he the last time I'd seen him two weeks before. It seemed whatever was wrong hadn't gotten any better over our time apart. He peered toward the house. "I gave Ruben the information. When the representatives arrive, they'll meet us back here."

Talk about a non-answer. Or, rather, an answer meant to keep on track about the subject and not risk us actually talking about anything important.

I kicked a rock with the toe of my boot, and it skipped across the dry sand, the white surface having a sheen from the moonlight. I hated the idea of going in general, but the idea of going with a bunch of people I didn't even know sat even worse. How could I trust them? Not just me, but Galen. I didn't love the idea of them having our backs, of us having to put our lives in their grubby little hands.

Nope. Bad idea.

I wasn't what anyone would think of as overly trusting, and this went to prove it pretty well.

It meant I had to deal with them, with what we were working on, with all this bullshit.

"You know," I pointed out, "I've never actually seen you shift. I've seen you shifted, but not the process."

"Are you worried about it?"

"Are you?"

He didn't make that weird, didn't imply I should or shouldn't be, only posed what was clearly a concern of his.

I snorted. "Do you have *any* idea what I've seen by now? No, I'm not worried, not one bit. Why would I be? A little good old-fashioned bestiality is nothing anymore."

He laughed, the sound soft and missed. It felt like a moment of the old us, the way I much preferred us, with Galen slightly annoyed and me impossibly charming.

Or at least I thought so.

"So, you ready to tell me what's been bothering you?" I asked when I couldn't help it anymore, when I couldn't stop myself from broaching the topic. I often hated to do that because I didn't always want the answer.

What if the answer was one I'd be happier not knowing? What if he decided to tell me things I'd much prefer to stay ignorant about?

But I was supposedly an adult — or so my age said — so I tried to act like it and address the issue between us.

Except, before he answered, the side gate opened and four shadows appeared.

Which meant we were interrupted by whoever the clan heads had sent. I had no doubt that they'd be good — they wouldn't dare send anyone half-assed, not if it was with me. In fact, I'd bet that Kelvin would have well-threatened whoever he sent to ensure they knew better than let anything happen to me. Porter wasn't a threatening type, but no one would want to piss him off. Any Justice Ruben sent would be no fun, but capable, as they all were. The fourth had to be a mind, though I didn't have a clue who Harrison would send—if he'd even send anyone.

I sort of expected him just to ignore Ruben's request, given that's how he'd reacted to anything having to do with me since everything had happened.

Galen pressed his lips together, his jaw tight. It seemed he wasn't a fan of having others around even if he acknowledged that it was a good idea. Accepting something and liking it were a big fucking difference.

The figures got closer, and when I could identify them, I didn't quite understand what I was seeing.

In the front was a cocky gait I'd recognize *anywhere*, and Kelvin had the smirk to match. Beside him was Porter, dressed in a pair of loose pants and a white shirt, something that made him look almost entirely normal. The third was Ruben, not smiling, but was he ever? The last, for a moment, I thought was Harrison.

The idea hit me so hard, I smiled at first. If he came, that had to mean he'd forgiven me, right?

Except, when they shifted from behind Porter, I saw that it was a stranger. A man, in his thirties perhaps, rather unassuming. He showed no sign of recognition as he approached, appearing to be the exact sort of errand boy I'd expect to be sent on such a mission.

It left me standing there, confused, as the four approached.

"What the fuck?" I asked as they reached me.

"Come on, Birdy, is that any way to react when people come to help you?" Kelvin said.

"You were supposed to send a representative—not come yourselves."

"We were told to send someone. I'm just going to be my own representative. Nothing says I can't do that."

I turned to glare at Galen. "Did you know about this little plan?"

His glare said he hadn't known, and that he wasn't all that happy about it.

"It wasn't a plan," Kelvin added. "I didn't know that Porter or Ruben were going to be here until they showed up tonight."

Which meant that they hadn't all gotten together to work this out? This wasn't some joint plan to annoy me?

That led me to only one obvious option.

Kelvin, Porter and Ruben had, on their own, decided to show up for me. They'd had the ability to not come, to send others, to keep themselves safe, but instead they'd each determined that coming for me was the right thing to do.

I set my hand on my chest at the realization, at the weird warm fuzzies I got from it.

"Careful now, she just might swoon," Kelvin said with a chuckle. "You want me to catch you?"

That woke me up.

I didn't need to act like some idiot in front of them all, like someone who needed romance and reacted like a teenager over it.

"Shut up," I muttered, warmth on my cheeks. I could only pray the light was low enough that they couldn't see it. I did pause and shift so I could see all of them at once.

"So if you're all going to come, what happens here? Can things go on without you?"

Galen shrugged. "I have Matt taking care of things while I'm gone."

"I've put someone in charge," Kelvin assured me.

"We don't really have 'in charge,'" Porter denied. "But should anyone have issues, I've put someone else in place to receive any such requests."

"I've already assigned another Justice to take over while I'm gone. The Justices are able to operate well no matter who is removed from the group. They will be fine without me."

I looked over at the last one, the one I didn't recognize.

He shrugged. "I'm not in charge, so no one will miss me. I just go where I'm told." He peered around. "I also have a feeling I'm missing a lot of details here, but honestly? As long as I get paid when I get back, I don't think I need to know."

He tucked his hands into the pockets of his sweater as though he didn't really care anymore, and I had to admit, I rather liked that.

I didn't trust people who were *too* eager, or even too curious. I'd take a good hired gun who admitted that they were here for the money over someone who proclaimed their allegiance to me.

Plus, it meant I didn't have to act like we were best friends.

"So, is this it, then?" I asked, looking around.

"I believe so," Porter said. "Now, I am the only one who has been here before. That means it's important for you to listen to me. Trust *nothing*. This is not our world, no matter how it feels."

"You sound paranoid," Kelvin said. "We're some of the most powerful Spirits in the world. I don't think a little hike is going to pose that great a difficulty for us."

Porter shook his head. "You don't understand. This isn't a little hike. The area we will be isn't Earth, and the things there are pure Spirit energy. We are half-breeds compared to what resides there. It means we need to watch our step. It also means we will feel a certain pull or affinity in a certain direction—you must ignore that. We have to follow Galen to ensure we end up where we need to be. Do you understand?"

"Don't get eaten by the wildlife, ignore the call of nature, follow Galen. Got it." I listed the items like a to-do list, using a finger to mark off each one. "Let's get this over with. The sooner we go, the sooner we're back." I peered at Porter and Kelvin who, surprisingly, had nothing with them. "You packed a little light, didn't you?"

Porter crossed his arms. "I am rather at home in natural spaces like that. I have no worries about needing anything."

"And you?" I lifted my eyebrow in Kelvin's direction.

"I brought food."

I twisted to see if he had a hidden backpack when his meaning hit me.

He means me.

He was lucky he stood a few feet away or I might have kicked him in the shin for that stupid joke.

And worse was the fact it wasn't a joke. So long as he had his personal feed-bag around, he didn't have to worry about much else. I was sustenance, medicine, everything all wrapped into one sarcastic package.

"That's enough. Come on, Galen, do the thing." I waved my fingers at him, already regretting this whole thing.

We hardly managed to survive council meetings together, but now we were going on a trip? What the fuck was that all about? There was no way we'd make it through this mess without someone killing someone else.

In fact, I wouldn't past it being me that lost my temper and offed one of these men.

Still, as we took our spots, I had to think that…well, I did look sort of bad ass. If there was a superhero team made up of moody, ill-adjusted, morally gray characters, we could fill that spot pretty easily.

Galen packed his items, then stripped. It amazed me he could manage it without looking nervous. Well, he *did* glance over his shoulder just once, at me, as though *I* made him nervous.

I'd think baring his ass to a group of Spirit men would be the more dangerous position, but maybe that's because I knew exactly how *that* went.

He shoved the clothes into his backpack, then held it out to Ruben, who took it without a word. No doubt he'd picked Ruben because he was less likely to make a stupid joke.

Galen turned his back to us again, facing the full moon that sat just above a mountain range, appearing larger because it was closer to the horizon. He rolled his shoulders, the action causing the muscles in his back to shift. It went to show just how built he was despite the fact he spent so many hours before a computer.

He spoke softly, his voice deep, just as his body started to twist. It happened differently than it did for me, lacking that rush of flames, the power, the magic. Instead, a Were's change was more brutal, with the popping of bone, the rending of flesh as it went from one form to another in quick succession.

He kept speaking as he shifted, though the words became more difficult to make out, to understand. They deepened, turned rougher, and as he fell forward to all fours, as he took that plunge into the final transition of his change, the words broke into a howl.

I froze, wondering…had it worked? Maybe we were too far gone. Maybe the tiger had gotten it all wrong?

A spark of electricity danced through the air, however, and a shimmering doorway appeared. It wasn't perfectly arched—messy and glowing amber instead.

Galen jerked forward in a leap, as though drawn to enter, but froze and looked back at us.

Right, it might close after him.

Which meant we had to go first.

I stepped up, ready to take the plunge, when a hand on my chest pushed me back and Ruben crossed it first. The shimmering made it difficult to tell what happened on the other side, but his figure showed through and he appeared to still be upright.

That was a good sign, right? It meant he probably hadn't died or anything.

I figured it was the best we'd get, so I crossed that line next, heading into the unknown, into the shimmering amber that led somewhere I'd never been, somewhere I didn't understand, that none of us knew much about.

On the other side, I took a deep breath and instantly knew what Porter had meant.

It didn't feel like home at all…

There were trees, and in some ways, it reminded me of the jungle Galen and I had gone to. Part of me wondered if that was why the weretiger had gone there, like some desire to return to this place?

Not that it mattered, really.

Despite the similarities, there were too many differences to ignore. The trees weren't right, with jagged lines to their leaves and a few that had feathers growing across them as well. The ground was covered with rocks that were smooth and had flecks of colored crystals in them, so many colors that it appeared like confetti.

I was used to the colors of the council, as though the world were made up only of those, but here had every color and shade imaginable, all of them sparkling from sunlight even if I spotted no sun.

After I came through, Kelvin crossed, then Porter, the Mind and finally Galen. As soon as Galen crossed, the portal closed with a sharp snap, trapping us here.

It gave me the chance to look out at the sprawling space before us, the world unlike anything I'd seen before, and wonder just what the fuck we'd gotten ourselves into…

Chapter Seventeen

"This is really boring." I knew I wasn't helping, that my whining wasn't making anything better, but that didn't stop me from doing it.

Anything that kept me at least mildly entertained.

"That's good, isn't it?" Ruben asked.

"Porter got me all ready for us to be avoiding danger at every turn and shit like that. I was ready for action. This is more boring than when my mom makes us take walks after Thanksgiving dinner because she read it was good for people."

"I said to be cautious. We've been here for two hours. Are you really this impatient for chaos?"

I turned around to look at Porter, amazed as ever at how natural he could look out here. "Do you recall what clan I belong to? Come on, what's it called?"

He sighed but repeated it as though he knew I wouldn't shut up until he did. "Chaos Clan."

"There you go. So no, I can't help it, and yes, I am that impatient. This is terrible—it's just waiting for something to happen." I looked forward, toward Galen who walked at the front. "Are you sure we're going the right way still?"

"Yes. I can feel it," Galen said without turning. "It's up that way, toward that mountain."

"That one?" I pointed at what had to be ten miles away. "Why couldn't we open the fucking portal a little closer?"

"It's not that far," Ruben said. "We'll reach the base by tonight." He looked over at me. "Well, by tomorrow at least."

"*Wow.* Rude much? I'll have you know that I'm not that useless."

"Yes, you fought a weretiger—I heard."

"She what?" Porter asked.

"Oh, you didn't hear?" Kelvin perked up as though amused. "Yes, apparently she fought a weretiger *while naked.* Our little bird right here is quite the live wire. You're still new to this entire scene, but I can assure you, no matter how ridiculous something she does seems, she can make it worse."

"I didn't mention I was naked! Who told you?" As soon as I asked, I got my answer. There was only one person who was there, only one person who could have told him about that little detail.

I glared at Galen's back. "You snitch. I had no idea you all were so close."

"We're best buddies. We spend hours on the phone every night," Kelvin said while Galen ignored me.

The conversation was good for one thing, at least, which was distracting me. It didn't seem so bad when we had this banter going back and forth, after all. In fact, it almost felt like a family outing.

A weird family, sure, and a super incestuous one, but still a family of some sort. I wasn't sure if the bantering was natural or if they did it to help me out, to keep me distracted, but I appreciated it all the same.

"What was I supposed to do? *Not* fight the tiger? Because that option led to death and I wasn't aware you all wanted me dead that much."

"You know the real problem?" Ruben pointed out. "Most people don't have to make decisions like that. They don't live their lives in such a way where fighting a weretiger naked is even an option they have to choose between."

I didn't argue back that time because what was the point? The fact I was *here* at all proved that my life was a little fucked up, a little messy, and they sure didn't mind when they benefited from it. That meant I thought it was crazy for them to get so upset when it went a little sideways.

Our back and forth went on, however, as we walked. It relaxed me, helped the time to pass.

Much of the greenery around us seemed the same as when we'd first gotten inside this place. Each time I glanced around, however, the fact we weren't home became more painfully obvious.

The smells were wrong, the sounds off. It was like that uncanny valley thing, where things that were almost human but weren't freaked us out the most.

And, yes, ignore the terrifying idea that there was something that looked *almost* human that posed a big enough threat that that shit got hardwired into our DNA.

The fact was that this place was close but not right. The trees were here, but different. The breeze existed, but seemed to switch direction so much that it was impossible to follow. Light covered the space, but it had no source, no sun, nothing that created it.

It all told me that I did *not* belong here.

That light—wherever it came from—started to dim as we walked.

Porter peered around, slowing his steps. "We should probably wait here. I don't know how dark it will get and trying to travel without light isn't ever a good idea."

Galen stood near the front, stopping but not turning toward us. Just staring at him told me that he wanted to go, that he didn't want to stop. In fact, I suspected it took all his control not to go at a full run—and I'd seen just how fast that bastard could run.

I called his name as I approached, but he didn't move. Did he even hear me?

I reached out and touched his back with the flat of my palm, trying my hardest not to scare him, but he didn't seem to even notice me.

Sure enough, as soon as I made contact, he jerked away and spun. Pain echoed through my wrist, and it took a moment to realize he'd swung his hand to knock me away.

His eyes were wide, the color having shifted to a bright amber, which was so *not* a good sign.

I tucked my hand behind me, not wanting him to see that it hurt, that anything had happened. "Hey." I kept my voice steady, as though everything were fine despite the fact that he looked as ready to take my head as a Karen who couldn't use her coupon. "We're setting up camp until the light comes back."

He blinked rapidly, as though the action could clear his head. After a long, tense moment, he nodded. "Right. Sure."

His gait was uneven, forced as he turned to follow Ruben, trailing behind the Justice like a puppy who'd gotten in trouble. It would have been funny at any other time.

It wasn't that funny right now, not with the throbbing of my wrist.

"Let me see." Kelvin's voice was dark.

"See what?"

His expression proved to be darker still. "Come on." He turned his back and headed off in the opposite direction as the others, and I had a feeling if I refused, he'd just put me over his shoulder.

Of course, not having to walk any farther might have just been worth that. I didn't understand people's hatred of being carried. Seemed like a benefit, if anything.

We didn't go far, just enough that the trees would muffle our voices and give us some privacy.

Kelvin pointed at a rock. "Sit."

I did so, like a good little pup, and even managed to keep the smart-ass comments inside my head.

He kneeled before me and held his hand out, waiting. His grip was cool, as usual, when I put my hand in his.

He turned my hand, examining it, running his fingers along the wrist joint, moving it to see what hurt. He didn't ask me anything, seeming to instead take his cues from my reactions—no matter how hard I tried to keep them from occurring.

Finally, he sighed. "It isn't broken, but it'll bruise. Why'd you hide it?"

"You saw him—he didn't mean to."

"So? If I dared to bruise you, you wouldn't just let it go. You're far more vindictive when it comes to me."

I blew out a long breath as I stared down at where Kelvin held my wrist. "It's not like that."

"Isn't it? You've always held me to a higher standard."

"Or maybe you've just always managed to fall beneath that line of acceptable behavior time and time again?"

He held my wrist, and I realized after a moment how nice the coolness was against the throbbing. Was that why he did it?

Then again, that felt quite like Kelvin. He was rarely outright kind, rarely did things anyone would think were romantic or sweet, yet he managed to be there for me in a way that actually mattered.

Not that I trusted much else he said or did...

It got me speaking more honestly. "You've never been out of control," I said. "You've never been out of your mind like that, so I've never needed to forgive you for something like that."

His gaze lifted to my neck. "I was once."

"And I forgave you."

"Did you? You still haven't accepted me after that, so I'm not really sure you can say you're over it."

I pressed my lips together, unable to deny it. I hadn't slept with him again, hadn't agreed to it before he'd bitten me. That meant I still had something holding me back, some part of me that refused to give into him fully.

Maybe he was right. Maybe I was still angry.

My crow seemed to flutter her wings at that.

Right. He *had* bound me to him against my will, or at least attempted it. He'd done it to save my life, of course.

I thought back to that night, to how lost I'd been, how devastated by my inability to fix any of this, how I'd realized that even if he hadn't meant for it to go that way, he'd been behind it. Once I put that aside, however, once I looked past it and to *him,* I had to admit... he'd seemed just as lost.

I recalled his pinched features, his pained voice. He'd been facing losing me, and he'd done the only thing he knew to try to keep me alive.

Was he really not just as out of his mind as Galen was now? Maybe for a different reason, maybe in a different way, but it wasn't that different.

It had me moving forward, the action pushing Kelvin backward so he sat on the ground. He was careful with my wrist, ensuring I didn't accidentally put pressure on it, always mindful no matter what else was going on.

It was like a portion of his brain was always locked on me, always on my well-being regardless of the chaos around us.

He lifted an eyebrow, but didn't stop me when I straddled his waist. I used my free hand to tip his face up toward me, to take his lips in a deep kiss. I didn't hold back, didn't stop myself.

Kelvin had fucked up—more than a little—but hadn't I, also? We'd both screwed things up, over and over again, and there was no good reason to keep beating us up over it.

Why destroy my future because of a blip in my past?

"I don't need to feed yet," Kelvin breathed out softly.

"So? I don't want to do this again for the first time just because you have to feed. We need it to mean something more."

That seemed to flip some switch in him, like they were the words he'd wanted to hear, had needed to hear.

He kept one hand on my wrist—never too tight, just enough to cool the injury and keep me from hurting it worse—and used the other behind my neck to pull me closer, to deepen the kiss. He teased the seam of my lips with his tongue, the touch somehow gentle despite how not gentle everything else about him seemed.

His aggressive hand at the back of my neck, his hard cock that ground into me—or, wait, I might have been grinding against him, actually—and the deep sound that rumbled from his chest.

Wasn't that just like him, though? The dichotomy between him, the fact he was dead, yet in many ways was more alive than anyone else I knew. He was constantly moving in the shadows to gain control, yet walked around as though he had no secrets at all. He was the last person I would believe a word from, yet I trusted him more than almost anyone else.

And just like that, I knew the truth. I couldn't ignore it anymore, couldn't pretend that it wasn't true just because it wasn't all that convenient.

I loved this idiot. I had for a while, and I was tired of trying to act as though I didn't. Sure, I might very well regret it at some point, but fuck it—I regretted lots of things in my life.

"The others aren't very far away," Kelvin whispered, though he didn't pull away from the kiss, the words muffled by my lips.

"So?"

He groaned and pressed his forehead against mine, as though grappling for some shred of self-control. His chest rose and fell in quick succession, another sign that he wasn't holding himself back easily.

Which was perfect for me.

I didn't care if anyone heard. It wasn't like anyone didn't know we were fucking at this point. We could keep our voices low — maybe — but we were adults and if anyone didn't like it, well, they should have brought earplugs.

So I reached with my good hand and yanked at the laces of my boot until I could slide it off, then undid the button of my pants with a flick.

It seemed all that self-control didn't last long, because when I pulled back enough to stare into Kelvin's eyes, I knew he'd lost that battle.

His eyes glowed red, bright, intense. *This* was the real him, behind all the games he played, behind his schemes and manipulations. Maybe that was one of the reasons I actually did like being like this with him, because I got to see a side of him I had a feeling few ever saw, the person beneath the power and the ambition.

This man wanted me — nothing else mattered.

And that was one heady feeling.

Kelvin

I fucking give up. Every time I tried to stand against Grey, it never worked. I could bend the rest of the world to my whims, could make it all dance for me if I just pulled the right string, if I leaned on the right note, but Grey?

Nothing ever worked as I expected it to. She defied all attempts to control, to even push in a certain direction.

For example, I would have never thought fucking her in a strange realm not more than a hundred feet from others would be a good idea, yet here we were, prepared to do exactly that. No matter if I resisted, I'd give in at the end.

She got the best of me in every situation, and, to be fair, at the end of it I wasn't even mad about it. Somehow, she led me in the direction I wanted to go.

I mean, we'd ended up bonded at the end of what was arguably her biggest fuck up.

I'd had a perfect plan to get rid of that old man, to take over, to finally get into power, and what did she do?

Put herself right in the middle of the crosshairs.

And yet, in the end, it brought us closer than I thought possible.

It meant that now that she wasn't resisting, now that she wasn't trying to escape it, I couldn't hold myself back. The best I could manage was to ensure I didn't hurt her, to keep my hand in a loose brace around her wrist, to keep track of my strength. That was easier than I would have expected, as though her safety were part of my own instincts.

I used my free hand to help pull her jeans off, taking her panties with them, stripping them off the leg that had no boot on. They hung on her other ankle, which was fine. We weren't in the sort of place where we had the luxury of laying her out, of teasing her to my heart's content.

When we got back, however, the next time I fed from her, there was no chance of me resisting that. I wanted to spread her thighs, to ensure not a stitch of clothing could obscure an inch of her body, and I wanted to explore every last part of her. I wanted to trace my tongue along her body, to find every last crevice, every mountain, every valley, every spot she felt self-conscious of and lavish attention until she understood just how much I adored it all.

Since that wasn't in the cards currently, however, I kept her in my lap. She undid my pants, and I lifted myself just enough to expose my cock, shifting up so I rested my weight on my knees, so my shins were flat against the ground. It offered a better position, for her legs to spread around my hips as she hooked her free arm around my shoulders for balance.

I guided my hard cock into her, and she lowered herself at the same time. It made this feel like a dance, like we both worked toward the same end, that we both wanted the same exact thing, that we craved it with equal hungers.

Which was nice.

I was an orphan in the vampires, a vampire born to no sire, an outcast, someone without family. Most of us didn't even survive because we didn't have the ability to grow as strong, didn't have anyone to protect us. Me, however? I'd scratched and struggled and made a name for myself even if I didn't have someone to give me one. I'd dug my own place, hollowing it out of those who had thought they could take me down, who thought me not worthy of survival.

I didn't give a fuck what they thought, not anymore, and I had been content to live on my own, to do as I pleased without thought or care toward anyone else.

When Grey moved like this, though, when her snug cunt swallowed my shaft, when her arm held me tight, it was the rare time I didn't feel entirely isolated. It was when I thought there was a place for me in the world beyond the one I'd made for myself. *She* was the only creature beyond myself who had ever made space for me, made room for me in her life even if she got nothing out of it.

She hadn't accepted me because she wanted something from me. In fact, in many ways, I'd made her life more difficult over the years. Still, she welcomed me, her warmth, her humor, even her temper, it all made me feel less alone in a very large and empty world.

So I set a hand on her hip, my other holding her wrist still, almost as though we were holding hands, and I fucked her. I didn't do it gently or sweetly — though we'd never been those things to start with. Instead, I took her with an intensity that I hoped she understood, a need that I'd tried to leash for so long but couldn't anymore.

I took her roughly, quickly, bottoming out with each thrust so I could ensure that there existed no space between us. I bit at her full bottom lip, then moved my mouth to her throat. Her pulse danced just beneath the surface, but I held back.

Her words echoed in my ear, the desire to have me like this, to have *us* like this, not clouded by biology, by a feeding, by my venom, but instead having it just be us, just our wants, just whatever we had cobbled together out of bad decisions and good jokes.

She took every thrust and moaned, her voice nowhere near quiet enough to even hope that the others wouldn't hear. I didn't care, and she didn't seem to either, so I took that as a win. I'd accept that everyone could know — fuck, I rather liked it to be honest. I wanted to claim her in some way, to ensure that at the end of the day, she was mine and everyone knew it.

I could share, but I wouldn't be pushed out. And, that petty part of me didn't mind the idea that others would want what I had, that I would be the enviable one.

I wanted them to be jealous, to recognize what I had with Grey, mostly because it had been so hard fought to get here. Despite all the things I had in my life, I doubted any meant nearly as much to me as this woman, so I wanted people to know.

I took her hard, fast, rough, and she rolled her hips to ensure I didn't miss anything, to keep going no matter what.

Words stroked the back of my lips, desperate to escape, to tell her exactly what she meant to me, that I wouldn't let her go, especially not now. Despite the problems with the Graves, the vampires making ploys against me, no matter all the dangers going on, only she really mattered.

I could let the rest of it go for her. I didn't think that was a claim I would ever be able to make, that I could ever care for anyone that much, that I could ever need someone in this way, but I did. I would let the rest of the Graves burn, would hand it all over to someone else if that was what it took to have her, to keep her safe, to keep her with me.

I kept the words inside, not because I was afraid of them. She already knew how I felt, how serious I was, but I didn't want to burden her, didn't want to force her to take on that sort of pressure.

Grey was the sort of girl who liked to run, and I was sick of chasing her. So I swallowed those declarations, not wanting to risk sending her running again just because I was a little too upfront. She required slow movements — after all, it had taken us five years to get here, to reach this point.

I could wait as long as it took to go further, to have more of her.

So I raked my teeth across her pulse, my end close, chasing the little sounds she made. I held off just long enough to feel her cunt tighten around me, to feel her squeeze down on my shaft.

She held me closer with that arm, her fingers digging into my shoulder, gripping me as though afraid I'd disappear if she didn't.

Stupid woman. Nothing could have dragged me away.

I followed her over that edge, came deep inside her as though that were a claim. It had taken far too long to get back to this point with her, to achieve this level of comfort again, and this felt like some sort of final proof that things had returned to normal.

No, better than normal.

I wasn't hiding anything from her.

Well, nothing important, at least, nothing that was going to get her killed.

I pressed my face against her neck, riding out the aftershocks, the way her still-squeezing cunt tightened around my cock and made me wonder if round two was possible.

No matter what we faced here, I knew I'd do everything it took to make sure we got back safely.

That was a promise I damned well intended to keep.

Chapter Eighteen

The worst thing about spur-of-the-moment sex was just how filthy it got a person. Without a shower afterward—or enough wet wipes—proper cleanup proved impossible.

I wondered for a moment if I could have shifted to my crow form. Wouldn't that work? Those flames that licked across my skin during my change might destroy anything that didn't belong, right?

Except, I'd changed before and still had blood on me, so that didn't seem like it would work.

I sat on the ground, my fingers tracing a crystal in the boulders around us. We'd set up in a spot just outside of a cave entrance—Porter had said he sensed nothing had been there in the past week or so. A fire roared and we circled around it, the warmth helping as the temperature had fallen with the passing hours.

No one had mentioned my little outing with Kelvin, either. I wouldn't say they weren't aware of it—they all had exceptional hearing, after all—but they hadn't addressed it.

I'd prefer that, of course. I thought I'd been able to stay quiet, but that was probably not that realistic. I wasn't quiet at the best of times, so there was no way I could have managed it during *that*.

And who could blame me? It had felt way too good for me to even think I could hold back.

"You're blushing," Porter said from across the fire, sitting on one of the boulders rather than the dirt as I was.

"Just the heat from the fire," I lied.

He lifted an eyebrow but said nothing.

Ruben cast a glare in Kelvin's direction—so much for people pretending they'd heard nothing.

Kelvin, of course, didn't look sorry. If anything, he seemed even prouder as he was scolded for his behavior. He was probably that kid in class who always got himself in trouble and only grinned through the lectures because he knew damn well he was going to do it again.

"Why are there so many crystals?" I asked to distract us as I pointed at the shimmering gems inside all the rocks around us.

"They hum with power," Porter said. "I think they help to contain it here, to hold it."

"There are so many different colors, though."

"Haven't you come to terms by now with the idea that council only represents a very small fragment of what is out there?" He gestured my way. "You, for example. Did you think you were the only clan not represented?"

"So that means that every single shade of crystal here is a different Spirit?"

Porter shook his head. "No, I don't believe so. Just as there didn't seem to be any of your type until you were changed, I think some of these powers aren't represented on Earth. I can sense the type of power, and there are many I have never felt before. Of course, that could mean there are just so few of them that we don't realize."

"Or they don't cause as much trouble as you, so we never notice," Ruben said.

Which was a rather fair point.

It made me wonder what my life would have been like if I'd just stayed quiet, if I hadn't put myself at the center of so many disasters. Would I have just gone on like normal?

Would I have even realized what I was? My changes weren't controlled by the moon or time, not like Weres, so what would have happened if I'd never been in danger? If I'd had no reason to escape that wolf, to turn into a crow, to meet Galen?

It felt like all those things led one into another, each spilling over so that the next event was even more ridiculous. So if I'd never gotten on that rollercoaster, if I'd never stepped onto that path, would things have been different?

"What are you thinking about?" Kelvin asked.

"What if I didn't get attacked that day, what if I never met Galen and so never went to the council and never met any of you. It's weird to think how different my life might have been. I won't pretend like it was amazing before, like my life was perfect or anything, but it was pretty normal."

No one spoke at first, as though my question had sucked all breathable oxygen from this entire realm.

It was Ruben who responded. "Is that what you would have wanted?"

"Yes. No?" I sighed and shook my head. "I don't know. Don't get me wrong, I'm not saying I'm unhappy with where I am. It's not like I regret a lot of it or anything. I'm just saying that I think about it, you know? I can't be the only one who wonders what other life we might have had. I mean—*look at where you all are.* If it wasn't for me, most of you wouldn't be *here.*"

At least the men looked at each other, as though considering my words.

They were true, though. Galen might be here, sure, because I hadn't started this problem myself.

Or, I was pretty sure of that, at least. Maybe we'd find out differently, but for the moment, I hadn't started this mess and I couldn't be blamed for it.

Yet.

But Ruben, Kelvin, Porter and the Mind rep were all here because of *me.* They'd come because of their connection to me, because they didn't think this was safe, because I'd talked them into it. I'd altered the course of each of their lives drastically, and it made me wonder—*what if.*

The expressions they each wore implied they thought the same, that they considered the differences.

No one spoke for a while.

I wasn't sure I minded that, though. I didn't want to hear them tell me about how they really wish they hadn't met me. I'd heard that enough in my life that I didn't want to hear it from them.

Especially not these men.

Well, the Mind could say that.

I didn't care if he liked me or not. In fact, he sat farther away, quiet, as though he didn't want to participate more than he had to.

I didn't mind that. I wasn't sure I had room in my life for *another* man who could piss me off. Sure, I was a mess, but to think they weren't was a huge fucking mistake.

They caused their share of problems, after all, and I didn't need another—especially a Mind strong enough for Harrison to pick for this job—bugging me. Harrison had been able to crawl through my head if he wanted, was far too good at working out what I thought and felt, so why the hell would I want that from someone else?

No thanks.

My brain was a strict *no crossing* sort of place. I didn't need all these muddy footprints in there, causing problems and fucking up my shit.

A glance his way made me wonder who he was, though. Harrison wasn't exactly trusting.

Him sending someone was nice, I guess, but the fact it didn't matter enough for him to even reach out to me stung.

It felt as though he were making it clear that he really didn't want to see me, that this wasn't even enough for him to just speak to me.

Fuck, this wasn't exactly a safe trip, and I didn't expect him to forgive me over it, to rush over and protect me—I wasn't some damsel.

Was it really that much to ask for him to just tell me that he hoped I was okay? To just show me that I mattered still, even a little?

I sighed as I realized maybe it really was too much. Maybe things had gone too far.

"I'm going to get some sleep," I said when I knew this conversation wasn't going anywhere good.

Kelvin stared at me, a tightness in his expression that implied he caught some of my distress. "Okay," he said instead of pressing it.

Like I really wanted to bare any of this in some weird group share like we were at a support meeting.

I headed into the small cave. When Porter and Ruben had checked it, they hadn't found any exits, anything that went off in another direction. It meant the entrance should be the only way in or out, making it easily defendable.

I was one of the few who actually needed sleep regularly, and I was long past the time of worrying about that, of feeling bad about it. It was a basic human need — that was all that really mattered.

So I dragged myself inside the cave. I'd tried to open my personal bay earlier, but the color had sparked then died, like a car that couldn't quite turn over to actually start. It meant I didn't have access to all the extras I would have preferred, but the sleeping bag I'd brought was enough to make me pretty happy.

The cave was warmer than the air outside of it, sheltered as it was from those breezes. It wasn't that dark, which wasn't all that conducive to good sleep, but at least I wouldn't have to listen for every last sound.

I stayed dressed because a person never knew what exactly they might face in this sort of situation, removing only my shoes and socks, then crawled into the sleeping bag. I used a sweater I had packed for a pillow, letting the sleeve fall across my eyes to shield them from the light the crystals gave off.

No sound came from outside, but I didn't know if that was because the men didn't speak or if they just kept their voices low enough that I wouldn't hear them. Either way, I appreciated the attempt.

"He didn't abandon you."

I frowned at the voice, moving the sweater to be sure that, yep, it was the Mind. "Pretty sure that isn't your business. Besides — stay out of my head. I don't like people poking around in there."

He stood near the entry to the cave, staring at me as though he were trying to decide something. Finally, he sighed. "You think that Harrison threw you away, huh?"

"I think that is between he and I, not you. Besides, you know shit about any of that."

"I know that Harrison has been holed up in his place for weeks, and that he sent me out with clear instructions."

"*Ruben* ordered the clans to send someone. Don't get it twisted."

"Ruben suggested it, but Harrison could have just paid me and sent me on my way. He didn't. He sat me down to explain the job."

"So he gave you an overview? Well, that proves fuck all."

The mind shook his head. "You don't get it. He explained what the job would be, that it was coming here, what we might face, all of that. I said, 'so my task is to make sure the mission succeeds? That we fix whatever is wrong with the Weres.' That's the right answer, right? That's what the fuck we're here for. He couldn't tell me that, though. Instead, he answered quietly that *you* were my top priority. That if it came down to completing the mission or getting you back safely, I was to pick you without hesitation."

The words sank into me, feeling almost too nice, too much like what I really wanted to hear. How often was that the case, though? When people took away what they liked because it made life easier.

Here he was, offering me exactly what I needed.

"Why are you telling me this? I doubt Harrison would want you to."

"He paid for my work, not my silence. Besides, call it a bleeding heart. I didn't like seeing you moping all because you misunderstand a situation." He shrugged, then tucked his hands into his pockets. "I've seen people be stupid for too long for me to just ignore it, not when I can do something about it. Take that as you want, but that's the truth." He turned to walk out.

"What's your name?" I asked.

He paused. "Blake." As soon as he gave me that, he left.

His words made it harder to sleep, as I weighed them, as I tried to decide their truth. Was he right? He had no reason to lie that I could tell, no reason to tell me something like that unless it were true. I didn't see an upside to it.

But if he *was* right, what the fuck was Harrison doing? Why ignore me if he still fucking cared?

Because I hurt him.

I thought about how I'd reacted to Kelvin, how hard Kelvin had worked to fix the situation, to wait for me. Was I being the unfair one? Was I expected too much from Harrison too fast?

I curled into the blanket and put the sweater back over my eyes, trying to ignore the light, the questions, the uncertainty.

Whatever the reason, whatever it meant, I couldn't do anything about it right now, not until I got back from this fucking place, not until I solved the immediate problem.

The rest would have to wait.

With that acceptance, sleep finally came.

Chapter Nineteen

I woke to a sound that my brain couldn't identify.

No, wait, it wasn't *couldn't*, it was wouldn't. It was like seeing something that was just too fucked up to even consider it could be real. It was like if humans suddenly saw a huge face in the sky speaking to us — we'd find a reason to believe it was a hoax just because we really fucking hated the idea of it being true.

We were excellent at lying to ourselves, after all.

So the skittering, the tiny little taps against stone that echoed through the cave was far too telling a sound for me to think deeply about. Instead, my brain protected me and told me it was the wind. It was anything other than what it sounded like — which was a million little spiders all rushing toward me, all creeping around me, close enough that it sounded as though they crawled just above my head.

When something brushed my cheek, I knew I couldn't ignore it anymore, no matter how nice that seemed.

Instead, I forced my eyes open, wishing immediately I hadn't.

The crystals in the cave had changed, still glowing, but now the teal shone bright while the others dimmed. It bathed the stone, tinting everything that color.

Of course, staring at the color was just an easy way to ignore the huge fucking centipede-like creature that spanned the length of the cave, curled around itself like a game of snake. It was made of joints that didn't make any sense. Nothing about it made sense, in fact. It was the same teal as the glowing crystals, and I would have sworn its eyes were gems as well. Near the face it had mandibles that came away from its cheeks, and more legs than I could count lined down each side of its long, agile body.

Just when I thought this nightmare fuel couldn't get any more disturbing, it reared back, using the end of its body as a counterweight, so it stood upright, tall enough that it could have easily looked Ruben in the eye.

Yeah, fuck this.

I didn't like randomly calling for help, but I was pretty sure a huge crystalline bug creature was so outside of my wheelhouse it wasn't even funny. This was *not* what I was cut out to deal with. I was made for other jobs — like eating a lot of tasty food, or mouthing off against things larger than me — but certainly *not* for fighting huge bug-like critters.

"A little help?" I called out.

The thing swiveled its head like an owl, the clicking of the parts moving even more unnerving.

"What the fuck is that?" Kelvin asked, the first to rush in. Despite his seemingly careless words, his attention had already locked on the thing, his eyes redder than before. He might seem casual, but he was ready to deal with the problem at hand.

"You said there was nothing in here," Ruben snapped at Porter.

"I said nothing had moved here in weeks. There was plenty of residual energy. I have to assume that beast hibernates here for long periods."

"Can we skip the science lesson?" I asked. "This isn't a fucking documentary. We don't need commentary. What are we going to do about it?"

"Try to come this way," Ruben said. "Move slowly, inch by inch. If you don't seem like a threat, it might let you pass."

I did as he said, moving in the smallest shuffling steps I could, my hands down to show I wasn't doing anything threatening. For the first time, I was thankful I seemed pretty harmless. It shouldn't have any problem with me, right? "Nice bug," I whispered, my voice soothing, as though I could talk it down from the ledge of wanting to bite my face off.

Except, before I got more than a foot or so, it twisted in a wide jerk, those legs working in tandem to move it around. It came closer but didn't attack, instead closing off my path, further placing it between me and escape.

"Got another plan?" I asked. "Because this one doesn't seem to be working too well."

No one responded right away, making me think that, no, they didn't.

And it wasn't so much a question of how to kill it. The truth was that I'd bet they could easily rush in and tear the thing apart—no problem. The problem was more that it could probably do a lot of damage before they managed to get hold of it.

Seeing as that damage was directed at me, I didn't really want to see that happen. I was not on board for any plan that had me playing up close and personal with Mr. A Million Legs over here.

"Can you stop it?" Porter asked, and for a moment I thought he meant me, until Blake answered him.

"No. I can't sense its mind. It's too different, or maybe it doesn't really have a mind." The frustration in Blake's tone made me think he cared a little. Or maybe he cared about his paycheck. If he let me die, I suspected Harrison might not tip.

"We don't have a lot of options here," I called out. "It doesn't seem to like when I move around much. What if we try to just run for it? Like, overwhelm it?"

"It has venom," Porter said. "Look at the fangs near its mouth. They're dripping something, and I would suspect you do not want to see what that might do to you."

At his words, I focused in on the fangs that I hadn't even noticed before, so distracted by the clicking mandibles as I'd been. I immediately wish I hadn't looked. Yep, they were dripping something at a steady pace, as though almost salivating, and I was pretty sure Porter was right.

Nothing had fangs that dripped anything good.

Well, Kelvin…

I shook the thought away, because it was so not the time for that nonsense. Nope, I needed to find a way out of this situation, because if I didn't, I wasn't going to get to feel the *good* venom ever again.

However, I felt like we'd hit that bad spot in a plan, where nothing sounded good, and the idea of doing anything felt overwhelming. People over thought because they had no idea what else to do, because they didn't want to risk making things worse.

Lucky for them, I was an expert at making things worse, so I didn't much mind being the one to do this.

"Okay, we go on three."

"Wait, go?" Porter asked.

"What does go mean?" Kelvin added.

"One," I counted.

"We have a plan?" Blake asked, a bit of panic in his voice.

"No, but she's always like this," Ruben explained.

"Two."

"Just figure it out," Kelvin snapped.

"Three!" I called as I dove toward the sleeping bag, pulling it in front of me just as the creature lunged. I got the fabric in front of me in time to see those dripping fangs tear through the bag as though it were as thick as tissue paper. Worse, it drenched it in whatever dripped from those teeth.

A roar echoed through the cave loud enough to hurt my ears.

And I fucking recognized that as Galen. It was the unhinged Galen I'd seen more and more of, the one didn't seem to know what the fuck he was doing or what was going on beyond his anger, his rage. I didn't love that sound before, but right now I didn't mind it.

The creature moved away from me, and I scurried backward to put distance between us. With the sleeping bag out of the way, I could see Galen — fully shifted — with his jaws around the midsection of the creature.

That really had no right being as hot as he made it out to be, right? Like, how unfair was it that he could look sexy as a fucking monster attacking a bug?

Completely ridiculous.

He twisted around it, but the creature was bigger. It wrapped part of its body around him like an anaconda, tightening and using the grip to gain the upper hand as it snapped with those fangs.

Kelvin and Ruben rushed in as well, quickly trying to help. Ruben grabbed the thing near the head, from behind, while Kevlin wrestled to get Galen free of the tail. It took all three of them before they got it somewhat restrained.

It thrashed still, managing to move them despite how strong the men were. It went to show the amount of power inside that thing. There wasn't much that could stand against just one of these guys, let alone three of them, but this thing made a pretty good effort.

A hand thrust into my line of vision. Porter waited for me to take it, and when I did, when he pulled to help me up, I hissed.

What?

I looked toward the pain, the stinging in my upper biceps, near my shoulder. It was only then I noticed a large wound.

How had I not felt it? It wasn't deep, but rather long, like a scratch just deep enough to bleed.

Porter's eyes went wide and he pulled me closer, holding my arm up to examine it. He didn't touch it, instead inhaling deeply and frowning.

A loud crack echoed through the cave, drawing my focus for a moment to see Ruben drop the creature, its heavy body striking the floor in a still heap. Neon teal blood poured from the wounds Galen had inflicted, and clung to his fur.

"She was infected," Porter said, his voice careful and flat.

"Are you sure?" Kelvin asked, rushing over to grasp my arm as well. He held it gently. "Maybe it was just from the fall? Or she was scratched by it?" Even I could tell that he was reaching for anything that might explain it, that he didn't really believe it.

"I can smell the venom in the wound."

"Can we disinfect it?" Ruben didn't give me the chance to even tense before he poured water right onto the wound, the chill causing me to let out an entirely undignified yelp. "Maybe we can flush the venom out."

"That won't work," Porter said. "I can smell it's already mixed into her bloodstream."

"So what's it going to do? Am I going to get superpowers? Because I wouldn't mind also having a bug form…" I laughed at the stupid joke because I wasn't sure how to deal with any of this. The nerves hit me hard, the uncertainty. I did what I always did, just going with humor to cover it up.

"I don't know," Porter answered. "None of these are creatures I know of. This one is connected to Natures, but not part of that clan. I have no idea what its venom might do. It could do nothing, it could shut down all her systems in ten minutes."

"That's a pretty fucking big selection," I pointed out. "You really can't narrow that down at all?"

"No. I wish I could, but creatures have venom for a number of reasons—mostly to slow down prey and to be able to take down creatures larger than themselves. Because of that, it could do any number of things."

"We should get her back," Ruben said. "There are healers we can take her to."

"How are we supposed to get back?" Kelvin pointed out. "The entire plan was that the Weres were always returned after they did whatever they were supposed to do. We don't know *how* to get back on our own. Even her bay portals aren't working."

"I'm really not feeling too bad," I said, though no one seemed to hear me.

They kept speaking like I wasn't even there.

"So what? We just pretend it didn't happen? We ignore it?" Ruben asked.

Galen growled, still in his other form, that serving as his addition to the conversation. I didn't understand what it meant, but the others responded as though it made perfect sense.

"I know that," Kelvin snapped back, "but we don't have another choice."

I yanked my arm away to make them pay attention to me. "There's no reason to just keep arguing like this, is there? We're stuck here until we deal with the problem at hand, so let's get to it. The sooner we finish this up, the better. It isn't doing anything right now, and maybe it won't. I'm weird and different, so who knows? Maybe it won't affect me at all." I shrugged, the idea nice even if I didn't really believe it.

I wasn't lucky enough for me to be unaffected by the venom of some other weird creature. In fact, it'd be a fucking miracle if I didn't end up in anaphylactic shock or something over this. Since I couldn't guess what would happen, however, I figured it was best to just keep moving. The sooner we worked this all out, the sooner we fix this and go back home, the sooner we could deal with whatever was currently sashaying its way through my body.

The men exchanged loaded looks that implied they didn't really believe that, that they didn't think I was being realistic, but none of them spoke up. Why would they? What would the point of that be? They might not like my idea, but it was all we had.

So we went about packing up our things, the light having returned. It was still a long walk and we had just been reminded that this place was far from safe, that we needed to keep our minds on our surroundings. Porter had warned us, the weretiger had warned us, but it hadn't really hit me that this place had the dangers it had.

Like huge fucking bugs that liked to inject unknown venom into people, for example, as just the first thing to fuck us over so far.

I left the sleeping bag—between the venom and the rips, it was pretty much useless now, and headed off again.

The aching in my shoulder continued, but I ignored it. I couldn't think about it, couldn't get bothered by it or the others would notice and worry. Sure, I saw their side-eyes, the concern, but that was fine. No doubt they'd do that the whole fucking way, but I couldn't show any signs of pain.

We just had to get through this, but the increasing pain in my arm made me worry we might have already been screwed...

* * * *

Ruben

"You need to get yourself under control."

Galen cast me a threatening glare.

It was strange to see him like this. I'd known Galen for many years now, had always preferred working with him over most of the other Clan Heads. He thought things through, reacting less based on instinct and stupidity. It meant he understood the intricacies of negotiation.

Many alphas before him had been no better than beasts, simply wanting to pee on things to claim them as their own.

Perhaps that was why I struggled so badly to see him in this state.

"You don't know what you're talking about," he muttered.

"Of course I do. You're entirely out of control. If you were anyone else, I'd say you had already gone feral."

He snarled instead of answering, which wasn't the best way to prove his point, all things considered.

"Is it that obvious?" he asked, lowering his voice. We walked ahead of the others, so Galen could lead us in the right direction.

"Perhaps not to everyone, but I have known you for a lot of years now."

Galen peered to the side, as though he wanted to look over his shoulder but didn't dare. The reason was obvious enough—Grey walked behind us, beside Kelvin. "Do you think she's noticed?"

She'd be a fool not to. Grey and Galen were even closer than he and I were, so there was no chance that she hadn't noticed the stark contrast in his behavior and attitude.

The only benefit of it all was that he didn't seem to take it out on her. I had a feeling that if he dared to so much as growl in his direction, he'd find himself on the wrong end of a few of us.

"It would be hard to miss," I said to lighten the blow. "How bad is it, really?"

He shuddered hard. "Bad. Worse since we got here. Before we came here, it wasn't good. I felt on edge, close to snapping, but I could still breathe slowly and work it through. Here, though? It's like my wolf suddenly has all the power, like I'm fighting to hold on to control of myself no matter what. It doesn't take me being angry, doesn't take anything and it's wrestling the lead from me. I've *never* felt like this before."

"It's probably this place. It's a source for Spirit energy, right? So it makes sense that there's more energy here and that might make your wolf stronger. I'd bet Kelvin's hunger is stronger, that Blake's Mind abilities are more powerful, that Porter can do things he never could before we got here."

"What about you?"

"Nothing new. I don't think I run off the same energy signals you all do, so I don't feel anything. In fact, I don't even feel a pull like you do, like they do."

Well, except for Grey. She didn't seem to feel any particular pull in any direction, either. I didn't know what that meant, why it would be different. She was a Spirit, after all, so why would she not feel the same? Wouldn't she be drawn to the source of her energy?

I would have been more bothered by that all if it wasn't for the fact that she never followed what she should have, that she was always breaking with the obvious constraint of how things should have occurred. It meant that when she yet again was different, it didn't surprise me that much.

Intrigued? Sure. I wanted to understand what made her different, but I accepted that she was.

So instead of thinking much about that, I focused on the problem at hand—Galen.

"We need you to keep your head on straight so we can get through this," I reminded him. "If anyone can do it, you can. This is about more than you, more than us. This is about your entire clan."

My little pep talk didn't seem to do a damn bit of good. Galen appeared just as distracted, just as on edge as before.

It made me wonder for the first time if we could lose him, if he could lose himself before we were able to find the source or solve this problem.

Maybe...

"You need to keep it together because if you can't, it'll probably be Grey who pays the price."

And, yeah, the noise that left him was vicious.

Still, like it or not, that was the reality check he needed. He might not care if anything happened to him, if it happened to us, but Grey was another matter entirely.

It reminded me of what I'd already known, the thing he'd never had to tell me.

Had he told Grey that she was his mate? That his instinct had already picked her for him? It was only a matter of time before they bonded — if they could. The fact he hadn't given in yet was astounding, really. It was to a testament of his control, of his ability to resist what he wanted.

However, with his current state, it would be best not to leave them alone together if possible. A Were's instincts were strong, and I didn't trust him to resist forever.

The selfish part of me didn't want them to bond, either. The connection between her and Kelvin was bad enough, but to craft another such link?

As a Justice, I had nothing like that, no ability to lock her to me, no innate form of connection that ensured she remained mine. I lacked confidence that she might choose me for any other reason, that I had much of anything to offer her.

Worse, so far as I understood, Justices didn't *have* relationships. They didn't fall in love, didn't settle down. We worked, we held the peace, we upheld the rules until something got the better of us or we took our own lives. Those were our only futures, so far as tradition and history said, and neither were ones I wanted her anywhere near.

"So you'll keep yourself in line?" I asked, forcing myself to return to the subject at hand, to stay on task.

Galen didn't answer right away. "I'm going to try," he finally said, then added, his voice low and his gaze pinned forward, "If I can't, can I trust that you'll make sure she stays safe?"

"You should know you don't have to ask that."

He laughed, the sound tense. "Who would have thought we'd end up here, huh? After all those meetings, all those times we sat across from each other, yet here we are. Grey asked me one day what it all meant, that there had to be more, and I told her life was random. I told her that life was mostly what happened in the meantime. This really proves it, right? I wouldn't have thought this is where I'd end up, half a snap from feral and running around some other realm with the likes of you all."

"Are you sorry about it?"

He peered over his shoulder at Grey. "No, I don't think I am."

And I certainly understood that. It seemed the normal way that things went with Grey — it never went the way I expected, but I always found it worth it in the end.

Chapter Twenty

No more caves for me.

After what had lurked in that first one—the memory still crept around in my brain just like the creature—I never wanted to try spelunking. Who knew what might exist even further into the darkness?

Instead, we stopped at a small clearing. Porter had suggested the fire, since it seemed to push away other things that lived here, given that fire wasn't natural to this realm. I didn't know if that was true, or if Porter had said it only to make me feel better, but I decided to take it at face value.

I could use a little comfort after all.

The others had moved away to survey the surrounding areas. It seemed they didn't want a repeat of what had happened the night before, so they planned to make damn sure it was safe this time.

It left me by the fire, and I knew they'd created a good circle as they'd moved out to root out any threat that might exist. Occasionally I'd hear a yelp, something that wasn't one of us, telling me they'd found some unfortunate critter. Of course, after the last thing we'd run into, I wasn't a big fan of any of that.

My arm hurt, a burning and itching that could have been on any of those commercials for STI meds. I couldn't smell what Porter could, but I could still feel the venom spreading through me. I had no idea what it meant, what it could do, and it reminded me that I wasn't a fan of surprises, especially not bad ones.

My life was a collection of surprises, honestly. My crow meant I could take nothing for granted, that I had no idea what might happen next at any point. Maybe that was why I didn't like the unexpected when I saw it coming.

I sighed and kicked my legs out, sitting on a sleeping bag that had appeared when they'd set up the little spot. I had to assume it was Blake's, given no one else would need to sleep yet. He didn't seem to care if I used it, so I didn't plan to complain. I was okay with being a damsel now and then if it meant a more comfortable sleep.

I'd eaten a foil-wrapped sugary pastry — much to the annoyance of Porter, who claimed it wasn't real food — for my dinner. He'd stared at it as though I were eating bugs, but I'd packed the vital shit. If we were here for fuck only knew how long, I'd have the important stuff with me.

Like sugary pastries.

A rumble came from ahead of me, past the fire, but the dancing flames obscured my sight. I pictured all sorts of things — none of them good — from that sound. It was low, dangerous, easier to feel than hear.

Before I found my voice, the source of that feral noise came into view, through the flames, as two amber eyes glowed in the darkness.

Galen.

He was human, at least he seemed to be, but those eyes were all wolf. They were vacant, nothing of the man I knew in them. He crouched there, on the other side of the fire, his head tilted slightly as though he wasn't sure what was before him.

I'd think he didn't recognize me, except no one had that much intensity in their gaze unless whatever they saw interested them very much. Unfortunately, I wasn't sure if it was a, 'hey, I like her,' interest or more of a 'I wonder what her small intestine tastes like,' interest.

"Hey," I said, my voice soft and coaxing. Maybe hearing me would help him decide? Help him get a grip on his own control? It could serve as a link between his currently fucked-up brain and the man I'd known for so many years.

He blinked slowly, but came no closer. Did my words get through to him?

Fuck if I knew, but at least I could try again. It was better than nothing. "You want food?" I held up a piece of the beef jerky like a dog treat. That was how I won over stray dogs, so maybe it would work with Galen, too?

Except, the way he stared at me suggested it wasn't food he was after. If he wanted to eat me, I was pretty sure it would be in the way that would leave me boneless but not tiny bloody chunks.

And why the hell did that turn me on? Was I an idiot?

Yes, I really am…

He growled lowly, then leaped forward, through the fire. Despite the fear, the realization that this could go very badly, I could admit that looked really fucking cool.

At least, I thought that before his weight slammed into me, shoving me backward, pinning me beneath him. He somehow felt heavier than he had before, even if he were human. Why? More muscles? Maybe he'd always been heavy, but I'd never had him on top of me like this, so I'd never realized it?

He leaned down, his face inches from mine, his expression unreadable. It made me recognize that he'd always been difficult to read.

Many of the men I was involved with were hard to read, but Galen was different. With Kelvin and Ruben, I had to worry about what they were up to, how it might affect me. While neither would do things outright to cause me harm, they both liked to trick me, to use dishonesty or non-answers to get what they wanted.

I never had to worry about that with Galen. No matter what happened, I'd always had absolute faith that he was on my side, that he was looking out for me. It meant even if I couldn't read his expression, if I couldn't work out what was in his mind, I didn't fear it. Nothing inside of me believed that he'd hurt me — even now.

He leaned in and pressed his nose to my throat, inhaling deeply. A more contented rumble left his chest, at least until he frowned and moved his nose down, over my shoulder, then to my arm and the cut.

His narrowed eyes became bright amber slits, casting out light brighter than the fire. It was as though this place took him over, like the Spirit energy that existed here drove him mad.

"Call for them," he said, his voice so deep and guttural that I hardly understood the words at first.

Call for them? Did he mean the others?

"Why?"

He tilted his head again, the action reminding me of a dog. Whether he understood the question or not didn't matter, because he crossed the scant space between us and took my lips in an aggressive, consuming, claiming kiss.

Galen had always been gentle, careful, sweet, but none of that rested in this touch. Instead, it felt like something between punishment and starvation, and he crowded me so closely I doubted there was any escape.

Which was probably exactly why he'd told me to call for them, to ask for help. The meaning hit me all at once, that he wanted me to understand that he had no control, that he couldn't stop himself from anything.

"Call," he repeated before nipping at my throat, his teeth sharp, telling me that they had at least shifted. The points pressed into my flesh, but he didn't break the skin. This delicious pain sparked from that place. It wasn't like Kelvin, like when he bit me — that was quick and brutal, a flash of agony before ecstasy took over.

This was entirely different. It wasn't quick, more like a threat, something torturously slow that forced me to wait, to endure, to submit. He raked his teeth across my skin, and to my own astonishment and shame, I moaned.

Yeah, I really am a pervert.

He pressed his forehead against my chest, over where my heart raced. "Call, please." Desperation saturated his words.

But I couldn't do that. Calling for help would prove I didn't trust him, that I needed saving, and I refused to do that. This was Galen, and better or worse, I accepted him — all of him.

"I won't."

He let out a snarl that sounded nothing like him, and when he moved, I expected him to back off. He was bluffing — I was sure of it. Just pushing me to prove a point.

It shocked me when he didn't go that way, however, when instead he gripped my waist and flipped me over. I gasped at the strength he used, the way he seemed to one handedly turn me over like that. I found myself on all fours, the fire to my left, far enough that I didn't risk getting burned even though the heat warmed that side of me. The other side had a chill, but my back?

Well, given the way Galen mounted me, it wasn't cold at all. In fact, his skin felt feverish against mine, even through my clothing.

And the way something hard pressed against me, I was pretty sure I knew exactly what was on his mind.

Even so, he didn't do anything more. He wrapped his fingers in my hair and tipped my head back, shifting so he could look into my eyes, his body leaned to the side to let me see him. "Call them."

"I'm not going to," I assured him.

He let out a low sound of frustration. "Do you know what I want to do to you?"

"I feel your little buddy poking me — I've got a pretty good idea."

"They'll protect you."

"I don't need any protection, not from you."

He tightened his grip in my hair, the action making my scalp sting in the best of ways.

I laughed, the sound breathless. "Is that supposed to scare me? Jokes on you — I'm into that. Look, it doesn't matter what you try, what you do, I'm not going to go running scared."

"You don't understand."

"Don't I? Whatever fucked-up thing you want to do, I've probably done a dozen times already, so stop worrying so much. I'm not afraid of you and that isn't changing."

He rolled his hips, the action causing his erection to grind against me. Damn, that was a nice sensation. It excited me, made me want to press back against him. It distracted me from the pain in my arm, from the questions of what was going to happen.

Fuck, it felt like I had *him* for a moment, at least. Despite the questions, the fears of losing him, for right now, he was here with me. Sure, he was half-crazed — and that was probably being generous — but he was here.

So I pulled against his grip and kissed him, the touch gentler than what he'd done before. In fact, I hardly could reach due to how he held my hair. He let out a rough, warm breath, the tension leaving his body, before he sagged on top of me. I nearly toppled under the sudden weight.

He must have realized it as well because, just as fast, he turned, twisting us both until I rested on my side, him behind me, the fire before me, my head pillowed on his arm. He trembled, as though more energy coursed through his body than he could make use of. He held me tightly, and I had to admit, being the little spoon wasn't so bad.

Sure, getting fucked would have been a pretty good way to spend the rest of the night, a good send-off to sleep, but amazingly...I didn't mind this, either.

So instead of asking anything, instead of trying to get him to talk to me, I just let us have this moment and fell asleep. He might not understand it, no one else might get it, but I knew that this was the safest place in the world.

Galen

Her body was soft against mine, and she'd somehow fallen asleep. Even after what I'd done to her — what I'd almost done to her — she'd never rejected me, never pushed me away. Was she foolish or brave?

Was there a difference?

She'd fallen asleep an hour before, her breathing evening out, somehow able to let her guard down around me.

It made no sense. Instinct guided me, and that instinct told me to never turn my back on anything that might attack me. I would never allow something as dangerous as me in this position, yet she'd not only done that, but also just fallen asleep?

I often ended up wondering what happened inside her head. Was she naïve? Clueless? Did she trust me because it was me, or was she just foolish enough to not recognize danger even when it rested this close to her?

My cock was still hard, as though trying to reassert itself. I knew, without a doubt, that if I'd kept going if she'd have allowed me to.

That terrified me more than anything, that she wouldn't have fought me even when she should have. It wasn't that I thought I wouldn't harm her, that I would have stopped, but I knew that even if I couldn't, she wouldn't have.

The idea made me want to pull her closer to me and shove her away all at once.

Hours passed, with the others coming up to check in. Even if I could feel their disapproving looks, no one bothered us. Even Kelvin only snorted, leaving me like a dog with a toy he didn't want to risk taking away. Normally it would have bothered me, but I didn't know what I'd do if they tried it, either.

When light bathed the space again, she still hadn't woken.

"We need to get moving." Porter crouched in my line of sight.

My fingers curled around Grey, hating the idea of anyone else getting close to her. I'd suffered with this same feeling for months—for years. Wolves were extremely territorial, known for our possessive nature when it came to our mates, but that was made significantly worse when the bond wasn't complete, when she wasn't *mine* yet no matter what instinct said. A part of me, the primal, wild part, feared that someone would take her from me. It made it difficult to focus, and without the normally logical part of me in control, it made it impossible.

I bared my teeth, but Porter didn't seem intimidated by it at all. Instead, he turned his gaze to Grey. "She's still asleep?"

I inhaled slowly, grappling with my instincts that demanded I tear him apart. *Calm.* I pulled away from her, sitting up to give Grey some space.

"Grey, it's time to wake up." Porter reached in and touched her arm, shaking softly.

The woman didn't move. Worse, the movement caused her head to loll slightly in an unnatural way.

Porter dropped from a crouch to his knees, then shook her harder. "Grey, wake up." A thread of panic bled into his voice.

The others must have heard that sound, because in moments, Kelvin, Ruben and Blake all rounded us as well.

"She's burning up," Porter said as he pressed his hand to her forehead. "You didn't notice?"

"Weres run hot," Ruben offered before I had to say a word. "He wouldn't notice a fever, especially in his current state. Is it the poison?"

The words were difficult to follow with my clouded thoughts, but I tried. It was important, I knew that much even if I didn't understand most of it.

"She reeks of the venom," Porter said. "Her breathing is erratic as well. We need to hurry—I don't know how long she'll last like this."

That I understood perfectly well. It had me looking forward, in the direction of where the power pulled me. It had called to me since we'd arrived, this promise of peace, of power, of everything I could want in that way. It was home.

It warred with Grey, with the pull I had to her, which was the only thing that had kept me from taking off so far. However, with Grey as she was, there was no reason to hold back anymore. We needed to move fast, to get to whatever called me.

I'd come here to save the Weres, but now that was the last thing on my mind. All that mattered was saving Grey.

Chapter Twenty-One

Porter

I held Grey against my chest, my arms around her, as the scent of poison spread through her small form.

It had started just past the edges of the shallow wound, but now it even hung on her breath with each exhale. It was a sharp scent, acidic, and it was increasing.

I'd chosen to hold her—over the arguments of the others—because it made sense. I was stronger than the Mind, but less useful in a fight than the others. At least, that was how I justified the choice.

The realities were that I disliked harming others, had a distaste for killing, but that didn't make me incapable of it.

I just didn't care for the idea of handing her over to anyone else.

It was strange to see her this way. She shook in my arms, soft whimpers escaping her lips with each step.

In the time that I had spent around her — limited as it had been — she'd always seemed so much larger than she was. Perhaps it was the attitude, the zest for life, but something about her made her appear bigger than any of those she was around.

She never wilted, not for a moment, even when things got difficult. Even when faced with execution, she hadn't so much as flinched.

So having her trembling in my arms forced me to recognize her in a wholly different way. The truth was that I knew little about her, even still. I hadn't known her prior to when she'd sought my help after she'd been framed for murder. I was still trying to understand her, to understand what she was.

We reached the base of the mountain, our pace having picked up greatly since Grey had fallen unconscious. She'd kept us slower before, but now? Now we knew we had to hurry. Even Galen appeared more focused, as if this had helped him grapple control back from this thing that had infected him.

"We're close," Galen said, his voice rough, betraying how he struggled. He turned toward a path that wound up the outside of the steep cliff. The path had crystals on it, as though almost made out of them fully. No dust coated the path, nothing that made it seem as though it had gone unused, but that didn't mean much.

I hadn't tasted dust on the breeze, either. Perhaps there wasn't any here. This place didn't follow the rules I knew about, so I dared to take nothing for granted.

I headed up the path, moving quickly, with Galen and Ruben at the front and Kelvin and Blake behind us. Even with our speed, I knew they watched for danger carefully.

It only took another ten minutes or so to reach a large cave opening, an amber glow spreading out on the path outside the entrance.

Galen's eyes were wide and empty, nothing showing of the person he had been, of his human side. It seemed the wolf spirit within him had taken over entirely. There was nothing else left of him inside.

I'd never seen a Were come back from this far, but Galen was unlike most Weres. This was not a case of a Were losing his mind naturally. I could only hope that once we finished this, it would resolve the problem, that it would fix him as well.

I hoped that not only because I wanted to avoid the upcoming war, but because I didn't want to see the Weres fall. Even if we solved the Were problem, I didn't trust that an alpha other than Galen would manage to keep them in line, that he would avoid war and violence as best he could.

Those weren't the only reasons, though. I thought about the pain Grey would face if we failed, or if we succeeded but Galen didn't pull through. I didn't want to watch her suffer in that way, the way she would blame herself, the way she'd hold that all on herself. None of that was what I wanted, so we *had* to find a way to bring him back.

Galen stepped first into the large cave, his gaze upturned like an acolyte ready to meet a god. It was strange to see him that way.

The inside of the cave was similar to the one Grey had spent the night in — the one with the creature — but this one had amber crystals everywhere, bathing it in that light, instead. It was larger, as well, with an opening near the back.

In the center of the cave was a pool of amber liquid, as though molten gold simmered there. The beauty stunned me, while it also warned me away.

It was the same part that felt that pull to go in another way, that warned me *this* wasn't for me. Did it want me to follow the path to my own source? To the thing that had given me the energy that made me a Nature?

I ignored it. That didn't matter, not right now.

What I carried in my arms was so much more important to me than whatever might rest at the end of that path.

Galen shifted into his wolf form, the stitches of his pants giving way, the scraps of fabric left behind, forgotten as he moved toward the water, drawn forward by something greater than him, than any of us.

That was one of the benefits of being a Nature—I didn't tend to fall under the same delusions of grandeur as the other clans. My connection to the rest of the world made it far easier to understand my place, to see how grand other energies were, and how both great and small I was in comparison.

Just as he approached the water, when I wondered if he would leap in, if he would drown in the gold, a flash of light filled the space so bright I had close my eyes to escape it—and even then it felt as though it seared my skin.

"You idiots."

I didn't recognize the voice at first, even if it felt familiar.

Then, when I could open my eyes, when I could look across the space, I wouldn't forget the man who stood there.

I held Grey tighter as Ruben stepped between us and Knot, the mysterious man who had created Grey, who had shown up to her trial to save her.

Even if he had saved her before, none of us trusted him.

"How are you here?" Ruben asked.

Knot scoffed as if the question were stupid as he came forward, not seemingly concerned at all about any of us.

When Ruben again got in his way, Knot raised his hand and swiped it. It wasn't a physical hit that got Ruben moving, though, and instead seemed as though a wave of power struck out, knocking everyone back except me.

I had a feeling it wasn't that he liked me in particular, it was simply that I held Grey. If he struck out at me, I might drop her.

He continued to come forward, his red hair bright and shimmering as though the amber glow in the room didn't touch it at all. His eyes were the same stark blue as before, locked not on me—as though I were no concern of his—but instead on Grey.

"What did they do to you?" he asked, his voice soft, a tone I suspected he saved for her and her alone.

And it immediately made me wonder just what was between them. This was not the tone used between two barely connected people.

Did he show this to her? Or did he hide it, only exposing this side when he knew she couldn't take notice?

He reached toward her, and I took a step backward, unwilling to let him touch her in this state.

He lifted his gaze to mine, any softness gone in an instant. Funny, given the way Grey had spoken about him, it had seemed as though he were a joke. If you listened to her, he never was serious, never clear, more like an annoying little brother than anything else.

Did that mean he hid this side of him?

Because there was no doubt that the man before me was nothing if not a hell of a threat. His gaze was steady, rage simmering deep inside his blue eyes, eyes the same color as Grey's hair.

"Is this your fault? You let one of the pests bite her?"

"You know what bit her? How do we cure her?" All the questions about what he was and worries disappeared, because at least Knot appeared to understand what had happened. That was better than we'd had so far.

He cast me a withering look. "If you weren't an idiot, you wouldn't have brought her here in the first place. Do you have *any* idea what kind of place this is? The things that would kill her the moment they saw her?"

That made me think about that creature, the way it had locked onto her — not us.

But why?

"Why would anything care about her?"

"You don't know anything but you come traipsing here, dragging her with you. *This* is why I told her to never get herself wrapped up in the problems of fools — it always ends badly and I knew she would end up paying the price." He reached again, and this time I didn't move away.

I didn't know how to save her, and I was at least smart enough to let someone else try.

He stroked his hand over her cheek. "She's burning up. If I didn't sense her pain, if I didn't come here right now, she'd have been dead within ten minutes." He leaned forward, his lips pressing to hers.

At first, I nearly knocked him away. She wasn't even awake, so how dare he kiss her like that? From what little I knew, even if he saw her that way, she hadn't said or done anything that indicated she felt the same.

Except, just when I went to react, I noted something blue floating between their lips. It was like a fine mist, sparkles in it, like so much of what was here. The color matched his eyes and her hair, and it passed from his lips to hers.

The more she breathed in whatever that blue was, the less she shook, the more stable she seemed.

After a long, tense moment, she started to cough, shifting so much that she nearly fell from my arms. I guided her down to the stone floor, and she coughed so hard she gagged, then spat out something made of that teal color.

It shimmered on the floor, thick and smelling strongly of the venom. However, just as quickly, it fizzed and dissolved until only a damp spot on the ground remained.

Knot crouched, balancing on the balls of his feet as he rubbed his hand on her back. "Better?"

His voice had changed, from the rough threat he'd offered to me, and from the gentle tone he'd used with her when she'd been unconscious, to something much shallower and more joking.

Grey pressed her palms against the ground and lifted her head, looking as though she hadn't just been moments from death. Her gaze found Knot, and a crinkle beside her eyes said her feelings about his appearance were complicated at best. "You always show up at exactly the right time."

He smiled. "It's part of my charm. Now, little crow, you want to explain to me just what the fuck you're doing *here*?"

By this point, the others had gotten back up, circling around. They had to see that he'd helped her as well, which was the only reason they weren't going for round two.

Plus, round one hadn't gone that well.

Even Galen had pulled his focus from the water, from the chaos in his mind to Grey and Knot.

"I told you the Weres are sick. *You* were the one who told me how to get that book."

"I told you so you knew what to expect, not so you could try to change it. You needed to know it's happened before, that it'll happen again." He shook his head and flicked her forehead. "You're always taking the wrong lesson away from every situation. You know that? Instead of realizing that you're helpless, you decide that means you should come here?"

She swiped at his hand but missed when he pulled back. "I told you I wasn't going to just let it happen. And besides, is *now* the time to get mad? We made it, didn't we?" She gestured at the pool. "There it is—the source of the power!"

Knot turned his head to peer at the water, froze for a moment, then started to laugh. "You think *that's* the source?"

"The story said it was a lake."

"The story is a fable, Little Crow, it isn't meant to be taken literally. That's just a puddle. Sure, if a Were goes swimming, they'll probably feel pretty good, but isn't the source."

"So what is?"

Knot turned back toward Grey, looking straight into her eyes without flinching. "The source is just past that doorway. Think carefully about the old stories, about what they all say created Spirits."

I knew, of course. The Natures had *always* known the truth, even if we didn't like it, if we tried to ignore it.

Knot smiled, though the expression was tense, as though it hid the deeper feelings beneath. "That's right. Just that way is a god, the one who created the Weres, and I really would suggest we not wake him."

Chapter Twenty-Two

I wasn't sure exactly what had happened after I'd passed out, but seeing Knot was both welcome and annoying.

He often managed to show up at the exact moment everything was going to shit. I appreciated it, of course — I hadn't wanted to die from whatever that was that had infected me — but I also knew damn well that if he wasn't always fucking *gone*, he might have kept this all from getting so bad.

That was the part that got to me, that he helped make the mess by not being a part of this shit from the start.

Like *this*, for example. He was so vague, to send me to find a book instead of just fucking telling me what was going on.

"A god?" I asked, incredulous at the information.

"Did you think that a pool of liquid could create Spirits? *Really?*"

"Oh, and talking about fucking gods is more realistic?"

"After everything, that's the hard thing to accept? Werewolves and shifters and vampires and mind readers are all okay, but thinking that something more powerful than you is crazy?"

I hated that he was right. That wasn't anywhere near the craziest thing that I'd heard or dealt with, so why was it so hard to believe?

Because I didn't like the idea.

Also, because it made me think about Knot, about what that made him.

Nope.

I couldn't agree with that nonsense. I couldn't accept that he was a god. That just wasn't possible.

"You said the god was sleeping," Porter said. "What do you mean?"

Knot lifted his gaze toward Porter but he didn't look thrilled at all about the idea of talking to the other man. He didn't rise, didn't appear bothered at all about any of them around him.

He turned his attention back to me as though he didn't see the men as being worth speaking to. "Immortality is long, and longer still for those who have the most power. When it becomes too long, when gods grow tired, they like to sleep. Sometimes they feel forgotten by the world, and that is their next best option."

"So the Weres are going crazy because the god who created them is napping?" I spoke slowly, the words clumsy in my mouth, like a sentence that my brain rejected because it made no sense.

"Basically? Yes. Spirits are created by the introduction of energy into humans. That energy is connected to the god, but if the god slumbers, the energy stops flowing. It turns bad, the energy corrupting, and the Spirit ends up going mad and dying from it." He shrugged as though it was expected, like it wasn't a big deal.

"So we just have to wake the god up?" I got to my feet.

Wakey, wakey eggs and bakey, bitch.

Knot grabbed my arm to pull me to a stop. "It's not that easy. Let me just say that this god has been hibernating for a long-ass time and we should *all* be happy he is. He isn't exactly friendly, after all. He isn't going to see us here and be thrilled by it."

"Aren't you a god?" Ruben asked, his dark eyebrow lifted.

"I hate that term. If you're asking me if I can deal with him, the answer is a big, fat no. He isn't a huge fan of mine." His expression didn't seem to have any fear, but it was pretty fucking clear he wasn't a fan of this god, either.

"We can't just let the Weres die," I said, even though I felt as though that should have been obvious enough that it didn't require actually saying it, but then again, I'd found people didn't pick up on what seemed obvious.

"Look... I don't want to see the Weres die either, but I'm telling you, you don't want to meet this guy. He's an asshole. He's a *much* bigger problem overall than some crazy Weres. The last time he decided to wake up and take a stroll around our world...well, there are a lot of cities that didn't survive it."

His warning silenced me for a long moment. It didn't matter the risks, though, or what he had to say about it. The truth was that no matter how dangerous he was, how bad an idea this might have been, I wasn't going to just let Galen die. I recalled the pack, the families, the children. I couldn't just walk away.

"Maybe he's right." I expected that statement from Ruben or Kelvin—they were both heartless when it came to the were clan—but I sure as fuck didn't think the words would fall from Galen's lips.

"Excuse the fuck out of me?" I turned to nail him with a glare. "After all this work, after I fought a weretiger—"

"She did what?" Knot asked under his breath, and I ignored the question.

"You are not about to just lie down and die now. Not a fucking chance." I held out my arm, the wound still there. "I got bit by a weird fucking bug! Worst of all, I *hiked.* Twice! So there is no opting out at this point."

He crouched, but it wasn't like Knot. Where Knot was balanced on the balls of his feet, his stance lithe and graceful, Galen's was more of a squat, his weight on the flats of his feet, his hands up, his fingers wrapped in the strands of his hair. He looked down, not at me, and for the first time I really saw the weight on him.

I crept toward him.

Knot set a hand on my arm. "He's feral. Maybe don't cuddle up with him?"

I knocked his hand free. "I'll be fine. He wouldn't hurt me."

I believed it, too. Even like this, even if he lost every sense of himself, he wouldn't hurt me. I knew it, a truth that ran deeper than anything else. He was lost to his instincts, to the wolf that lived inside his body, and that wolf wouldn't do a thing to harm me. So I crossed the rest of the distance until I kneeled right there with him.

"What if it hurts you?" he asked in a small voice.

"It's a part of you, right? Your wolf came from it. Your wolf isn't so bad, so I don't think it will be."

Knot snorted loudly behind me, but I ignored him.

"You don't know that," he pled. "What if you're wrong? You don't know that side of me, don't know what it's capable of. What if I sacrifice you and everything else just to try to save myself? To save my clan? What if the world is better off without us?" He paused, then lifted his gaze to me. "You asked me a long time ago what any of this meant. Why did things happen the way they did? I gave you some answer to make you feel better, but I thought about it after that. What if we met and I was human? What if I wasn't a Were, wasn't alpha. Maybe I would have been better off, and maybe the world is better off without us." His voice cracked, words that I had a feeling he never would have dared admit any other time. It went to show how close to broken he was.

"He's got a point," Kelvin said softly. "None of us want to see what will happen to the Weres at this rate, but we might be doing something right now we can't take back. If anyone understands what that's like, I do. I almost saw you die because of my choices, because of plans that I ended up unable to control. This is Galen's choice, at the end of the day."

"We can help the Weres as they go through this, to ease the burden. Maybe that is the kindest thing we can do," Porter said. "I can assure you that there are things here we don't want to find. If the dangerous things here are only tiny examples, then none of us may survive a run in with something as powerful as this god sounds. We have more to think about than just us."

I shook my head, refusing to listen to them.

No. I couldn't stand the idea of just losing him, of losing them all.

Galen reached out and set both his hands on my cheeks, pulling me in so his forehead was pressed to mine. "It's okay. I'm sorry that I didn't get more time with you, that I'm not going to get to keep seeing you grow into the person you're becoming, but that's all right. I got to save you once before and I can't see a better thing to do than save you now, again." He tipped his head slightly and brushed his lips to mine, the kiss sweet and sad and enough to make my eyes water.

It was a goodbye—no two ways to think about it. He was telling me it was okay, that he was okay with this, that he accepted it. He kissed me like a sorry for the end, like it was more about reassuring me than what he wanted.

Hands pulled me back, but I wiggled free of them, throwing myself forward.

Until Knot himself grabbed me. That was different, stronger, and no matter how I yanked, I couldn't get free.

"I'm sorry," Knot whispered into my ear, pulling me backward, toward the door of the cave. "He'll stay here—it'll be better that way. This place will feel like home to him. Once we're out of this cave, I'll be able to use my powers to bring us back home."

"No," I said, shaking my head.

Galen stared back at me, still crouched on the ground, as though he wanted to see me for every last moment he could.

It took me back to that first time I met him, when I'd had no idea what he was, who he was, nothing. I'd been lost, frightened, alone, and he had managed to not let me feel that way. In a world that felt so large, so different, he'd always given me a place I could go.

He'd always given me what I really needed, no matter what it meant to him, no matter the risk. Even when his own world was heavy, when it seemed to fall apart, he never wavered.

He'd been there for me every bit, always willing to step up when I needed it.

I'm going to do the fucking same now.

If I'd learned something, it was that sacrificing some for others was *never* the right choice. Even if it was easier or safer, it wasn't right.

My crow squawked in my head, enraged at the idea of *anyone* holding her back—even the one who made her.

I didn't care if he was a god, if he'd created me, none of it. I shoved him, a rush through me as my power—my inability to be trapped—kicked in. He caught his foot on, well, nothing physical I could see, and he tumbled backward.

I rushed forward, not toward Galen, not toward any of them. Instead, I hurled myself toward the doorway at the back.

"Grey!" Knot shouted my real name, not what he called me, but I ignored it. The other noises didn't matter, either. I had a goal, and that goal was saving Galen and the Weres.

The doorway wasn't solid but it wasn't empty, either. Instead, it was like throwing myself through water. I passed through it, tripping at the other side to find myself in a strange space. The doorway closed behind me, solidifying into solid rock. There was no wall, just a sheer cliff that overlooked the valley. It was lovely, a sight that people would have traveled across the world to witness.

I swallowed. I wasn't a huge fan of the heights, especially after my last disaster at flying, and when my arm still ached.

When I turned, I found a man asleep on a stone slab. He had long, wild hair and wore nothing.

Which was not how I expected to spend my day, seeing nude gods.

Of course, it wasn't that bad a thing, all things considered. He was built and pretty damn good looking.

No, focus!

I needed to wake him up, right? How did one wake up a god?

Surprising them was probably *not* a great idea.

"Excuse me?" I asked.

No response.

I crept closer. "Um, Mr. Were God? Rise and shine." I tried to sing a stupid song my mother used to sing to me as a teenager, when I really didn't want to wake up. No doubt I sang it off key and horrible, but maybe that would get him up faster.

I set a hand on the side of the slab and leaned forward, giving me the chance to peer into his face. It was younger than I figured, making him look like he was in his twenties or so. "Time to get up," I whispered.

His eyes snapped open, and I immediately regretted everything in my entire life. He had no iris, no pupil, nothing but the amber color, brighter than a flame, nothing human or soft or kind there. It was like seeing a feral Were, seeing something driven by instincts and desires I couldn't understand.

Yeah, maybe waking a grumpy sleeping god wasn't the best of ideas…

Chapter Twenty-Three

The man sat up slowly, his gaze locked on me. He sure woke up well, not a bit of grogginess in his features.

I backed away, wanting more distance between him and me. He did *not* look like the sort of person I wanted to spend much time around.

"You smell of chaos," the man said.

"I get that a lot," I answered, trying to inch back toward the doorway.

He was awake, right? That's all I needed. According to our best guesses, all he needed was to be aware and the energy would correct itself. It would flow correctly now, which meant I didn't need to get all chummy with this guy.

And everything about him drove me backward, step by step. It felt like a deeply buried instinct that said I should *not* be here, that I should get away from him.

My crow told me that, even older instincts than that told me it.

I reached the doorway, but it was just as solid as it had looked. I turned my gaze back on the man, to find him standing now.

"You shouldn't be here."

With the open wall, I didn't have a lot of places to go. I didn't have much room to maneuver, to get clear of him. Still, I tried to keep space between us. "You're just confused. Sleeping a long time will do that. Maybe some coffee? I know a great place."

"I missed the scent of fear. You reek of it." He sounded as though it turned him on, like he had some weird kink for it. That let me know everything I didn't already know, made me suspect Knot had been totally on point.

This was not the sort of person we really wanted to deal with much.

"Well, we don't kink shame here," I said with a rough laugh, my hand patting along the wall behind me, searching for *some* way out.

I couldn't hear the men from beyond the doorway, giving me a feel for just how thick the walls must be, the doorway still solid and uncrossable.

Still, even if I was starting to wonder if this had been a good idea, I was locked in. So why exactly hadn't I found a way out? Maybe because the wall was open?

The man came forward so fast, I couldn't track his movements. He went from across the room to just before me, his hand on my throat, pinning me to the wall.

He didn't close off my airway, didn't stop my breathing, but his hand was like a band around me, unwavering. He didn't even shake as he held me, as though it took no effort at all from him at all. "I can *feel* how long I've been asleep. Centuries."

"We all need our beauty sleep."

He tilted his head, staring at me. "Where is he?"

"Who?"

"Your master. What has changed that he would be foolish enough to make you, that he would *dare* to allow you to stand before me? Has so much time passed that he's forgotten his place?" He leaned in, smiling to show teeth that weren't in the least bit human. Instead, they were sharp, like wolf fangs. "I might have gone right back to sleep if I hadn't seen *you* here."

I tried to shove him away, but I had no luck getting him to budge in the least. He held tight, his eyes brighter than ever, something dark inside of them, something crazed and hollow and terrifying.

This was what Galen had tried to warn me about, what he hid. It was the energy of this being but, untempered by Galen, it was so much worse.

For the first time, I understood *why* Galen was so careful around me, why, as he'd lost himself, he'd pulled away. He'd struggled against this, against the instincts inside this thing.

My crow objected, and after a moment, he yanked away as though burned. He stared down at his hand, his brows furrowed as though he didn't understand what had just happened.

Usually, my crow went for more random options, but this time?

It seemed she *really* didn't like him touching us and had gone for a more direct reaction.

"You dare?" he asked, his voice vibrating with an anger that made the ground shake. "Clearly, I've slumbered too long. I am going to tear through this world again, remind you all of just how small, how insignificant you are. I'll plunge my teeth into your flesh and tear it free, picking everything from your bones and maybe, at the end of it, if any of you still survive, you'll recognize what true power is."

I stared up at him, entirely unsure how to respond to *that*. If it had been just anyone I might have laughed at the villain quality of the monologue, but unfortunately, it wasn't just anyone.

It was a god who I was pretty sure could carry out that threat if he wanted to.

"I'll start with you," he said, his voice so deep that it didn't sound human at all anymore. "When I'm done with you, he'll remember why he hides, why he crawls among lesser beasts, to escape *my* gaze. You can remind him with your broken body."

He reached for me again, but before he touched me, I found myself on the other side of the room, as though torn from one place and deposited in another.

"Don't look, he can pull you in with his gaze." Knot's voice warmed my ear, soft and oddly calm as he set his hand over my eyes.

"So you were around?" The man's voice eased, though an undercurrent of hatred rushed through it. It was as though he were more comfortable dealing with Knot but hated him all the same.

It was a deeper hatred as well, something that spawned from many more years than I'd known Knot. Of course, given how much he annoyed me even in the years I'd known him, I could see why someone might hate him.

"You know me—I always show up when you least expect it." Knot kept his hand over my eyes, and for once, I didn't struggle, didn't fight. I didn't feel the need to.

"You've grown bold since I've been gone."

"I like to keep people guessing. You have a nice nap?"

"I did, but I certainly didn't expect one of *yours* to be the one to wake me."

"What can I say? She takes after me — a bit brash, a bit ridiculous."

"As strange as it is to see you create one, I am even more surprised to see you *here*, trying to protect her from me. You've never given a damn about anyone else."

"I'm a quality over quantity sort of person. This one's worth the risk."

"Be careful you don't overestimate your abilities, Loki, because you have had to be taught that lesson time and time again."

Loki?

The name made no sense to me, and for a moment, I wondered if that was some nickname of his. I didn't have time to think much about it, however, as I stayed put.

"You should hand her over, now. Maybe that will appease me, at least for a while. See, I've been slumbering so long that I feel ready to stretch my limbs, to bathe this realm in blood again. I can *feel* how many of us slumber, how many have grown weak. I will wake them, now, draw them together again, and we *will* remind this realm who truly rules it. I'll start now with *her*."

"Not a fucking chance," Knot said, voice amazingly strong.

An angry roar echoed around as a familiar floating sensation ran through me, something similar to when I visited Knot in my dreams. When Knot removed his hand, I found that we weren't there anymore. Instead, I stood in my own living room with just Knot.

Epilogue

Panic struck me when I didn't see the others. "What about—"

"I pulled them out as well, don't worry. They're all safe and sound at the Justice Complex. I just thought you might want to talk privately after all that." He stepped away and looked around my place. "You know, this is the first time I've come to your house."

"Yeah, you're like a deadbeat dad."

He laughed softly as he went around picking up random items, examining them.

Which gave me the chance to ask what we both knew I wanted to. "He called you Loki."

"I figured you wouldn't just let that go."

"He doesn't mean, like, *that* Loki, does he?"

Knot turned back toward me and leaned against the edge of a side table, crossing his arms, somehow looking less like the childish guy I was used to. Maybe it was what happened, maybe it was the name, but something caused him to appear different. "I never liked that name, but yeah, that's me."

I swallowed hard, feeling weird all of a sudden. I'd known him for years now, was used to how I saw him, but to think he was actually a real, honest to fuck *god* was something I struggled to grasp.

"And that makes him…"

"There are a lot of names for him, but the one you probably know the best? Odin."

I frowned, unable to quietly sort through that mess. My Norse mythology wasn't exactly up to snuff, and the idea that the Odin of those stories — or at least the being they were based on — had just nearly killed me didn't sit well.

"Are you afraid of me now?" He kept his gaze locked on mine, not giving me any space to escape it, to lessen the impact. It went to show how even he behaved differently, as though he'd been careful to not expose me to this side of him. Was this some sort of dare? Was he testing me?

"You know me," I offered with a crooked smile. "I'm not smart enough to be afraid. I'm a bit annoyed. If you were a god all along, why the fuck have I had to still work? You should have been a better sugar daddy."

He stared back at me, still and silent, until he busted out laughing. "You know, you really were the right choice. Sometimes I worry, think I made a mistake with you, but then you open your mouth and I know that I you were the only choice."

I lifted an eyebrow as I thought back to my Norse mythology education, which I hadn't really paid much attention to. "So, are all gods from Norse mythology?"

He shook his head. "No. We've been in most civilizations in one way or another, so most cultures have some story about us under different names, different descriptions. Some stories are complete bullshit, too, so you can't trust a word of most of it."

"Is that man really going to do what he said?"

Knot sighed, his expression screaming that he really would rather *not* tell me the truth. It made me wonder if he would. Finally, his shoulders sagged. "Yeah, he will. He always has. I warned you that the old ones weren't what you were used to. They aren't human in any way, don't care about humans or Spirits."

"You're one of them."

"Technically, yeah, but clearly, I've never fit in. They'd never seen me as one of them, either. I'm not human, not a Spirit, and the others like me, well, they suck, so I've never really had a place where I fit. That's why I tend to just wander, staying just as long as something is fun."

"I don't think what we just went through was fun," I pointed out.

"No, it really wasn't. I guess I wasn't just kidding — you are special. You're the only one I'd do something this not fun for." The words were quiet, serious, not a speck of humor in them.

It took me back to what he'd said before, to Odin, how he'd told him I was special. I'd never understood where exactly I fit with Knot, what we were, but clearly it was far more complicated than I'd even figured. What did I think about that?

My brain seemed to short circuit at that, unwilling to work out exactly what I thought about Knot, to see him in a way I wasn't prepared for. It was going to take *much* longer to come to terms with that.

"So what now?" I asked.

"Odin slept for a long time — he won't be able to do much right away. It's gonna take some time to get his power back. I'm pretty sure he'll seek out some of his old allies as well. They don't play together much, but when they do, it's a problem for everyone. In short? We've got some time. It's a problem, but it won't be a today or tomorrow problem." He came over and sat on the couch beside me, a bit less carefree than he usually was. "I'm serious, little crow, what does this all mean for us? Are you going to treat me differently? Because I didn't tell you because I didn't want that to happen. Maybe I should have told you sooner, but I thought you'd never find out and then we wouldn't have to have the conversation."

I knew he wanted a real answer, and I owed him that much. Even if he was absentee—he always showed up exactly when I needed him. It felt like he was always watching over me in some way, even if I couldn't see it all the time. "It means I'm going to expect you to pull your weight more and get me better birthday presents. Other than that?" I leaned against his side. "We're good."

He let out a long, slow breath, a shuddering like he couldn't believe I'd agreed, that I'd accepted him. "Seems like a pretty good deal to me. Besides, with Odin sniffing around, I'll be sticking pretty close by, so you'd better get used to that."

I chuckled and leaned my head against his shoulder, exhaustion wearing on me.

"Get some sleep. I'll make sure the others know everything's fine," he said.

I closed my eyes, figuring that sounded like a damn good idea. At least, until one of the things I *had* learned about mythology stuck out. "Wait, did you really fuck a horse?"

He snickered. "Technically, it was the other way around. Go to sleep, Little Crow." A warm press of his lips to my temple helped erase the last bit of frustration hit me, the worry, and sleep took me.

I hadn't expected this to end with me waking up a god — who now wanted me dead — but it didn't shock me as much as it should have. Did that show how fucking weird my life was?

I'd fucked around, I'd found out.

I'd started to build what was actually a happy life, had people to protect, to watch out for, to care about, and if anything threatened that?

I might have just been a crow, but I'd take on anything — even a god — to protect what I'd found.

* * * *

Galen

It was good to think clearly again, but I wished I couldn't recall everything that had happened while I'd lost my mind. It was strange to come that close to my other side, to see that part of myself that I always kept such tight control on.

I'd been helpless against its wants, its reactions, all of it.

We'd gotten back the night before, and Knot had come to tell me — and the others — that Grey was sleeping at home. I'd touched base with all the Weres I could, only to find all those who had gone feral had returned to their old selves.

I understood the cost, perhaps better than most. If there was a being who spawned all the Spirits inside the Weres, that was not a benevolent spirit. And because of us — because of me — it had been awoken and unleashed.

"You look better." Grey's voice unknotted all the tension inside of me.

"What did I tell you about breaking into a Were's house?" The words left me automatically, the familiar back and forth helping me feel at ease, as though things were okay between us.

"That you find it impossibly charming?"

I turned to find her smiling, standing just past the porch in my backyard. She'd probably hopped the fence, but with her, who knew for sure?

It took me back to just how much she meant to me. I'd held off before, held back the instincts that made me want to bind her to me, to make her my mate. Even after I'd nearly lost her twice, I'd resisted it all.

This time was different. I'd come face to face with my own demons, with the beast inside me, and I'd watched Grey risk it all to save me.

"I really do," I said. "So I'm going to give you one more chance, Grey. If you don't want this, if you don't want to be my mate, you need to leave. I can't pretend like I can keep things like this, not anymore." I gripped the edges of my chair, using that to keep myself in place, to not reach out and grab her as I wanted. I closed my eyes, because I wasn't sure I could let her go if I had to watch her walk away.

The waiting nearly broke me, my senses straining for any sign of what she would choose, fully expecting her to walk away. Why wouldn't she? I didn't think I had anything to give her, not really.

The unexpected gift of her warmth struck me harder than anything else when she crawled into my lap, when she pressed her lips to mine. I immediately let go of the armrests and wrapped my arms around her, clinging her to me, letting my beast go just a little, letting myself grasp her so she couldn't escape me.

"You're sure?" I asked, unable to believe my good fortune.

"I mean, I don't know what it requires, so if there's anything weird, we'll see."

"Too late," I said and kissed her deeper, slipping my tongue past her lips, tasting her, letting it soak into me, to ease those parts of me that had craved her so badly for so many years. I pulled back to stare at her, needing to see her reaction. "You're mine. Next full moon, we make it official."

"You keep focusing on what I want, but you've seen the messes I've gotten myself into. You sure you want to have that disaster as a mate?" I heard the question in her voice, the uncertainty, the fear. It reminded me that she hadn't rejected me so far because she didn't care for me, because she didn't even love me, but because she truly didn't think anyone could love her.

It broke my heart that even this far into knowing me, she still didn't realize the truth.

I slid my hand to the nape of her neck so she looked into my eyes. "You are a mess, Grey, but there is nowhere I want to be more than right next to you in whatever disaster you find yourself in. That's exactly where I belong."

She took her lip between her teeth, her eyes bright as she stared back at me. I could see the way she struggled to accept that, to believe it.

Which was fine by me. I pulled her in for another kiss.

I'd spend the rest of my life proving to her that she was the only choice for me.

I'd told her once that thinking someone's life had some grand purpose was pointless, but I'd been lying back then. The truth was that the more time I spent with her, the more I knew the truth. My whole reason for life was loving this girl, and that sort of certainty was good for me.

It sounded like a damn good way to spend a life to me.

She might be able to escape anything, but that wouldn't include me, because Grey was my mate.

Sign up for our newsletter and find out about all our romance book releases, eBook sales and promotions, sneak peeks and FREE romance books!

Want to see more from this author? Here's a taster for you to enjoy!

Flocking It Up: For Flock's Sake
Jayce Carter

Excerpt

Sure, food was great and all, but I'd rather if one particular werewolf would just take his clothes off and fuck me already.

I huffed and popped a bite of fruit into my mouth. The pineapple caused my mouth to sting from the tartness, though the sweet dip he'd added cut into the sharpness.

Galen sat across the table from me, a shallow, wide green bowl of fruit before him, the dip in the center.

He'd proven his skill in the kitchen, but that was so *not* the skill I'd thought we'd be exploring when he'd invited me over.

"Do you not like that fruit?"

I dropped my gaze as though I'd forgotten what we were even eating. "No, it's good."

"You're not eating much." He said as though it were just a random statement, but I knew better.

I blew out a long breath, then set my fork down, the clink of it against the bowl sharp and loud. "I just thought we were doing something else this evening."

"Did we have something else planned?" He frowned. "I said dinner."

"Yeah, but I thought dinner meant dinner in the same way that coffee after a date doesn't at all mean coffee." I didn't mean to, but surprised myself when I felt my own lips pursed forward in a blatant pout.

He blinked slowly, staring back, and the little wheels behind his eyes spun as he tried to work out what that meant. His cheeks tinted red. "Oh…"

I groaned and shook my head. "That makes me sound horrible, doesn't it? It's not like I don't like having dinner with you normally. Damn it, I sound like a man who gets mad when his date doesn't put out. I just assumed that, after our talk, you know…" I gestured with my hands wildly, as though that went to explain how I felt about the whole thing.

"Well, it'll happen," he hedged.

"When? You know I'm not exactly some wilting flower here. You don't have to worry about that."

"I don't want to rush things."

"Rush them?" I choked on my own saliva, thankful I hadn't tried to add in food with the whole ordeal. Fuck knew I'd probably end up dying if I added a single other thing to this mess.

I thought back to Kelvin, to Harrison, to Ruben, to the many men who warmed my bed at any given time. Was Galen seriously trying to act like I needed romance like some teenage girl? What bullshit was that?

Once I caught my breath again—the action aided by slamming my fist against my own chest to get my lungs back on track with their job—I looked across the table at a wide-eyed Galen. "Who exactly do you think I am? I don't know what you're picturing, but I don't need wooing here. I don't need to be broken in slowly."

Way to make yourself sound like a whore…

It forced me to snap my lips together, to pause. I hadn't thought much about my behavior—life was easier if I never did that.

Yes, my love life was a bit weird, and not headed toward anything more normal anytime soon. If anything, it was turning far stranger as we went. The reality was that I was fucking men when I wasn't entirely sure how to define our relationship.

Kelvin was the closest to a boyfriend? The term sounded far too juvenile for what we were. We were bound by blood, with me as his thrall, something that, so far as I understood, we had no way to break. Ruben and I hadn't had sex, but we weren't exactly innocent, either. He'd spent a good amount of time between my thighs, after all. I'd slept with Harrison, but then he'd walked out of my life, and now?

What about Galen?

"Why is it a problem if I want to take it slow?" he asked, the words almost hurt. "You're going to be my mate, so why do we have to jump straight into anything?"

I opened my mouth to tell him that was one of the dumbest statements I'd ever heard when nothing came out.

He...wasn't wrong.

Why was I in a hurry?

Well, the way his ass looked in a pair of jeans was a pretty good reason, but there had to be more to it, right?

Because you can't imagine someone would stick around without it.

The whispered thought dragged sharp claws across my mind. It was one of those inside thoughts that never dared leave the safe confines of one's brain, in case they ever had to come to terms with them. I didn't know that I could deny it if forced to, if I could find enough evidence to say it wasn't true, so I preferred to ignore it entirely.

Instead of speaking, I dropped my gaze to the table, hating how uncomfortable the question made me. It wasn't shaming me.

If he'd said I was acting like a slut, I'd have told him off and stormed out of the house — no problem. Instead, this forced me to take a look at myself. It wasn't about jumping into sex too fast, it was about rushing to it, about trying to force it because I was afraid of losing Galen.

He let out a soft rumble, a noise that was very animalistic, one that reminded me of the beast inside of him. Except, it didn't scare me, not anymore. I'd seen that beast, had watched as even it hadn't fought the idea of dying just to keep me safe. He'd worked so hard to keep me safe — so I didn't mind it one bit. It did force me to meet his gaze.

He held out his hand.

I didn't have to think about it before I set my hand in his. No matter how difficult I could be with him — with everyone — I had no doubts that I trusted him, that I needed him.

Hell, I'd risked us all to save him. I'd been so unwilling to lose him that I'd woken a sleeping god just to prevent it.

His expression softened, a crease appearing in his cheek just before he smiled. It seemed as though he let out a soft breath he'd held, proof of his worry. Did he really think I wouldn't give in?

He tugged me around the table and into his lap. My legs spread around his hips, leaving me to rest all my weight on his thighs. He placed his hands on my waist, and the action giving me a rare chance to look down at him. Usually, given my height, I rarely had the chance to look down at people. It was forever my place to have to look up into people's faces, which made this both strange and welcome.

"Is this what you wanted?" His tone was soft and sweet, as though coaxing me.

Yes. It really was.

"It's what I expected. I figured saying yes to the whole mate thing would mean we'd move past the 'just friends,' thing."

"You haven't been just my friend since I first met you. I wouldn't do what I've done for you for just a friend, wouldn't feel the way I feel about you for just a friend."

"Then what was the whole mate thing?"

"That was me needing to make it official. I'm a were, and that means I have certain instincts. Those include needing to mark you as my mate."

"And what does that involve?"

He reached up with one hand and slid his thumb across my bottom lip. A shiver raced through me. How could a single touch be both chaste and extremely filthy? "We'll spend the entire night of the full moon, along with the following day. I'll leave the rest up to your imagination."

"So why wait?" Fuck, didn't *that* sound like whining?

"Because you matter to me, and I want to do it right. I want you to be *mine* before we go that far. Is it really so unthinkable that someone would want to hold off until that?"

I nipped at his thumb, which still stroked along my bottom lip like the biggest fucking clit tease I'd ever seen. "Yeah, it is unusual."

He laughed, showing no annoyance over my childish attitude or my little bite. Then again, when it came to a man who had fangs some of the time, my blunt little teeth probably couldn't do much damage. "I want to do this right—you deserve that. Please, let me cherish you?"

And *fuck*. I never thought I'd be a sucker for romance. Normally, I was allergic to the very idea of it. Flowers and sweet words, things like that had never settled well for me. I'd always waited to see when they went bad, when the person who uttered them proved themselves false. It always happened, after all. Eventually, if given time, people failed.

It meant those sweet words always felt like a quick spit before attempting anal—not enough to help before the main event. It frustrated me, always put me on edge, just waiting until the person let me down. That explained why I'd moved to physical relationships, because I understood them.

Sex was easy, after all. It was simple to do, didn't force anything complicated. I much preferred that compared to anything else.

And here he was, trying to convince me he was different, that he'd treat me better?

I struggled to believe it, but for the first time, I *wanted* to believe it. Something inside me craved him proving it.

So I nodded, just before he pulled me in for a kiss— sweet and deep and so much more teasing since I knew it wouldn't go further.

Talk about blue ovaries…

* * * *

A few hours later and I'd come to find that an actual date was oddly endearing.

I stretched out on the couch, my head in his lap, a movie playing on the television and a bowl of popcorn in my lap. It wasn't piping hot anymore, since I'd popped it at the start of the previous movie. This was about a park with dinosaurs, that obviously goes horribly wrong because why wouldn't it? We were on the second movie in the series, which in many ways was just a rehash of what had happened previously.

Still, I had to admit…

This wasn't so bad.

There was a quiet niceness to it. When had I gotten to just be normal? To watch a movie? To have a night in with another? That seemed so far away from the life I'd led recently, from the chaos and mess of it all.

Galen would run his fingers through my hair now and then, his gaze locked on the screen, the room dark.

It made me wonder if he watched it the way dogs watched television, a slight twitch now and then implying he wanted to give chase to something.

The idea made me chuckle, and Galen offered me a lifted eyebrow in response.

I opened my mouth to tell him the nonsense going on in my head when the air shifted, when tension sparked through the room.

Galen's body went rigid, the dangerous stillness of a predator on alert.

I didn't know what he heard, what set him off, but that didn't change the obvious reaction.

It gave me time to sit up just as a dark figure appeared in the space beside the television. Red eyes glowed — *a vampire?*

Galen didn't wait to identify them — why would he? No vampire would have any good reason to come here, especially *inside* his home. Only bad things could come from this. Instead, he spoke with a strong, low, threatening voice. "Leave, now."

The vampire didn't move, didn't blink. The light from the still-running movie bathed the figure in dark, meaning I could spot almost no details about them. The size made me think man, but only the eyes were easily seen.

Galen seemed to hold back. He was generally level-headed, willing to talk things out, but I had no doubt he could take on this vampire. Why didn't he?

Because I'm here.

He didn't want to risk me. I was far more fragile, and one good swipe could end me. It didn't bother me that much anymore, since it was simply a way of life for me. I was a handicap in a fight, but it wasn't like I could do anything about it.

"Last chance," Galen said, his voice even rougher, as though his throat had started to change. I didn't shift my gaze to Galen, but I knew if I had, I'd see his eyes that eerie amber color.

The vampire sailed forward, so fast I could only stumble backward just before he struck Galen. The clash of their massive bodies was dreadful, making an absolute joke of the fights I normally saw.

This was more like a dogfight—two capable apex predators doing whatever they had to to survive. It also reminded me just how capable Galen was.

I felt pretty confident in Galen's odds—he was alpha for a reason, after all. His wolf was not one to fuck with, and he sure as hell showed it off, then. He gained the upper hand quickly, proving his superiority.

I went to take a relieved breath when another shadow sailed across the dim room, knocking Galen backward, rewarded with a furious roar.

Something grabbed me, yanking me against a hard plane of muscle. An arm wrapped around me, holding me tightly, letting me know that the person restraining me wasn't human.

"Don't hurt her."

Another?

It was up to four vampires, and the odds of winning didn't feel so certain, anymore. I had a lot of faith in Galen, but there was a limit, especially because I had no idea how old or powerful these vampires were.

"Who cares?" the vampire holding me asked.

"You know the rule. No one touches her."

Really?

I had to assume that was a Kelvin order. I was, technically, his thrall. It made sense that no one was supposed to fuck with me. I almost wanted to feel flattered until I recalled the exact situation I'd found myself in. Now was not the time for swooning.

However, it gave me more room to maneuver, knowing that they were at least reluctant to hurt me.

Galen fought the two, holding his own even as they worked together. The third joined in there, probably figuring I wasn't a concern worth their attention.

One deep breath centered me before I moved. I let my weight shift forward, going limp. It wasn't enough to throw them off balance—not for a vampire—but Spirits tended to get jumpy when people passed out, especially people who they didn't want to die.

It was like as soon as someone turned into a Spirit they forgot what being human was like.

Sure enough he leaned forward, guiding me to the floor, his motions panicked. It wasn't about *me,* but probably worry he'd get blamed for accidentally killing Kelvin's thrall. I'd take it as a win even if it wasn't really about me.

When he got me down, I shook.

Sure, it was the worst fake seizure anyone had ever seen, and any human would have wondered what shitty basement acting class had taught me such nonsense, but for a vampire?

"Shit. Something's wrong with her."

Bingo.

"What?" one of the others asked.

"She's like...shaking."

"Did you snap her neck? Shake her too hard?"

"I don't think so." The vampire stood, panicking enough he was probably balls deep into what excuses he'd use later.

Which was exactly where I needed him.

I took that chance to fling myself sideways, getting my feet beneath me. I wouldn't have long — vampires were too fast — but surprise was a hell of an advantage.

So was not being seen as a threat.

They wanted me *not* dead, but if they didn't think I could hurt them, they wouldn't worry much about me getting away.

I got to the kitchen just as the vampire came up behind me.

Too late.

I'd already grabbed my goal, the long knife that Galen had used to slice dinner.

"Come on, thrall, don't misbehave."

"But that's what I'm best at." I turned, keeping the knife hidden, the handle against my palm, the blade up against my forearm.

This time I got the chance to actually see the vampire. Not a surprise, but I didn't recognize him. I spent more time with the vampires than I used to, but I still avoided interacting with them best I could. They brought me nothing but trouble, after all.

"We don't want to hurt you. This isn't about you."

Another angry roar from the other room told me Galen was still fighting. *Good.*

"Just stay put and it'll be over soon."

I smiled widely, trying for innocence. Anyone who knew me knew better than to believe such bullshit, but something about my big eyes and vacant stare seemed to help—especially when I pulled my shoulders back and stuck my tits out.

His gaze dropped, making me thankful I still wore my slutty, low-cut shirt from when I'd thought a certain werewolf would be taking it off for me. Even dead men liked boobs, after all.

So I took the chance to shift the blade down, out of sight, then swung the knife in a wide arc, burying it between his ribs. A metal knife wouldn't be enough to kill him—I needed wood for that—but fucking up a person's heart, even a vampire's, would slow them down until they healed. It still caused the blood to not travel through the body, would make them sluggish and lose consciousness until they healed.

I twisted the knife, angling it around best I could to do as much damage as possible as he yanked backward. Blood poured from the wound, and he stumbled almost instantly, clutching the counter as I darted away. He'd go down pretty fast, and it was more important to help knock enemies down than worry how long they stayed down.

Inside the living room, I found one dead vampire— because I was pretty sure they couldn't heal from a lack of a head. It again went to show the vast difference in the way I fought compared to how Galen did.

I didn't bother with waiting, throwing myself instead into the fray—but with a bit more thought than before. A few years ago, I would have just gone in swinging no matter how stupid it was. This time, however, I'd gotten a weapon and only moved in for a quick attack then retreat.

See, I learn!

I sank the blade into the back of one of the vampires, meeting with a vicious look from Galen that said he didn't approve of my getting involved.

Too bad.

I went to do it again when the vampire twisted and grabbed my wrist, the action causing pain to scream through the joint. As soon as it started, however, Galen raked claw-tipped fingers across the vampire's face, opening it up like cutting through the film that covered tubes of hamburger.

I am never eating ground beef again…

The skin tore, the grip on my wrist disappearing, but it gave the last vampire the distraction he needed.

He sailed forward, shoving Galen back, pinning him against the wall.

My knife had fallen to the floor after the vampire had grabbed me, leaving me with no weapon, no way to help. All it would take was one good grasp and the vampire could tear Galen apart.

Suddenly, all the time I'd vacillated between a relationship or not came back to me, all the wasted years, the times when I could have had sex with him and hadn't.

My brain clung to that stupid comment because it was easier than thinking about actually losing him, than not having Galen in my life.

Fear crept along my skin, time dragging by, so slowly I wondered if it wasn't giving me just another moment with him.

I locked eyes with him, that amber painfully familiar. I had no fucking idea what he was saying with that look, but I suspected — knowing him — it was an apology. It was him being selfless, as always, telling me not to worry, that it wasn't my fault. The fucking asshole, taking his last moments to reassure me?

He just has to one up me, doesn't he?

A loud crack echoed in the room just as I closed my eyes, the action automatic, my brain refusing to see any of it, unable to witness my loss in real time. My legs gave out, my knees striking the ground so hard my teeth rattled together.

I threw myself forward, opening my eyes at the same time. It seemed some habits never quite went away.

No weapon, no real chance, but anger fueled a hell of a lot of bad choices in life and it was one hundred percent behind this one. I'd take the fucker apart with my bare hands or die trying.

Either way was fine by me.

Except, when I slammed into the figure, I froze.

What?

My brain made sense of the scene best it could, fitting together the pieces. The body on the floor, with no head, wasn't Galen but the vampire. Galen stood against the wall, still, and the person I'd flung myself against, the one I'd been ready to attack, was Kelvin, the other vampire's missing head gripped in his hand.

Galen lifted his lips, his teeth sharp, his voice deep. "It looks like we need to have a conversation."

"Seems that way," Kelvin answered and dropped the head, the thud of it sickening.

Well, that solidifies it. This date isn't ending in sex...

About the Author

Jayce Carter lives in Southern California with her husband and two spawns. She originally wanted to take over the world but realized that would require wearing pants. This led her to choosing writing, a completely pants-free occupation. She has a fear of heights yet rock climbs for fun and enjoys making up excuses for not going out and socializing.

Jayce loves to hear from readers. You can find her contact information, website details and author profile page at https://www.firstforromance.com

ENTWINED PUBLISHING